ladies' night out

Also by Electa Rome Parks

The Ties That Bind
Loose Ends
Almost Doesn't Count

ladies' night out

Electa Rome Parks

 NEW AMERICAN LIBRARY

New American Library
Published by New American Library, a division of
Penguin Group (USA) Inc., 375 Hudson Street,
New York, New York 10014, USA
Penguin Group (Canada), 90 Eglinton Avenue East, Suite 700, Toronto,
Ontario M4P 2Y3, Canada (a division of Pearson Penguin Canada Inc.)
Penguin Books Ltd., 80 Strand, London WC2R 0RL, England
Penguin Ireland, 25 St. Stephen's Green, Dublin 2,
Ireland (a division of Penguin Books Ltd.)
Penguin Group (Australia), 250 Camberwell Road, Camberwell, Victoria 3124,
Australia (a division of Pearson Australia Group Pty. Ltd.)
Penguin Books India Pvt. Ltd., 11 Community Centre, Panchsheel Park,
New Delhi - 110 017, India
Penguin Group (NZ), cnr Airborne and Rosedale Roads, Albany,
Auckland 1310, New Zealand (a division of Pearson New Zealand Ltd.)
Penguin Books (South Africa) (Pty.) Ltd., 24 Sturdee Avenue,
Rosebank, Johannesburg 2196, South Africa

Penguin Books Ltd., Registered Offices:
80 Strand, London WC2R 0RL, England

First published by New American Library,
a division of Penguin Group (USA) Inc.

First Printing, January 2007
1   3   5   7   9   10   8   6   4   2

NEW AMERICAN LIBRARY and logo are trademarks of Penguin Group (USA) Inc.

LIBRARY OF CONGRESS CATALOGING-IN-PUBLICATION DATA:
Parks, Electa Rome.
Ladies' night out / Electa Rome Parks.
p. cm.
ISBN-13: 0-978-451-22025-7
1. Female friendship--Fiction. 2. Triangles (Interpersonal relations)--Fiction. 3. African American women--
Fiction. 4. Domestic fiction. I. Title.
PS3616.A7555L33 2007
813'.6—dc22   2006016660

Set in Bembo
Designed by Spring Hoteling

Printed in the United States of America

To my hubby . . . the one who fulfills all my fantasies

lexie

What's the freakiest thing you've ever done? Almost a month ago, that was the ultimate question, posed to me by one of my best friends, Meshell. The Crew, which consisted of Meshell, Tonya, Tracee, and myself, were all comfortably sprawled out on the polished hardwood floor and soft leather sofas in my midtown Atlanta loft apartment. After a night of partying, we were in the process of finishing off very expensive bottles of wine that Tonya had been so gracious as to provide.

Tonya is a head buyer for one of the largest wine distributors in the United States and Europe. Girlfriend always hooks us up with the good stuff, which by our definition means expensive. By the way, I'm Alexis. Lexie to my friends.

What's the freakiest thing you've ever done? That question took me completely off guard. It was a Saturday night, the second Saturday of the month to be exact, and we were participating in our monthly ritual . . . Ladies' Night Out. Our adventures were synonymous with getting buzzed (not drunk, mind you), being a little loose (not to the point of being a slut), having a wonderful time (limited drama and no work discussed), talking about men (or lack of), and keeping it real (we could say anything to each other and usually did).

Years earlier, Meshell, Tonya, Tracee, and myself had met at a historically black college in Atlanta and become instant friends when we pledged the same sorority. Being line sisters can create an everlasting bond, one that we have yet to break. Now, years later, we're all pushing thirty with exciting and demanding careers and various commitments without husbands or children in our lives. Once a month, the second Saturday, come rain or shine, we stop and put everything on hold, to rebond, regroup, hang out, and have a good time in between our weekly phone conversations with one another. We look forward to this monthly ritual.

As I said before, after a night out of dancing, drinking, and flirting with attractive men at one of the popular Atlanta nightspots, the Crew was now crashing at my loft apartment, which if I must say has an amazing view of the city. Just like old times, we were still hyped up after an evening out on the town. We were not quite ready to call it quits; the night was still young. In college, we'd hang out in one of our dorm rooms, change into our PJs, drink and talk into the wee hours of the morning about our dreams, ambitions, families, and of course men. This early morning was no different. Even through our alcohol haze, those four topics were still important to us and heavy on our minds.

After we left the club and grabbed something to eat at the International House of Pancakes down the street, we headed back to my place for our traditional sleepover. Before we could even make it into the living room, expensive shoes were tossed off at the front door as we chatted amicably about who the possible down low (DL) brothers were in the club. Nowadays, you just didn't know.

Tracee, the true drinker of the group, made herself at home as she stumbled into my compact kitchen and retrieved four cute wineglasses that I'd purchased for a great price at IKEA's One-Day Sale. In a swift, skilled motion, Tonya opened one of the bottles of wine that she'd brought over and joined us in the living room. We were full of chatter and laughter.

After everyone's wineglass was filled almost to the brim, Tonya captured our attention by lightly tapping her glass three times with her long, acrylic nails.

"Ladies. Ladies, please join me in a toast," she exclaimed, with a slight slur to her sultry voice.

As we looked from one to the other with big, genuine smiles, everybody raised their glasses high in unison.

"To my best friends. The smartest, sexiest, and most divine women I know. I love you divas!"

"We love you too, girlfriend," we shouted in unison, gently clicking glasses among ourselves and sipping. The wine was excellent.

Tonya continued. "I mean it. I love you divas so much, and I thank God every day for placing you in my life."

Meshell spoke up first. "Okay. Don't go getting all mushy on us. We know you love us—ditto—but this wine is making you say it just a bit too much. We heard you the first time."

We all laughed. I glanced around at my girlfriends from my spot on the floor, below my tan leather loveseat. With my feet curled underneath me, I had made myself comfortable. We are all so different, yet so good for one another. The Crew definitely complements each other in ways that only the rich spirit of sisterhood can.

I am the levelheaded, rational one of the group. I keep everyone balanced and centered and point out the pros and cons of every situation before they jump headfirst into them. My girlfriends call me for advice and an ear to bend when problems arise in their lives or they just need to vent or chitchat. Back in college, they jokingly nicknamed me "Miss Goody Two-shoes" and they still call me that from time to time.

It was unbelievable to them that I was a virgin until I was twenty.

They jokingly claimed I was the group's conscience; always trying to do the right thing. I admit, sometimes it's hard for me to cut off my counseling skills and techniques once I walk through my front door. By profession, I'm a psychologist working for a small practice in Midtown.

Of all the ladies, I am the closest to Meshell. She is a straight trip. What words can describe Meshell? She is loud, articulate, outspoken, and very confident. She doesn't hold back—anything. Most people either like her or hate her. Typically, there isn't an in-between. Meshell and I divulged some personal truths back in the day that weren't shared with the rest of our crew, and to this day she has not betrayed my trust. Meshell's personality is the perfect blend for her role as an assistant district attorney.

Tonya is most definitely the group member who has the most expensive and elegant taste for the finer things in life. She is a true diva in every sense of the word. Hell, we all are, but Tonya takes it to a whole other level. She is always dressed to the nines from head to toe in designer wear. Her weave is always fabulous and flowing down her back, and I don't think I've ever seen her without makeup since we pledged. I think she sleeps in full makeup just in case she has to wake up suddenly and dash out. Tonya is fierce and aggressive, but I guess she has to be as head wine buyer for a major distributor.

Last, but certainly not least, is Tracee. Tracee is outgoing, always has a smile on her pretty face, and is into karma, energies, spirit guides, and the entire metaphysical dimension. Her one vice is drinking. That girl can drink any man under the table in a matter of minutes. We joke that she is a closet alcoholic, but Tracee just shakes her head of long dreads, quotes some line from a famous poem, and declares she is a social drinker. Tracee is an associate professor of English literature at one of the colleges on the Atlanta University Center campus.

That's my crew. I love them with all my heart and soul. I'd trust them with my life. Oh, did I mention we are all gorgeous women? I'm not boasting, just keeping it real and breaking it down for you to give a clear, precise picture. We are a combination of the friends on *Sex and the City* and the popular sitcom *Girlfriends*. True divas. When we go out, heads turn from both men and women. I'll never forget the time this big-boned, Amazon-looking lesbian tried to pick up Meshell in the bathroom of a local club. Meshell calmly finished washing and drying her hands, freshened her lipstick, and told her off in no uncertain terms. I can't begin to mention the words that came out of Meshell's mouth. I almost felt sorry for the lesbian. Almost, not quite.

For as much as we have it going on, we are all turning or have turned the big 3-0 this year and none of us are married, have any strong prospects for marriage—or have any children—or even a man, at this particular point. My work is my life, and I am very good at what I do. However, I want it all! The husband, the career, and the family. Is that too much to ask for?

"Miss Goody Two-shoes, where is your mind tonight?" Tracee asked, filling her glass up to the brim, yet again.

"Uh, what did you say?" I asked, looking around in confusion. For a minute I was so lost in thought that I didn't realize Tracee had asked me a question and put on some soft, baby-making music, as we called it. By now, we were all in a mellow mood.

"Earth to Lexie. Can you hear us? Come in," Tonya chimed in, lighting the multiple candles of all shapes, sizes, and colors that were a permanent fixture on my marble coffee table. Candles soothed me, so I always had them lit and placed throughout my apartment in every nook and cranny imaginable.

"Tonya, you know Lexie is always thinking about or analyzing something or somebody. Y'all leave Lexie alone. She'll come back to us sooner or later," Meshell said, jumping to my defense. She was reclining next to Tracee. I threw a small pillow at her. She didn't even try to fend it off. We all laughed a hearty chuckle through our alcohol-induced buzzes.

"This wine is excellent," I said, lifting the half-empty bottle from the table to check out the label for future reference. I knew the price was probably too steep for my pocketbook. I didn't know that much about wines, but Tonya had dragged me to a couple of wine-tasting events so I knew a little something-something.

"Of course. Only the best for my divas. I don't do substandard nor do I do cheap. First class all the way," Tonya exclaimed with a toss of her wavy hair.

"Yeah, and it'd be even better if I had a man standing in front of me instead of you witches in my face," Meshell said from her spot on the sofa, with her eyes slightly closed, swaying to the soulful music. Some old D'Angelo song was playing.

"Meshell, I can't even disagree because I haven't had a date in two months. Two months, y'all," I said, stretching and changing my position on the floor.

The Crew nodded their heads in agreement.

"At this rate, we'll be fabulously single at forty," Tracee predicted. "Where are all the good men? Quit feeling intimidated by successful women. We don't bite—that is, unless you want us to."

Again, there were more nods of agreement and amens in between sips of wine and personal reflections.

"Diva, you know we're already married. Married to our damn jobs," Tonya said. "But I shouldn't complain because my j-o-b is providing for the lifestyle that I so enjoy."

"That's all true and good, but the last time I checked, my j-o-b couldn't make me have an orgasm," Tracee added. "There is nothing like the feel of a man deep inside you."

"It's been so long since I've been with a man that if one even touched me on the shoulder, I'd start quivering. The other day, I promise you, I almost had an orgasm at the water cooler when this new associate, fine as all get-out, twenty-something, walked up behind me and accidentally brushed against me. He was smelling all good and looking like he stepped off the pages of the current issue of GQ magazine." Meshell sighed with a big smile on her face as she relived the moment.

"Meshell, you are so crazy," I said.

"I'm serious. If I hadn't been at work and baby boy and I didn't have to see each other every day on a professional level, I would have been on that. Believe me. Like jelly on peanut butter."

"Yeah, I believe it. You would have done some freaky shit like that," Tracee shared, pulling back her dreads.

"Damn right! I work hard all day. Every day. I work hard for the money. Hell, I need to get my freak on every now and then. I would have been working that dick in slow motion and showed baby boy some new tricks."

"I hear ya," I said, seriously feeling the wine. It was going straight to my head. I was definitely not a drinker.

"In fact, ladies, let's get real and live! What is the freakiest thing you've ever done?" Meshell asked, looking from one to the other. "If we can't get the real thing tonight, at least we can reminisce on when we did."

For a few brief moments, we were deep in thought as we tried to remember the freakiest shit we had participated in. As for me, I was seriously racking my brain and coming up nil. Nada. I mean, exactly what does freaky mean? In *Webster's II New College Dictionary* it means "something unusual or out of the norm." What sexual freakiness had I participated in? Straightlaced was my middle name.

"Oh, divas. I've got one of several that I can share. In fact, this is too easy. The freakiest thing I ever did happened with Michael Dobson. Y'all remember him? The guy I went out with about four months ago?" Tonya asked. She placed her wineglass down and sat back.

We nodded. I remembered him because Tonya had told us all the man's personal business. She didn't care. Tonya's like that: a true gossip and lover of dirt. Michael Dobson is a popular, and very attractive, local councilman that is always on the news for some outrageous behavior on his part in some form or fashion. Yet, he always walks away untainted and continues being reelected. Michael and Tonya met at a black-tie fund-raising event and hit it off immediately because of a shared interest. Tonya boasted that she had never met a man who loved to eat pussy as much as Michael did.

"Anyway, remember I told y'all how the man loved to travel *downtown* with a major passion? And divas, you guys know how that turns me on. Drives me crazy. To have a man with his head buried between my spread legs while he feasts on my womanhood and if he really, really knows what he's doing . . . Oh, hell yeah!

"Damn. This is making me hot just thinking about that night. Diva, pour me some more wine and then I'll continue my story," Tonya requested, leaning back and fanning herself in an exaggerated manner.

That was our cue to take bathroom breaks and then we eagerly waited while Meshell retrieved another bottle of wine from the refrigerator, opened it, poured more for Tonya, and set the bottle in the middle of the coffee table. Anticipation was high.

"Okay, witch. Spill the beans. What happened?" Meshell asked, focusing her total attention on Tonya as if she were interrogating a witness.

"Don't rush me! One Friday evening, Michael called me at home and asked me to pack an overnight bag. He said he had a big surprise for me, and he'd be over to pick me up in two hours. His excitement was contagious. You know how I love surprises, but I adore a man spending money on me even more. I quickly packed my Prada overnight bag along with some of my sexiest pieces of lingerie. I couldn't decide on only one outfit. They *all* look good on me. As I waited for Michael, I tried to speculate on what he had planned. We had only been seeing each other for a brief period and gone out a few times because I traveled a lot and his schedule was equally full.

"To make a long story short, Michael had his driver pick me up, and we checked into one of the luxury suites at this ritzy hotel in Buckhead around seven o'clock. The suite was breathtaking. It was so elegant and beyond classy, so you know I was in heaven. After ordering room service, we had a quiet, relaxing dinner on the balcony overlooking the city. The weather was nice, the stars were out, and Michael and I talked, got to know each better, and enjoyed ourselves immensely."

The Crew had been pulled into the story and we gave Tonya our full, undivided attention. The only other sound was the slow jams playing on the radio.

"Michael wasn't in a hurry to get me into bed. That impressed me because I knew he wanted me as much as I desired him. His body language told the story; he had amazing willpower. However, he seemed genuinely interested in my career, my thoughts, my life. That's when I realized why he made such an awesome politician. He made people think they were the most important person in the world at that moment."

I was vaguely aware that a slow song was playing in the background. After years of knowing Tonya and her peculiarities, it was a given not to rush her when she was sharing something. She was going to share her way: long, drawn-out, and dramatic.

"After dinner and relaxed conversation, Michael ran us a steaming hot, lavender-scented bubble bath in the garden tub. We climbed in together, arm in arm. He lovingly bathed me with his firm hands, gently caressing me all over. In between his getting to know my body intimately, we shared passionate kisses," Tonya said, looking off in a dreamy state.

"That's sweet and romantic, but not necessarily freaky," Tracee interjected, looking a bit disappointed and let down.

"Well, if you will let me finish. After the very erotic and stimulating bubble bath, Michael dried me off ever so delicately with a big, thick, fluffy hotel towel. In his arms, he then carried me to the king-size bed. After lotioning my entire body with lavender body lotion and giving me a wonderful full-body massage in the process, Michael spread my legs wide open, as wide as they'd go. He proceeded to eat my pussy like there was no tomorrow.

"The brother had serious, don't play with me abilities. Make you slap your own mama skills. Michael was the truth."

"No—you didn't say the truth?" Tracee questioned.

"Yes, I did! Personally, a man doesn't even have to have a dick to be with me. It could be cut off, chopped off, severed, as small as my baby toe, gone. Just give him a tongue, the use of his fingers, and it's on. Ladies, Michael put it on me and then some. I was ready to have his babies and tattoo his name on my lower back. I still have vivid flashbacks and my coochie starts to throb in eager anticipation. I saw him on the Channel Five news the other night and I started to tremble."

"Damn!" was all I could muster. I saw Meshell cross and uncross her legs a few times. Tonya and Tracee slapped palms.

"Every time I'd catch my breath, Michael would be all over me again. He couldn't get enough. Kept saying how wonderful and sweet I tasted. I don't even think he used his dick that night; Michael would come from watching me come. Seriously, I came so many times that I lost count after the first five times. He had me sitting on his face, hanging half on and half off the bed, on the floor, in the shower against the wall, you name it, we did it. My all-time favorite was when he had me sitting in this high-back, executive-looking chair, with my legs propped up. Michael was kneeling in front of me on the floor, sucking, licking, and stroking me with his fingers. He had my juices all on the sides of his face, and he looked like he was in heaven."

"God bless him!" Meshell screamed, throwing her hands in the air. Tonya was beyond lucky. I could mentally picture a butt-naked, gorgeous Michael putting it on her. Things like that didn't happen to me.

"Michael and I spent the entire weekend in bed. We'd stop long enough to eat lunch and dinner . . . to build our strength back up . . . and then go at it again with me being the ultimate dessert. It was like he was possessed. The man adored my pussy. By Sunday, at checkout time, I could barely walk. But you better believe a big, goofy smile lit up my entire face. I was beaming for days."

We sat up and exhaled at the same time. Michael and Tonya didn't work out in the long run, but just the thought of having a man do to you the one thing that sends you into a frenzy, and for him to be able to do it well . . . Yes, Tonya was a very fortunate lady. Lucky indeed.

"Whew. It's getting hot in here!" Meshell screamed, fanning herself with her hand. "Girl! How'd you let that one get away?"

"Conflict with schedules," Tonya said with an air of sadness.

"Damn. I would have worked around his. I wouldn't have let that mouth get away; I'd have him on speed dial like 9-1-1. Okay, who's next? Is anyone brave enough to follow that story?" Meshell asked, looking around, making eye contact for a few seconds with each of us.

"Sure. I'll go next," Tracee answered, raising her hand like a school student addressing her teacher. Her eyes were red-rimmed and half-closed. Our attention was fixated upon her in eager anticipation.

lexie

The candles continued to burn low, casting an alluring setting and providing a fragrant aroma to my apartment. As the music from the stereo flowed freely, the Crew got comfortable to hear Tracee's version of passion, sex, and freakiness. I was stretched out on the floor by now and Meshell was lying down, legs extended, with her head in Tracee's lap. Tonya sat above me on the loveseat with her legs tucked underneath her, arms propped up on a pillow.

"Two months ago I was casually dating Professor William Kessler over at Morehouse. There was nothing serious going on between us. I think I was attracted to him because of his intelligence and his relentless pursuit of me. Y'all know how I adore an intelligent man who is well-spoken. A man who can converse with a woman on any topic—that's a true aphrodisiac. And it didn't hurt that William was very attractive and had a sexy goatee."

I vaguely remembered meeting him a couple of times when Tracee and I had gone to lunch and Professor Kessler had stopped by our table to say hello as he was leaving the campus cafeteria.

"Well, he turned out to be one big bore with a capital Yawn. Professor Kessler was a big mistake. My mama used to say, 'Don't shit where you eat.' Even though William and I didn't teach at the same college, he was still too close for comfort. He was just across the yard. What was I thinking?"

"Uh, Tracee, we don't have all night, girl. Move your adventure along," Meshell playfully demanded. "We know what you were thinking. You were horny and you wanted some. The professor had a dick between his legs and you gave in to temptation. Plain and simple, girl. We've all been there and done that at some point in our lives."

Meshell's comments brought a round of nervous laughter because we knew she had spoken the truth. With us being highly successful black women, sometimes we intimidated men. Yet we have needs and desires too.

"It wasn't even like that," Tracee interjected, playing with a piece of her hair.

Meshell murmured, "Yeah, whatever. I don't know why you would want us to believe that Miss Intellectual herself doesn't get horny and want to do the nasty. Witch, I've seen that vibrator you keep hidden in the back, far corner of your nightstand. The big black one. Keep it real."

We howled in laughter. I was holding my sides, I was laughing so hard. Tears were rolling down Tonya's face.

Tracee just rolled her big doelike eyes at Meshell and continued. "You are one nosy heifer. Stay out of my drawers!" she teased. "As I was saying, William was as boring and stiff in the bedroom as he was in the classroom, yet I still had my freakiest experience with him."

"Do tell," Tonya exclaimed excitedly, pouring herself half a glass of wine and wiping away tears with her finger.

"One night, we'd gone to dinner at this fabulous seafood restaurant that served huge portions of crab legs, lobster tails, oysters, and shrimp. Y'all should check it out. Anyway, I ate like there was no tomorrow; I was stuffed. Afterwards, I suggested we walk to digest our food. There was a nearby park and it was a beautiful, star-filled night in the city. I wanted to enjoy the night air and embrace nature.

"William and I were walking hand in hand, admiring the stars and the full, luminous moon, and talking about students and academic issues. There weren't too many people in the park, just some joggers and a few other couples like us who were enjoying a leisurely stroll. One very attractive jogger with a runner's physique and a butt to die for was taking a break near us. We briefly made eye contact. He took a sip of his bottled water while he boldly checked us out, offered us a nod of his head, and then he moved on to complete his run."

"Stop. Hold that thought. Bathroom break. Who wants a snack? I think I have some red grapes in the fridge," I shouted, bolting for the bathroom. The wine was running right through me. Within five minutes, I had relieved myself, reclaimed my spot on the floor, and was happily munching on the seedless red grapes that I had picked up from Kroger earlier that morning. The rest of the Crew wandered back into the living room with various snacks in hand. Our attention soon focused back on Tracee.

"Where was I? Oh yeah. At some point, William stopped talking, cupped my chin, and proceeded to kiss me. Now, he is an excellent kisser; I'll give him that much. When our tongues met, I felt it all the way down to my toes. He knew how to do that little thrust with his tongue when he kissed, like he was seducing your mouth. It made me only imagine what he could do with another body part. I should have kept imagining.

"Soon, I felt familiar longings start to stir and my panties were moist. I pulled William's right hand up to my breasts, and he squeezed and fondled them. I moaned faintly. I swear I don't know what happened. Maybe it was the night air, the many drinks from dinner, or the relative isolation of the park, but I suddenly wanted to have sex with him. And I wanted to do it then and there."

"What? Bring it on," Tonya exclaimed, popping a grape into her mouth.

"I whispered my desire in William's ear. He was shocked and hesitant for a brief moment. Yet his lust-filled passion and hard dick betrayed him. I firmly pulled him by the left arm and we eased ourselves off the main path of the walking/jogging trail. We found ourselves standing in a secluded spot that was semicovered with long hanging branches with plenty of greenery from the massive trees overhead. We were probably fifty feet off the beaten path. There was one lone streetlight directly overhead that cast us in an eerie shadow. Of course, boring William protested and wanted to go back to his house, behind closed doors, to continue what we had started.

"When I swiftly unzipped his pants, released his dick from his boxers, and started to give him the best blow job ever, he came around quickly. Y'all, I had the man almost in tears. He was moaning so loudly that I'm sure anyone walking nearby thought a wild animal had escaped from Zoo Atlanta and was loose in the park. I started off sucking the head of his rod. You know, I played with it, taking it in and out of my mouth, slowly. Getting it juiced up. Then I took his entire shaft in my mouth as far as I could and repeated the process several times, slowly, not too fast, teasing William. At the same time, I was gently squeezing his balls and licking them in between sucking his dick."

"Damn, diva! Who taught you those skills?" Tonya teased. "Let me take some notes."

Tracee ignored her and continued. "William was groaning and probably wasn't even sure where he was. He had his head thrown back, eyes closed, and a tight grip on the sides of my head. I hesitated for just a moment because I thought I heard a sound nearby. I cocked my head to the side to listen and William swiftly pushed it back down and continued to squeeze and stroke my breasts. He had managed to open my silk blouse and release my breasts from my purple satin bra. The cool night air had my nipples hard and erect. They stood out like huge, ripe blackberries against my skin. William was gently tweaking them and I let out a soft, slow moan."

I imagined that sight because Tracee is not small in the breast department. The girl is more than a handful.

"I heard that crackling noise again. I thought maybe it was a squirrel or someone's dog that had run off the jogging trail. This time, I nervously looked over to my immediate left and there he was, less than forty feet away; the tall, muscular jogger was cooling down from his run and staring straight at us. Watching us. At first, I was afraid, then it switched to embarrassment; lastly I realized my pussy was dripping wet. As I continued to suck off William and place my fingers under my skirt and inside my panties to touch my throbbing womanhood, the jogger and I never broke eye contact. Just the thought of this handsome, complete stranger watching us get off was turning me on. Big time. The stranger didn't say anything, and I didn't mention anything to William about him. With his back to the jogger, William was still lost in ecstasy as I continued to work him over. If a herd of wild horses had run through, he wouldn't have noticed it.

"William had managed to pull my skirt up and panties down to my ankles and had inserted his thick fingers inside me. I was so wet already and his fingers were going in and out of me, and I was squirming around, moving up and down to their rhythm. His dick was slipping in and out of my mouth. Yet, my eyes never left the jogger's. As the jogger licked his lips, he had a slight smile on his face. It was obvious that he was breathing harder and was totally into what he was witnessing.

"The jogger placed his hands inside his pants and was touching himself. Amazingly that turned me on even more. Next thing I knew, he pulled this big, huge black dick out, the largest I have ever seen on a human, and started to jack himself off in front of me. I had seen enough and couldn't take any more. I was about to explode. I begged William to take me then and there. Right there on the ground, I got down on all fours with my skirt hitched up to expose my round ass and William started pumping in and out of me, hard. Apparently this was turning him on too. He had never been this aggressive before. I was crying out, moaning and cursing for William to do me harder, and in the distance I could see the jogger watching every thrust as he jacked off. He never uttered a word, just watched the live sex show.

"Finally, when William exploded his warm juices inside me, and I fell to the ground completely spent after two orgasms, we heard muffled moaning. William was like, 'What was that?' I secretly smiled and said I didn't have any idea. Shortly afterwards, we composed ourselves, redressed, picked the leaves out of our hair, and headed home. Get this. On the way out of the park, we passed by the jogger—walked right by him. We made eye contact; he said good evening to us in this deep sexy voice and jogged right past us. I instantly felt heat and couldn't wait to get the professor home for round two."

This time, Tonya, Meshell, and myself sat there breathless and speechless. I broke the silence.

"Girl, why didn't you tell us about that sooner? That was wild."

"A lady has to have some secrets to fantasize about to get her through the dry spells," Tracee giggled.

"Sounds like an episode out of a Zane novel. Did you ever go back to the park looking for the stranger? Just out of curiosity?" I asked.

"Hell no! No, I didn't go back out of curiosity. That was all fantasy. I wouldn't want to date or formally meet a man who was a freaking peeping Tom. That dude actually stood there and watched us fuck. I will admit, at that moment he got me off."

"Damn, Tracee, Lexie was simply asking a question. Don't get all excited and bent out of shape. Hell, he may have been a peeping Tom, but you let him watch you get banged. Think about that. We all know you are an exhibitionist. You've told us how you walk around your house buck-naked, with the windows open, for your neighbors to see," Meshell said defensively.

Tracee didn't say anything else. Meshell's words rang too true.

I still hadn't come up with anything that was near freaky in my opinion. Compared to the two stories I had just heard, I was Miss Missionary, beyond straightlaced, the preacher's wife in the bedroom. All of that translated into borrring! Hell, I might as well have Tracee hook me up with the professor. Sounds like we were made for each other. Two peas in a pod. Dull.

I have yet to experience an orgasm, let alone find my G-spot. Maybe God forgot to give me one at birth. Only Meshell was aware that I had never experienced the so-called big O. I was almost thirty years old, but had never been formally introduced. One time I had her try to describe how it felt. I rationalized that maybe I had had one and didn't realize it for what it was. She was like, "If you had had one, you'd know. Believe me, you'd know."

My toes had never curled up, nor had my legs opened involuntarily with a mind of their own. My breathing hadn't accelerated like I was flying solo to the moon nor had I suddenly learned to speak in foreign languages, nor had a sudden desire to pull a grown man inside my body. No, I can't say that I wanted to bow down to a man and worship him because he gave me an explosive orgasm. But man, how I desired to have one.

"Do you want to go next, Lexie?" Tonya asked. "It's just you and Meshell left and we are anxiously awaiting the juicy details."

"No, you go, Meshell. I'm still thinking."

"No problem. Listen, before I even get started, you witches go handle your business. Go grab your snacks or do whatever you need to do before I start my little drama. I'll need your full, undivided attention for this one. Trust me, you'll be hanging on my every word. Those other two stories were mere child's play. I'm about to explain to you how the adults get down."

We looked at each other, glanced back at Meshell, and burst out laughing and high-fiving each other.

"You are so full of it. Tell us how the adults get down . . . Whatever," Tonya said, smiling.

"Yeah, we haven't seen you with a man in so long that I thought you were practicing celibacy," Tracee piped in, laughing.

"Okay, ladies. Everybody got jokes. We'll see who gets the last laugh. You witches have five minutes to handle your business."

"Oh no, she didn't call us witches again," Tonya said in mock indignation as she dashed to the bathroom.

lexie

I glanced at my gold-trimmed clock hanging on the kitchen wall and couldn't believe it was almost four o'clock in the morning. Time always flew by quickly when I hung out with the girls. Suddenly, everybody decided they wanted to change into T-shirts and shorts. After rummaging through my dresser drawers to find something to sleep in, the Crew converged back into the living room. Meshell had moved front and center, like an actress on a stage, to tell her tale. This wasn't *The Vagina Monologues*. Girlfriend had pulled up one of my kitchen chairs and was seriously looking at her watch and back at each one of us.

"I said five minutes, not fifteen, damn it," she said, holding up five fingers.

"Girl, I think you need to put that wineglass down. You ain't no drill sergeant up in here," Tracee said in a joking voice.

"Is everyone comfortable and ready to hear my tale?" Meshell asked, ignoring her.

We nodded our heads and leaned forward in anticipation. We looked a mess in our head scarves and mismatched sleeping attire. We all knew how crazy Meshell could get and wondered what she'd been up to and with whom. Of the Crew, Meshell was probably the most sexually uninhibited of all of us. She spoke freely of her sexcapades. I am the most inhibited, with Tracee and Tonya falling somewhere in between.

"Last year, do y'all remember when I was in DC for that conference?"

"Yeah, I do because it was around your birthday," Tonya interjected.

"Exactly. I was bummed out because I was away from home on my twenty-ninth birthday.

"Ladies, I never told you this because I didn't want you guys to think I was a complete, total slut, but I celebrated my twenty-ninth in grand style."

"Really now? Do tell, darling," Tracee said, with a raised eyebrow and smirk. "Give us all the dirt."

"How did you manage to keep this a secret?" I asked out of curiosity.

"I can be secretive when I want to be. I don't have to share everything with you witches. Damn."

"Well, we are anxiously waiting to hear the juicy, graphic details," said Tonya, barely able to contain her excitement. "Don't leave out anything."

"I was in DC on business, attending this boring-ass conference, pissed that I wouldn't be celebrating with you guys on my birthday—my last year in my twenties. My third day there, I ran into an old friend at a local restaurant. Do y'all remember Charles Bailey from college?"

"Charles? Charles Bailey? You mean that fine Omega that you had a fling with during our junior year?" I asked.

"More like a one-night stand. But, yeah, girl. That's him. Well, he hasn't changed. He's still sexy as ever. He works in DC as a corporate banker. Charles and I exchanged numbers and agreed to hook up during my downtime, which turned out to be few and far between."

With a delayed reaction, Tonya screamed out. "Oh yeah, I remember him now! He was the Que Dog who was screwing every female on campus! He loved popping the cherries on the freshmen girls."

"Yeah, he did have sort of a reputation as being a BHOC," Meshell confessed.

Out of curiosity I asked, "What is a BHOC?"

"It means Big Ho on Campus," Meshell explained, laughing. "Yet, I still wanted to sample the goods. Had heard it was delicious. I wasn't in it for the long run.

"Anyway . . . that Thursday, much to my surprise, the conference came to an end around lunchtime and my flight wasn't due out until early Friday morning. So I quickly called up Charles and asked if he wanted to meet me for lunch or drinks later that night. I informed him it was my birthday, and I didn't want to spend it alone if I didn't have to."

"I bet you didn't," I stated, smiling and looking at her knowingly.

"Lexie, I'm never going to finish if y'all keep interrupting me."

"Okay, sorry. Go on."

"Well, Charles couldn't meet me for lunch because he had a big meeting or something, but he agreed to meet for drinks and dinner. He was going to pick me up at my hotel at seven o'clock and take me somewhere nice. I spent the remainder of my day pampering myself. Hell, I deserved it. I found this chic hair salon, got my hair hooked up, had a relaxing manicure and pedicure, and then went shopping and purchased this gorgeous outfit. I arrived back at the hotel in time to take a nice, restful nap and a long, hot bath. When Charles knocked on my hotel door promptly at seven, I knew my efforts had paid off. I instantly saw that lustful, 'I want to screw you' look in his eyes.

"Dinner was delicious. We talked, laughed, laughed some more, and had an all-around good time. Charles caught me up on what some of our former classmates were doing. Come to find out, several were living and working in the DC/Maryland area. By the time dinner and dessert were over, it was obvious that there was still a strong sexual attraction between us. Throughout dinner, we had flirted shamelessly with one another. At one point, I took off my shoe and rubbed my foot across the merchandise, under the table. Asked him if the merchandise had grown and improved with age. Charles even remembered a sexual fantasy I had told him about in college; he asked if I had ever fulfilled it. I had forgotten that we had a few deep conversations back then because as much of a ho as he was, Charles was very intelligent and compassionate. He wasn't simply a ho. He was an intelligent ho.

"After paying the check and leaving a generous tip, Charles was honest with me. No bullshit. I liked that, appreciated it even. Hell, I'm almost thirty years old and tired of the dating games. He confided that he wanted to celebrate my birthday with me by making love to me. Charles said that he wasn't going to lie, he had a girlfriend, and he'd understand if I didn't want to sleep with him.

"I knew Charles was running game, but ladies, I was selfish. I didn't care, I didn't want to be alone on my birthday, and I wanted to sample the goods one final time. As I recalled, he definitely knew his way around the bedroom. To hell with his girlfriend—as long as he didn't have a wedding band on his finger, he and his dick were legally free in these United States of America. As I made my way to the restroom, I saw Charles pull out his cell phone and make a call. I figured he was checking in with the girlfriend and lying about his whereabouts for the remainder of the night. A few minutes later, as we walked arm in arm out the door to his car, Charles informed me that he had a big surprise in store for me. Of course, nosy me asked what it was and why he didn't bring it to the restaurant. He smiled secretively and told me to be patient, that I'd find out soon enough."

"Damn, why do y'all get the surprises?" Tracee asked, without expecting an answer. I glanced over at her and she was seriously pouting.

"The drive back to my hotel was stimulating. Charles couldn't keep his hands off me. He kept touching my knee or cheek or hair. At one point, he had placed his hand in between my thighs. By the time he parked the car, Charles and I were holding hands. We were like two pieces of dynamite ready to ignite. In the elevator up to my room, we exchanged heated kisses in anticipation of things yet to come. I was already heated and flushed. I could barely contain myself. As he kissed my neck, my breasts were straining to be released from my bra.

"Once I'd opened the door with my scan card, we didn't waste any time. We knew what time it was. Charles and I were all over each other before we barely set foot in the room. We had just got into it, when there was a firm knock at the door. Then another. I looked at Charles and told him that I had no idea who that could be because I hadn't ordered room service. As he proceeded to walk over and open my door, he looked at me with this big grin on his face.

"As I was attempting to rebutton my blouse and wondering what the fuck was wrong with Charles, opening my hotel door, this god walked into my room with a dozen long-stemmed red roses. He said, 'Happy birthday, Meshell.' And then he strolled my way and leaned down and kissed me on the cheek. I just stood there with my mouth wide open. The man was simply gorgeous. He had muscles in all the right places, beautiful eyes, a sensual mouth, strong, lean hands and fingers, the smoothest, darkest chocolate skin, and a Crest smile.

"Charles finally identified him as his friend KeVon. Then KeVon said, 'I have another gift for you.' I murmured, 'What?' He didn't say another word. He simply grabbed my arms, gently, and led me over to the bed, got down on his knees, massaged my legs up to my thighs, and then proceeded to pull up my skirt, around my waist. I was almost speechless, for once.

"Knocking his hand away, I asked him, 'What are you doing? Stop!'

"KeVon responded, 'I—we—want to make you feel good on your birthday. That's all. I'm not going to hurt you, just love you.'

"As Charles stood there watching, KeVon proceeded to pull my panties down to my ankles and then off. He opened my legs wide and played with my pussy for a while. Man, he had me open for the whole world to see as he manually stimulated me and sucked on my clit. Charles, not wanting to be outdone, walked over and started to unbutton my blouse. He threw it on the bed, and sucked on my nipple as he squeezed and caressed my other breast. I didn't know what to do. There I was, hemmed up by two gorgeous men who were doing wonderful things to my body. I was in disbelief. I thought I had died and gone to heaven.

"Without missing a single beat, Charles disrobed himself, with his eyes never leaving mine, while KeVon went down on me and ate me like I was a gourmet meal, savoring every morsel. The man's tongue was stroking me like an expensive violin, while the rhythm of his finger, then fingers, left me moaning and begging for him not to stop. As he opened me up to get a better view of my clit, Charles came over and took over at the helm. He started sucking and squeezing my clit so deliciously. I was actually crying, it felt so good. Words couldn't describe it.

"KeVon undressed quickly and I finally got to view that spectacular body. Kid you not, the man looked like one of those Greek gods we see in glossy magazines and history books. He looked like he had been double-dipped in Nestlé's chocolate. He brought those thick lips over, pulled my head back, and proceeded to kiss me and stroke my neck. Mind you, Charles was still feasting like he was having his last supper. When my legs started trembling uncontrollably, I knew I didn't have long before I let go. Charles rose up, licked his lips, and kissed me. Just to push me over the edge, KeVon reached down and stroked my breasts with one hand and inserted his fingers inside me with the other. That took me over the top. I came like a gusher.

"It wasn't over yet. After I had calmed down a little, KeVon lifted me up and pushed me down on all fours and fingered me some more and then put all ten-plus inches of himself inside me with one thrust and started pumping away. The entire time, the two of them were talking to me. Saying all sorts of dirty shit. Charles spanked my ass a few times and said, 'Oh yeah, man, she likes this shit. Give it to her. Harder. She likes it harder.' I was moaning so hard and breathing frantically, trying to hold on to the spread while KeVon went to town on my ass. He was pumping in and out and making me moan so savagely that I didn't realize it was even me. I heard him say, 'Man, put something in her mouth. Shut her up.'

"Next thing I knew, Charles had his tool in my mouth, pumping it in and out, holding the back of my head while he tweaked my nipples. Y'all, by then, I didn't even know where I was or what my name was. It was amazing. I've never experienced that much pure pleasure in my life. I didn't know if I was coming or going. I felt like I was a hot, bubbling volcano ready to blow my top. This time I came at the exact moment Charles came and pulled out, and I collapsed on the bed.

"I remember us resting, with me sandwiched between them throughout the night. I lost track of how many times we went at it, with each time taking me to a higher plateau. I don't care if you call me a slut or whore. I had the time of my life, ladies.

"This one time, Charles did me slow and easy while KeVon watched and got off by himself on the other side of the room. The entire time KeVon was coaxing me in this calm, sexy voice to climax. I came so many times that it started to hurt. I think we finally fell asleep in the wee hours of the morning. Totally exhausted. Charles was still inside me and KeVon suckled my breasts. The next morning, I slept through my wake-up call, but woke up just in the knick of time to shower and dress. I was exhausted but very satisfied. I'm glad I hadn't scheduled a very early flight back to Atlanta because I wouldn't have made it. Charles and KeVon were gone, their spots were cold, but there was a note propped up on the pillow. It simply read: *Hope you enjoyed your birthday present. Next time you're in DC, give us a call. Charles and KeVon.*"

With a smile on her face, Meshell looked around triumphantly.

We were fanning ourselves uncontrollably and crossing and uncrossing our legs. I know I felt a few sensations down there.

"Amazing," was all I could muster.

"You big slut," Tracee said jokingly, grinning. "You nasty diva."

"I wanna tag along the next time you go to DC," Tonya chimed in.

"Well, didn't I tell you witches that I had the story of all stories?" Meshell asked, pleased with herself.

"Was that really true?" I asked.

"Hell yeah! They got me off that night. Several times. Girl, I'm thinking about taking them up on their offer. Real soon."

For a few minutes, we were lost in our individual thoughts. I guess we were trying to imagine ourselves being satisfied by not one, but two gorgeous men. Things only happened like that for Meshell. I couldn't get one man. She approached sex the way men did. Sometimes I think Meshell thought with her invisible pair of balls.

"We still have one more story to go. Lexie hasn't gone yet," Meshell said, breaking our reflection. They turned to stare at me.

I shifted uncomfortably. "Ladies, unfortunately I don't have anything quite as exciting and provocative as you guys to share. I live a boring life compared to y'all. Remember, I'm the product of preachers."

"Diva, don't say that. I know you've done something that's considered freaky. I don't care what women say, at some point, we've all lost our inhibitions, stopped being the good girl, and crossed the line. Afterwards, you can blame it on the alcohol or whatever, but there is always that *one* man (or two men) who makes us lose our damn mind and do things we would never, ever admit to anyone that we'd done," Tonya volunteered.

I shrugged my shoulders.

"I love having a man going down on me. I don't know how to describe it. It totally gets me off to see him down there rubbing his nose and face in it and slurping me up. Tracee gets off being an exhibitionist; she likes to screw in public. It turns her on to have other people watching her; it makes her hot. Now, Meshell is straight buck wild. She gets off being handled by two men; one isn't enough for her. Because we are professionals by day and freaks by night, that doesn't make it wrong," Tonya said, on a full roll. "You can be an intelligent woman and still enjoy sex. One does not cancel out the other."

Pushing a lock of hair out of her face, Tracee continued. "Preach, sistah. Black women are some of the most inhibited women on the face of this planet. We have been so brainwashed by what *they* tell us, what they think of us, and the labels they place on us. Back in the day, white men thought we were sex-crazed and promiscuous. Huh, some still do. That label made it easier for white men to rationalize raping us anytime they pleased. They claimed we thought about sex all the time and lived to fuck like wild animals. I can only imagine some of the heinous acts our female ancestors must have endured on a day-to-day basis. On the other hand, our grandmothers and mothers have brainwashed us into thinking that sex and our bodies are dirty and we shouldn't touch or please ourselves. They want us to believe that sex is nasty and cheap, and only bad girls open their legs and actually enjoy it." Tracee, the college professor, was in full lecture mode.

"It all boils down to the fact that we need to free our minds so that we can emancipate our bodies. When we do that we won't have to worry about losing our men to other ethnic groups because their women will suck dick or take it in the butt or swallow when we won't," Meshell said.

After the tirade quieted down, they looked at me again. Silently, prompting me to share.

"Okay, like I said before, I'm pretty conservative compared to you guys. So don't laugh because I could only think of one daring thing. Daring for me, anyway."

"Girl, be for real. We won't laugh at you," Tracee said, seriously. "We are all adults. What is spoken here, stays here."

As they prepared for my scenario, they leaned forward and filled their glasses with the last drops of wine. The candles were all but burnt out and the sun would soon be making an appearance over the horizon. There was a calm and stillness to the early morning hours, a peace that could only be found at the end of a day and the glimpse of new beginnings. The perfect time for shared secrets and whispered misdeeds.

I hesitantly started. "When I was dating Joseph, something strange occurred."

They knew that Joseph, or Joe, as he preferred to be called, is a fellow psychologist that I dated for over two years. I thought he was the one for me, but things didn't work out between us. Basically, Joe found someone else, dumped me, got married to this waitress—yes, a waitress—and broke my heart. And that's all I'm going to say about that.

"One night, after returning from his parents' thirty-fifth wedding anniversary party, we decided to try something different in bed. Like me, Joe was considered pretty conservative. Doing it doggy-style was pretty daring for us. I don't know what Joe had been watching or reading or who he had been talking to, but he decided that he wanted to try anal sex."

I heard an intake of breath from each member of the Crew.

"Maybe I'd had too many glasses of wine earlier because I don't know what I was thinking or what got into me. Normally, I never would have considered such a disgusting act. But for whatever reason, I gave in that night and agreed. I drank another glass of wine to build up my courage. Joe put on some romantic music, lit some candles, and proceeded to get me in the mood. I didn't have any K-Y Jelly, so we improvised and used Vaseline. What a mistake! Joe scooped up a handful of the stuff and smeared it all over and inside my butt cheeks. Neither one of us knew what we were doing, so I have no idea why I trusted the man."

I took a big gulp of wine for the courage needed to continue my tale. In looking at my friends' expressions, I couldn't tell what they were thinking. Tonya wouldn't make eye contact with me.

"To make an ugly story short, after situating me in the proper po-sition, Joe proceeded to enter me. At first everything was okay, there was a bit of pressure, that was expected, and I was uncomfortable. After all, I was still a virgin back there. Joe was proceeding very slowly and being extra patient and considerate. However, I could feel Joe growing larger as he got more and more excited. By now, maybe two inches of him was inside me. Just to get that much had taken forever, and I wasn't sure if I was ready to accommodate more. In the next few seconds, a high-pitched scream escaped me.

"The remainder of my story is a little fuzzy. I can only speculate on what got into the man. I don't know if he got overly excited, but all of a sudden, he tried to cram the rest of his dick inside me. The pain had a delayed reaction, so Joe probably got another half or one more inch in before it, the unbearable pain, hit me. It hit me hard. I started screaming at the top of my lungs. My neighbors probably thought I was being murdered. I was crying big dinosaur tears. I started moving around on the bed, clawing at my sheets, trying to reach behind me to slap the shit out of Joe. The entire time I was screaming for him to 'take it out, Lord, make him take it out!' I'm yelling, 'You're killing me! Take it out!' and poor Joe didn't know what to do. For a minute, it got stuck inside me and the agony was indescribable. I nearly passed out. Circles and dots were spinning around in front of my eyes.

"Joe finally pulled it out, and I instantly collapsed facedown onto the bed, still crying. Joe simply dressed and walked out the door, with-out a word. After that episode, he didn't speak to me for a week, maybe two. So . . . so much for trying out new, freaky things."

When I finished, I turned and glanced at each lady in turn. I still hadn't gauged a reaction. Meshell, Tonya, and Tracee had blank, un-readable expressions on their faces. They were just staring back at me and then . . . they all burst out laughing so hard that Tracee started cry-ing. Tears were spilling down her cheeks, and Meshell spit her wine out. Tonya almost choked on a grape and I had to hit her back two times before she caught her breath. They thought it was so funny; I didn't think so. Ha, ha, ha, joke was on me. I got up to walk away, to go to my bedroom.

"Wait, wait, Lexie. We are not laughing at you; we're laughing at the situation. You've got to admit that just picturing the two of you is funny. I can see poor Joe now, trying to pull out while you are screaming like a banshee." Meshell howled between words.

A few seconds later, I had to admit it was actually pretty funny. At the time it wasn't, but yes, now it was hilarious. I joined in the laughter. Every time it settled down, we'd start up again. With our sides hurting, we finally calmed down. An hour later, we were knocked out on the floor and sofas, overcome with sleep, as, unbeknownst to us, the sun crested over the horizon. Another successful Ladies' Night Out was over.

lexie

That was almost a month ago. In fact, it's almost time for another Ladies' Night Out. Yet, it didn't end that night for me. Not by a long shot. That next week, the more I replayed that night and the stories I had heard, over and over in my head, the more I realized how sheltered I had been in my life. I am a "goody two-shoes," always trying to do the right thing and be the right person. But for whom? And why? Two words: my parents.

Even in high school, I never lied, never cheated, never cursed. Always hung with the right crowd, dated the right boys, spoke proper English, never slang, dressed the right way, said and did what my teachers wanted to hear and see. Kept my legs tightly closed and didn't give up my virginity until college, at the ripe old age of twenty. Even then, I thought I was in love, so it wasn't like I was just giving it away. I thought he was the one for me, the man I'd spend the rest of my life with. Ha! That illusion quickly vanished once he got in the panties.

I realize there is nothing wrong with my life and my choices. Others envy me, but sometimes I want to grab life by the tail and fully experience it, taste it, savor it, and not worry about what other people are saying or thinking about me. Most of the time, people are too scared to take chances themselves and are jealous that you are. For once, I want to truly embrace life and not play it safe . . . Is that so wrong?

I am almost thirty years old and have never experienced an orgasm, couldn't find my G-spot for a million dollars, and have never done anything considered anywhere near freaky. I don't do thugs, roughnecks, bad boys, scrubs, or whatever you want to call them. Don't give them a second glance; they are too dangerous and too unpredictable for my taste. They don't follow rules. I do. Yet, in my fantasies I've imagined what it must be like to be with one.

To put it mildly, I have never gone out of my element or safety zone. Never tried anything crazy or remotely considered stupid or unladylike. Never ventured off course and just lost complete, utter, undeniable control. The mere thought of relinquishing my power scares me beyond explanation. I never let go, just feel, and go with the flow. That's not in my calibrated formula for living. That's too liberating.

I know my world isn't going to come to an abrupt end, but as crazy as it sounds, I feel like I have missed out on something very vital and essential to living my life to the fullest. That scares me.

Sure, I am highly successful in my profession; I'm very proud of that. I love my job and I'm very passionate about what I do. I believe in people. I listen, analyze, and try to help my patients resolve their problems and situations each and every day. My patients look to me for guidance, advice, and the truth concerning their interpersonal relationships and emotional well-being. I go beyond the call of duty to seek out ways to make them better. I want them to live emotionally healthy and fulfilling lives. My colleagues respect me for my professionalism, expertise, and dedication to our chosen field. I give it my all and realize that I'm in the right field of work because it is very satisfying and uplifting. Many can't say that.

Yet, again, on a personal level, I feel that I'm missing out on something. Work isn't everything. It isn't the be-all and end-all. Hell yeah, work pays the bills, but at the end of the day, when all is said and done, I deserve to be happy and fulfilled on a personal level as well.

After carefully weighing the pros and cons, I made the decision to rectify my situation. I set out to do just that, the same way I attack all other problems: headfirst. With research, questions and answers, and an action plan. My deadline is thirty days. Due to the very delicate nature of my task, I decided to keep the details to myself. Translation: the Crew wouldn't know what I was up to; they'd be left out in the cold, even Meshell. Who could say? Maybe at some point down the line, I'd let them know at one of our infamous Ladies' Nights Out. Wouldn't they be surprised? So, like all other things that I do, I dove into this mission with both feet running and a take-no-prisoners attitude.

Here it is almost a month after the last Ladies' Night Out. I'm sitting in the parking garage of a hotel on the other side of town from where I live, scared and excited all at the same time. Too afraid to get out of my car, with my box of thin, extra-sensitive condoms, and knock on the door of room number 457, and then have sex with a complete stranger whose last name I don't even know. No strings attached. When it's over, it's over. I will never speak to or see him again. Ever. Those are my rules and conditions.

I met him over the Internet, on a discussion board, of all places. It's amazing how many of those sites exist on the Internet. The Internet really is the information superhighway. Yet, the thought of going upstairs, meeting this man and letting him touch me in intimate places excites me. How did I get to this point? Have I lost my mind? How can a rational, educated person like myself find herself in this volatile situation? It's a long story. So, let me explain myself. Maybe in the process I'll get my nerve up, because my secret lover is waiting. Waiting to take me to ecstasy.

———

After making the final decision to bring a little excitement into my otherwise dull life, I wholeheartedly started my research. I attacked this self-assigned mission as if it were a full-time job search. I surfed the Net at my desk, between appointments—even took copious notes. Man, I found all sorts of interesting sex sites, from straight-out porn to photos, chat rooms, even advice columns. I never realized just how much information was right at my fingertips. With two clicks of my mouse, I was in a totally new and different world from anything I had ever known. These people embraced sex like it was a religion. They believed in self-gratification and nothing was too far beneath them.

After I surfed into these new waters, there was this one particular Web site that caught my attention. It was an African American Web site called Freaksrus.com. I know, the name says it all. It was the type of site where you could write about your sexual adventures or mis-adventures, whichever the case may be, ask for sexual advice, order toys, and even read erotic stories by some excellent undiscovered writers. There wasn't really a moderator, so it was pretty much an anything-goes sort of experience. It was wild and untamed. Free and liberating.

I started reading some of the stories, questions, and situations. Who were these people? Smartchick. Heatedpassion25. Sexcee. Curvygal. Choc. They were totally off the wall. No inhibitions here. A lot of people, young and old, all across the world were doing some pretty freaky stuff at home, work, and play. Who knew?

I scanned some of the advice that participants were giving. Questions ranged widely: *Does it matter how long his dick is? How do I give good head? I'm having erotic dreams about a woman and I'm a woman—does that make me a lesbian? I enjoy anal sex—does that mean I'm a freak? Should I tell my best friend that I slept with her man, two times?* To my surprise, some of the advice was actually on point and intelligent. After a few days of checking out the discussion board, getting a feel for it, I saw some of the same names posting entries and responses day after day. Evidently, the site had its regulars. Some were real dimestore psychologists who got into dishing out advice; you could tell from the length of their responses.

After days of being an invisible spectator and reading the different entries and responses, I decided to post a question to the site. Even though I'd use an anonymous e-mail name, Mysterywoman, I was still rather nervous. Of course, no one would know me, but I felt vulnerable nonetheless. I finally coughed up the nerve to post my first question. It simply read:

```
E-mail: mysterywoman@msn.com

Message: Hello, everyone. I'm new to the discus-
sion board, and I need your help, guidance, and
advice. What do you think of a woman who has never
experienced an orgasm at almost thirty years old?
I yearn to experience one, but my body doesn't
seem to be willing and able. Help!
Desperately seeking answers!
```

Within thirty minutes, I had received over a dozen responses to my post. Some of the replies were hilarious. I received several straight-out propositions to remedy my situation. Two posts in particular stood out. The first read:

```
E-mail: sexyblackwoman@yahoo.com

Message: Sistafriend. I feel for you. Almost 30
years old and not one time. Not once? Damn. You
don't realize what you are missing. Maybe you
need to learn your body. Masturbate. Learn what
feels good to you. Check into a hotel and spend
the weekend, undisturbed, discovering your body.
Touch, taste, enjoy. Explore. Use a hand mirror
to check yourself out. Our pussies are beauti-
ful. If you learn what turns you on, then you can
guide and teach your lover. I wish you well. Good
luck!
```

Another one read:

E-mail: bigblackd@comcast.net

Message: Baby girl, you just haven't met the
right man. Fuck all that "explore your body" psychobabble. No disrespect, Sexyblackwoman, but if
her man is doing his job, and hitting it right,
Mysterywoman would be getting hers.
    Mysterywoman, you need to find yourself a real
man who knows what he's doing, has the right flow.
Baby girl, with the right combination of fingers,
hands, and mouth, you'll come. Believe me, you'll
come. I could have you squirting like Old Faithful. Guaranteed (LOL).

I excitedly read both posts again and checked out the others. I
didn't realize I'd receive responses so quickly. This was addictive. Time
flew by. I could hardly wait until my next scheduled patient was gone
so that I could get back to my computer. What Sexyblackwoman said
made perfect sense. And I intended to take her suggestion, because the
more I thought about it, the more I realized that I really didn't know
what turned me on. I couldn't say if I would go to the extreme and
check into a hotel. My apartment was sufficient. However, there was
something about Bigblackd's e-mail that captivated me. He was totally
different from the men I usually dealt with. I had chill bumps up and
down my arms. He came across as very confident in his skills and abilities; I wanted to hear more. So I posted two more quick messages.

E-mail: mysterywoman@msn.com

Message: Sexyblackwoman, thanks for the advice!
One weekend I'm going to try your suggestion.
I'll let you know what happens.

E-mail: mysterywoman@msn.com

Message: Hey, Bigblackd. So, it's that simple? I
just haven't met the right man who can take me
there. That's all it takes? A good flow and hitting it right? Are your skills really that good
or are you all words and no action?

Again, within five to ten minutes another response awaited me.

E-mail: bigblackd@comcast.net

Message: Baby girl, I have many satisfied "customers" who can verify that I come correct. No
doubt. If you're in my bed, you leave VERY satisfied. I haven't had any complaints yet. I love
'em and leave 'em with a big smile on their face.
In fact, I can guarantee you an orgasm. My tongue
on your clit, two fingers against your G-spot,
baby girl, I got you . . . got you creaming, back
arched and calling out my name. That's money in
the bank (LOL).
    I repeat, you just haven't been with a real
man before. You've been dealing with amateurs.

This message board thing was fun. I couldn't believe how easy it
was for me to flirt back and forth with Bigblackd. And you best believe, I was flirting. He didn't know me and I didn't know him. That
made it all the more delicious and exciting. I could say anything and be
anyone I wanted to. For all I knew, Bigblackd looked like he was run
over by an ice cream truck two times . . . yet . . . I was getting tingly
from just his comments.

E-mail: mysterywoman@msn.com

Message: Bigblackd, I love a confident, cocky man!
However, hypothetically speaking, I think I'd be
a challenge. It just doesn't work that way with
me. My body refuses to react. I get right there,
I can almost feel it coming on, and then . . .
nothing. Absolutely nothing. Nada. It's like I
get to the peak of the roller coaster, and then I
coast back down in the opposite direction.
    Even you can't perform miracles!

E-mail: bigblackd@comcast.net

Message: Baby girl, see, there you are wrong. Hypothetically speaking, I'd have you having multior-

gasms for me. One on top of the other. You'd be
begging me to stop. Your body hasn't been handled
properly. See, you're hanging with the knuckle-
heads who don't understand the anatomy of a woman's internal workings. I'd have you humming to
my touch and begging for more. Yeah, baby girl,
my women beg me for more.

See, you're probably used to those conservative types who don't know what the fuck they
doing because they're used to jacking off over
the thought of their next big business deal. But
baby girl, I'm real. I'm all man. I know how to
please a woman. I come correct. I break it down.
You like it rough, no problem. You like it smooth,
not a problem. You like me to spank that ass,
not . . . a . . . problem!

E-mail: sexyblackwoman@yahoo.com

Message: Mysterywoman, you need to jump on that
because Bigblackd has my panties wet down here in
Florida. If you don't, I may have to check him
out (LOL). And I'm married with four children and
two dogs.

I was beginning to learn that some of these participants did actually
hook up and do the do. They were all into instant gratification, not
relationships. This was foreign soil for me. My parents raised me to
believe that being sexually promiscuous was morally wrong.

E-mail: mysterywoman@msn.com

Message: Sexyblackwoman, thanks but no thanks.
Bigblackd and I are just dialoguing. I wouldn't
think of hooking up with him in person.

E-mail: sexyblackwoman@yahoo.com

Message: Girl, what are we going to do with you?
That's why you can't have the big O. You're too uptight, bent out of shape about everything. I'm not
asking you to marry the man, just fuck him. Chill.

E-mail: mysterywoman@msn.com

Message: Bigblackd, you are something else. What
does the D stand for? Why you dogging the professional men? Huh? Smooth, rough . . . you can be
whatever I want you to be. I'm sure you've had
your failures in the bedroom.

E-mail: bigblackd@comcast.net

Message: Now, Mysterywoman, I know you aren't
that naive that you can't figure out what my name
stands for. BIG BLACK DICK, baby! Oh, I get it.
You one of those sistahs who like your man to
talk dirty to you. You wanted to hear me say it,
baby girl (LOL)? I'd love to show it to you too.
You wouldn't be disappointed, just impressed or
maybe scared.
    Baby girl, evidently you weren't listening
closely. I don't have failures. I come correct. 100% of the time. Now, I can talk all day,
but like you said, actions speak louder than
words. Enough said. You read between the lines
(LMAO).
    As for the professional men, nah, I'm not
dogging them. I don't hate. I just call it as
I see it. I'm blue-collar, baby. Working class.
I work hard for every penny I earn. My finger-
nails get dirty and my hands aren't soft to the
touch. Now you, you come across as one of those
high-maintenance chicks that want to be pampered
and treated like a lady, but flat-out fucked in
the bedroom. And your $100,000-a-year men aren't
doing it for you. Am I right? Am I close?

E-mail: mysterywoman@msn.com

Message: Why all the judgment? You don't know me
like that. Yeah, I'm a professional woman, but I
work hard for my money too. And I'm not about to
throw all white-collar men into a category just
because I haven't been with one who got me off.
And there is nothing wrong with being pampered
and taking good care of yourself.

E-mail: bigblackd@comcast.net

Message: I'm not judging you, baby girl. It's just that I've seen women like you all my life. Nose stuck so far up in the air that if a good rainstorm came along, you'd drown. You don't even glance twice at brothers like me. Or if you do, it's when we are dicking you down behind closed doors. Always behind closed doors. And then you come onto these kinds of sites, wanting to get your groove on. Yeah, you have it all, the money, the clothes, the power, but you just can't get your pussy stroked right (LOL).

E-mail: mysterywoman@msn.com

Message: Behind all the macho words, you sound like you've been hurt! Don't take it out on me because I remind you of her. I'm sorry you couldn't or wouldn't live up to her expectations. She hurt you, not me! Typical transference of emotions.

E-mail: bigblackd@comcast.net

Message: Baby, you don't know what the hell you're talking about. You can hide behind this discussion board with your twenty-five-cent shrink mentality when in reality you are scared of me. Scared to death of me and what I have in my pants. Afraid of how I could make you lose control of that confined world you live in. Have you pulling the sheets and saying words that have never entered your Webster's Collegiate Dictionary vocabulary. You hate that, don't you, losing control? I bet you've never had a man talk dirty to you while he's fucking you from behind, while you are down on all fours. I mean say filthy, dirty shit to you. Bet you've never even had a man eat you while you sat on his face, and he gripped your thighs and ass so hard that it hurt. Yeah, you'd be scared shitless of a man like me. I'm like your worse nightmare and deepest desire combined.

E-mail: mysterywoman@msn.com

Message: Man, YOU DON'T KNOW ME! I repeat, you
don't know me and I'm definitely not afraid of
you. What is there to be afraid of? Having sexual
prowess doesn't make you a man! That's one hundred percent BS.
    Being a man is about so much more!

Email: bigblackd@comcast.net

Message: And you still haven't gotten off. So
we're back to square one. Mysterywoman, maybe you
aren't afraid of me. Hell, I don't know. I don't
care. Like you said, actions speak louder than
words. I know what I'm capable of. Unfortunately,
you are too inhibited, too uptight, too fickle,
and too narrow-minded to even realize a fourth of
what you are capable of sexually. In the words of
an erotica author, "free your mind," boo. I'm sick
of this back-and-forth sparring we are doing. If
you wanna talk further, woman to man, hit me up
off-line. I'm out of here. Peace.

Damn! I was shocked and pissed off. Bigblackd dismissed me. Just
like that. If I didn't have a patient in ten minutes, I would have given
him a piece of my mind. How dare he dismiss me? Who did he think
he was?

With Bigblackd still on my mind, I proceeded to ready myself for
my next patient, Mrs. Rogers. I had been working with this middle-
aged woman for over a year now. She was trying to recover from the
damage, both emotional and physical, that was placed on her from a
long-term abusive relationship. My patient had very little to zero self-
esteem and seemed to have a pattern of attracting very controlling,
possessive, and violent men into her life. Her father was an abusive man
and she grew up watching her mom being terrorized by him day after
day. Eventually her dad killed her mom and she was placed in foster
care. Her adult life had been a cycle of living out her mom and dad's

past mistakes. Huh, my life had been a cycle of living for my mom and dad. Always the good daughter.

After having a fruitful session with Mrs. Rogers and walking her to my office door, I reclined behind my desk, closed my eyes for a few seconds, and massaged my forehead. My sessions with her were sometimes taxing and always made me realize how much of ourselves we as women handed over to our men on silver platters. It's like we are saying: *I just want to be loved. Do whatever you want to me—cheat on me, spit on me, bring me down, stomp me into the ground—but never stop loving me. I need you in order for me to be someone. You complete me.* Sad. I've always said that a man doesn't do more than a woman will allow him to. I tell my sixteen-year-old niece that all the time because . . . it's true.

Starting to eat a late lunch at my desk, I decided, to e-mail Bigblackd again. I had weighed my pros and cons and decided, what could I possibly lose? He didn't know me, didn't even know what city or state I resided in. And I had control over my e-mails to him. I could stop e-mailing in the blink of an eye, take him off my e-mail list, block him, and be none the worse off. There was something about Bigblackd that was fascinating and raw and dangerous. It was obvious that he was a roughneck with a serious chip on his shoulder. This would be like an experiment. I could study and analyze him from a safe distance. Maybe he could teach me a thing or two in the process about letting go of my inhibitions.

Before I lost my nerve, I quickly typed off an e-mail to him. This time, I e-mailed him directly and didn't go through the Freaksrus site.

E-mail: mysterywoman@msn.com

Message: Hello, Bigblackd. I guess you are surprised to hear from me. I'm sure you thought I was too scared to e-mail you off-line. I hope this teaches you a lesson: you should never judge a book by its cover (LOL).
    If it's worth anything, some of the things you

said in your last e-mail were true. Other comments were so wrong. I am hesitant about taking
chances; that I will give you. That's just the way
I was brought up by my parents. Now as an adult, I
find it hard to break away from what I was taught.
I'm trying. Hard.

I nibbled and munched on my turkey on wheat sandwich, chips, apple, and drank my bottled water as I anxiously monitored my desktop to announce that I had new mail. I didn't have to wait long. Within fifteen minutes, I heard the beep that indicated I had a new message awaiting me. After excitedly clicking into my message box, I saw his name in bold letters. I smiled. His message was an apology of sorts:

E-mail: bigblackd@comcast.net

Message: What's up, Mysterywoman? Yeah, you have
more balls than I thought. Seriously, I was hoping you would e-mail me off-line. I like chatting
with you. You're refreshing. It's obvious that you
are intelligent. Some of those other posts come
across as straight-out elementary school. Straight
chickenheads. I think some of the participants are
simply young girls who don't know any better or
weren't taught any different. You challenge me.
    Where do you live? Tell me something about
yourself.

E-mail: mysterywoman@msn.com

Message: Why do you care where I live? Let's just
keep it like on the discussion board. Okay? It
was working before. I really don't want to get too
personal. We can talk about whatever, but I don't
want to bring personal info into the mix. Are you
cool with that?

E-mail: bigblackd@comcast.net

Message: Cool! Not a problem. If that's how you
want to roll, I aim to please. You really are a

mystery woman. Just so you know, because I have nothing to hide, I live in New York City and I'm 32. I don't think you can find me and stalk me on that bit of info (LOL).

So, you got a man? Looking for one? Talk to me. What brought you onto the discussion board? Everybody's looking for something.

E-mail: mysterywoman@msn.com

Message: No, I don't have a man and I'm not looking for one. Every woman in the world is not searching for a man.

I surfed into the discussion board for answers and out of curiosity. And by the way, I'm not a stalker.

E-mail: bigblackd@comcast.net

Message: Neither am I (a stalker). Why do you take everything I say in a negative manner? It's been my experience that everyone needs and wants someone to share his or her life with. I know I do.

What answers are you searching for?

E-mail: mysterywoman@msn.com

Message: Sorry, I didn't mean to come across so hostile. I guess I've been too busy with my professional life to focus on my personal life. My personal life has taken a back seat on the bus. I don't have time for love. As for my search, I'm searching for the answer to my little problem, the one I mentioned on the discussion board.

So, do you have a girlfriend?

E-mail: bigblackd@comcast.net

Message: Now who's being too personal? Yeah, I have a woman. I care for her. I don't know if I love her. I share parts of my life with her. I'm in her bed whenever I please. So I guess

that classifies her as my woman. My main woman
anyway.
    As for your search, I got your problem solved.

E-mail: mysterywoman@msn.com

Message: Your main woman? In her bed whenever you
please? Aren't we the arrogant one?
    Aren't you about ready to settle down at 32
and stop chasing skirts?

E-mail: bigblackd@comcast.net

Message: Are you the defender of women or something and what's with the fifty questions? There
is something you have to learn about women, about
your kind. I'm going to tell you a secret: *As long
as I'm dicking her down and got "good dick," I can
pretty much come and go as I please. My lady is
no fool; she's knows I'm out there messing with
other women. As long as I do for her, treat her
good, be discreet, don't bring trouble her way,
and continue to break her off some, all is fine
in paradise.* Don't get it twisted.
    As for 32 and unmarried, I'd rather sow my
wild oats now and then settle down later and be
faithful as opposed to cheating on my wife.
    You're almost 30 and not married. I assume no
children. What's your problem? Aren't you getting
close to being classified as an old maid? Isn't
that biological clock closing in on you? Tick.
Tick. Tick. LOL.

E-mail: mysterywoman@msn.com

Message: Oh, you got jokes today. No, I'm not the
defender of women and I'm just trying to understand and get to know you better.
    You think you got all the answers. Some women
aren't as desperate as you think we are. Personally, I wouldn't put up with you running around
on me, good dick or not.
    Like you, I choose to be unmarried. I'm not
going to rush into something with the wrong man

and be divorced, disillusioned, and bitter at
32.

E-mail: bigblackd@comcast.net

Message: Like I said, you got balls, girl. You
wouldn't put up with me running around on you.
Keep thinking that. Yes, you would. If I was
treating you like a queen and serving you up
right . . . yes . . . you . . . would.

E-mail: mysterywoman@msn.com

Message: YEAH, WHATEVER! Keep thinking that. If
you were treating me like a queen, you wouldn't
be running around on me.

Bigblackd and I talked, via e-mail, for the duration of my lunch
hour. He had me laughing, thinking about and debating him on various issues and getting pissed off on others. I learned even more about
him because he wasn't shy about giving up information on himself. He
claimed he had nothing to hide. However, I realized he could very well
be feeding me a bunch of lies and telling me what he felt I wanted to
hear. How would I know? It wasn't like I had hired a detective to check
him out. You could be whoever you wanted to be over the Internet.
For all I knew, *he* could be a *she*.

According to him, he was five-eleven, medium to muscular build,
dark brown skin with a goatee, green to grayish eyes, and a low-cut
fade. Oh, and let's not forget the tattoo on his upper arm. He had lived
in New York City, Brooklyn to be exact, his entire life. Never been
married, had a ten-year-old son by the "bitch from hell" (his words),
and he was employed as a fireman. One of New York's bravest. His final
e-mail of the day read:

E-mail: bigblackd@comcast.net

Message: Mysterywoman. Hell, I'm tired of typing Mysterywoman over and over. I'm going to call

you Mystery. Yeah, Mystery sounds cool. I haven't
forgotten your little problem (LOL). What are we
going to do about it? Notice I said "we." I bet
you are sexy as hell in a shy kind of way. You
shy women are the ones you have to watch. Make a
brother work and shit.

    You got me seriously wondering about you,
Mystery. Since you won't tell me anything about
yourself, I'll make up a description. I see you
at about 5'6", small frame, small/medium breasts
like I like 'em. Not too small, but not too big.
I bet you're a redbone with pretty, shapely legs
and an ass that I can just grab on to. Got a cute
little shape. You probably got shoulder-length
hair that you keep looking tight, and in bed
you're a moaner. One of those soft, barely audi-
ble, slow, sensual moans that come out every time
a brother strokes it right. Am I right?

    Anyway, listen. Let me call you or you call
me if that will make you more comfortable. I just
wanna hear your voice, just one time. That's all.
Bet it's all sexy and sweet as honey. Wait. Don't
say anything yet. Think about it. Don't give me
your answer today; let me know tomorrow. Okay? I
really need to talk with you. Just once. I promise
I won't ask for more of your time.

    Stay sweet. Peace.

I finished up my lame lunch, dumped the bag and my half-eaten
sandwich in the trash can, and logged out of my e-mail account with
my mind made up and my answer on my lips. There was no way in hell
I was giving that man, some stranger, my phone number. Hell no! You
could learn a lot about a person from just having access to their home
or work number. For all I knew, Bigblackd could be a scam artist just
waiting to get some personal info from me.

    And as for me calling him, that wouldn't work either. I could put a
number block on my phone, but what would I say to him? In an e-mail
I could say or be or do anything I felt like. No, Bigblackd and I would
continue to e-mail each other, if he wanted to, but that was all. I'd let
him down easy in an e-mail. I admit, I was curious as to how his voice

sounded. I bet it was deep and sexy, peppered with street slang and a Brooklyn accent.

The next day at work was more of the same. I saw patients through the early morning hours, then I juggled a quick lunch at my desk again and caught up on a stack of phone messages. Around two o'clock, my mind began to wander back to Bigblackd. I hadn't received an e-mail from him all day, but I saw where he had posted a new entry on the discussion board. He had responded to this chick who wanted to know what really pleased a man in bed. Bigblackd's response was almost poetic the way he laid it down for her. The man was fascinating. As for chatting with me, I guess he was waiting for me to make the first move.

The afternoon zoomed by in a fast blur. I didn't know where the time went. I had a couple of meetings: a staff meeting and one with my mentor and boss. Then it was back to more phone calls and one last patient for the day. By the time six o'clock rolled around, I was exhausted, mentally anyway. I pulled a Coca-Cola out of my mini refrigerator, which was also stocked with fresh fruit, water, and juices for my late evenings. I figured a hit of caffeine would give me a boost.

I was getting ready to log out of my PC when I decided, at the last minute, to check my mail. To my surprise, I found an e-mail from Bigblackd. My pulse sped up. His message had come over within the last hour. I smiled. It read:

```
E-mail: bigblackd@comcast.net

Message: Mystery, where are you? I've waited all
day to hear from you. You brighten my day, girl.
Call me on my cell at 917-555-1212. I just wanna
hear your voice, baby, that's all. I wouldn't do
anything to hurt you. Trust me. You are in com-
plete control. Think about it—you can always sim-
ply hang up the phone. Call me!
     By the way, my first name is Derrick.
```

I didn't know what to do. I was second-guessing my earlier decision. This was a first for me. I anxiously picked up the phone and then put it back down quickly, with a trembling hand, as if I had been burnt by it. I hesitated a few moments. Composed myself. Took a few deep, relaxing breaths.

I scooped up the receiver again and attempted to dial the first six digits of Bigblackd's phone number, then I slowly placed it back down. I couldn't do this. I had never done anything like this before. Ever. I didn't know this man from Adam. He could be on America's Most Wanted list for all I knew. There could be a ten-thousand-dollar reward leading to his capture at this very moment and here I was discussing my G-spot with him.

Then again, he was right. If anything went wrong or I was uncomfortable, I could simply hang up the phone. And . . . that would be that. After all, I was the one looking for answers and a resolution to my little problem. And . . . I wanted a bit of excitement in my otherwise dull, routine, and boring life. Bigblackd definitely brought me excitement. Even now, my heart was pounding away a mile a minute, attempting to pounce out of my chest.

To my amazement, I did something totally outside my realm. It surprised even me. Before I lost my nerve, I picked up the phone and dialed Bigblackd—I mean, Derrick.

"Talk to me," this deep sexy voice with a New York accent answered.

Damn, I thought as I quickly composed myself. "May I speak with Derrick?"

"Speaking. Who this?"

"Hi, this is, uh, this is Lex, uh, Mystery."

"Mystery? I can't believe you actually called. I was giving you a one percent chance," he said with a rich, genuine laugh. "Hey, hold on for a minute. Okay?"

"Sure."

In the background, I heard several male voices carrying on like they were having a good time. I heard Derrick call out to someone and words were exchanged. Then silence followed. He came back on the line.

"I'm back. Sorry about that. I had to get away from all that noise and distraction."

"Seems like y'all were having a good time."

"Yeah, those guys can be crazy as hell," he laughed. "But after almost twenty-four hours together, what can you expect?"

Silence.

"So, what's up, Mystery?"

"Nothing. Not much at all."

"You sound so professional and formal, baby girl. But you do have a kinda sexy, sweet voice. Sweet as honey," he whispered in a dreamy tone.

I laughed because I didn't know what else to do.

"You do," he repeated.

"Thank you."

"You're welcome, Mystery."

Silence.

"Does that make you uncomfortable?"

"What?" I asked.

"Me complimenting you."

"No, not really."

"Yeah, I think you are sorta shy. Remember what I told you about shy girls," he kidded.

I laughed nervously.

"Listen, so, have you been thinking about me today, baby girl?"

"No."

"No?" he questioned.

"No. I don't know you like that."

"Well, I thought that was what we were trying to correct."

I didn't say anything. He cleared his throat a couple of times.

"Don't get shy on me now."

"I'm not."

"Talk to me. Tell me something good. What are you wearing?"

"What?"

"You heard me. What are you wearing?" he asked again in a sexy, low voice. I could picture him making himself comfortable as he licked his lips in anticipation.

"I'm wearing a black skirt, white button-down silk blouse, and black pumps with fishnet stockings," I recited, feeling myself relaxing and being pulled in by his deep voice.

"Fishnet stockings? That sounds sexy. What color are your bra and panties?"

"Why?"

"Come on, Mystery. Just play along with me. Humor me, baby. Don't make everything so difficult."

"Okay. My bra is lacy black and I have on matching panties. The kind that ride up high."

"Umm. Nice. What's your bra size?"

"You are crazy."

"Just tell me, baby. Tell me," he whispered real soft-like.

"I'm a thirty-four B."

"I knew it. I like that; you're just a mouthful. I could suck those babies for hours. If you can't tell, I'm a breast man."

"If you say so."

"Do you have thick nipples?"

"I don't know," I said, nervously.

"Yes, you do. You know. You're a trip, Mystery. Are my questions making you that nervous?"

"No," I lied.

"Good."

"Are they making you hot?"

"No," I lied again.

"Well, I wanna make you hot," he whispered suggestively. "Does a man sucking your nipples turn you on?"

"No. Yes, I guess."

"Which one? I bet it does. I bet you get so wet."

As I gripped the phone receiver, I didn't say anything.

"Where are you? At work? Home?"

"I'm still at work."

"Do you have any privacy? Are you in an office?"

"Yes to both."

"Okay, cool. This is what I want you to do. Close your door if it's not already closed and dim the lights. Can you do that for me?"

I don't know why I played along with him, but I did. I wanted to see where this was leading. I had a pretty good idea.

"Hold on a minute."

I placed the receiver facedown on my desk, walked over to the light switch, and dimmed the lights. Everything in my office took on a ghostly cast. I took it one step further and closed the window blinds. My door was already closed; I made sure to lock it. Double-checked it. An hour earlier, my secretary had left for the day, so there wasn't a chance of her walking in on this scene.

"I'm back," I murmured breathlessly.

"Good. I missed you. Did you do what I asked you to?"

"Yes."

"I want you to do something for me. Trust me. I know you don't have a reason to, but I think you are feeling me. I'm definitely into you. Like I said before, I want to help you with your problem," he said as I heard him shifting around. Probably leaning back and getting comfortable.

"I don't know about this. Maybe."

"Mystery, come on. Just go with the flow. I want you to close your eyes and imagine I'm there with you, doing intimate things to you . . . feeling you, touching you, loving you . . . like you want to be loved. Okay?"

I didn't say anything.

"Mystery, you've got to trust me for this to work."

"Okay."

"Now, close your eyes and relax. Let go. Put me on your speakerphone and turn it down low enough for you to hear my voice. Relax. Imagine me touching you."

I quickly breathed in and out.

"Now, I want you to slowly unbutton your blouse for me. Don't rush. Imagine me watching you from across the room."

As I listened to his sensual words, my fingers started to undo the buttons on my silk blouse one by one, ever so slowly as instructed. My breathing sped up.

"Let me know when you are finished. I bet your skin is so soft and silky. Imagine me running my hands down and across your slender neck. Down to your breasts. Barely touching them."

"I'm finished."

"Good. Take your blouse off and place it on the back of your chair. Now, I want you to lower the shoulder straps on your bra. Don't take it all the way off, just move the straps to the sides. I want you to tease me. Imagine me slowly and softly kissing your neck and massaging your tender shoulders. My hands are learning your body and my mind is memorizing it as I inhale your sweet fragrance. I unsnap your bra and release your twin mounds.

"The cool air hits them and your nipples instantly become rock hard. I take in their beautiful sight as your chest heaves up and down. The tiny hairs on your arms stand up. You anticipate my next move and you tremble slightly. My mouth begins to water at the thought of tasting them, one by one. Savoring them like fresh melons on a hot summer day. I know you want me even though you don't say so. It's all in your body language. Your eyes won't meet mine. Your body leans forward, offering them to me. My mouth finds one breast, then the other. So sweet. I gently but skillfully run my tongue across the tips of your nipples and gently suckle and caress each breast with loving care. You moan a little to let me know you are receiving pleasure. You still there?"

"Yes," I stated, barely able to get the word out. My eyes were still shut tightly, and I could feel Derrick through his words. His invisible hands were molding me, touching me, seducing me.

"You alright? I don't want to lose you."

"Yes, I'm fine."

"I wanna hear you moan. Moan for me. Just a little. Keep touching your breasts, run your fingers lightly across the nipples. Lick your fingers and firmly squeeze your nipples. As my other hand runs up and down your thighs, imagine me sucking your breasts over and over. First one, then the other. I have your entire breast in my mouth. Now open your legs for me. Wider. Don't be shy."

This time I moaned involuntarily.

"That's it. Oooh yeah, keep moaning for me, baby. Open them wider, as wide as they'll go. I wanna get all up in you.

"That's a good girl. It feels good, doesn't it? I want you to push your skirt up around your waist and pull your stockings and black lacy panties off. Open your legs again. Spread them wide and imagine me looking at your womanhood with great admiration, lust, and appreciation."

It was absolutely amazing. I actually felt him. My body started to get hotter and respond to his voice. I was yearning for him. I continued to touch myself with no shame. Derrick continued on in his sexy voice.

"You getting hot, Mystery? I can hear your breathing change. Imagine my fingers as they touch your spot. Yeah, right there. You like that, don't you? Oooh, you're wet now. Slippery. I'm down on my knees, in front of you. I've inserted a finger inside your creamy walls. Let me hear you moan again. I move my finger around, up and down. Side to side. Slowly. Yeah, you like it slow and easy. You're getting even wetter; that turns me on."

I moaned a little.

"Mmm, you feel so damn good."

My eyes were still closed and I was trembling. I felt flushed.

"Baby girl, you feel better than I ever imagined. All hot and wet and tight. I wanna taste and kiss your pussy so bad. I open your legs wider with my hands and pull you to the edge of your chair. Do you feel my tongue as I taste you?

"Hmmmm. Oooh yeah. I insert two more fingers and I'm going in and out of you at a frantic pace. You're biting the back of your hand so that no one will hear your cries. You're afraid to touch me, but you give in. You throw back your head and move your body against my hand, making my fingers go deeper. I reposition myself and start loving you with my tongue. I'm sucking on your clit, while my fingers work diligently inside your pussy.

"You taste so sweet. Sooo . . . sweet. Your hands are now touching your breasts. Gently pulling your own nipples. The feeling is so wonderful that you almost cry. You grasp the back of my head and moan when my tongue hits that spot again. I thrust my tongue deeper inside and hold it there. Wet your fingers and touch your clit for me, baby. Gently rub it back and forth. Oooh yeah. Can you feel the sensations?

"Tell me how it feels."

"Oh yes. It . . . feels . . . so . . . good! Oooh."

"You are almost there. Come on. Let go. Give in to it, Mystery. Let it go. Ride it out."

"Oooh. Damn. Oooh, that's sooo good."

"My finger is on your G-spot and the pressure is quickly building. You're almost there. You can't take much more. You feel like you are about to explode all over the place. Come for me."

"Oooh, Derrick, I'm almost . . . about to . . ."

And then I heard it. The janitor turned on the high-powered vacuum cleaner that he used to clean the carpet. I almost jumped through the ceiling. Seriously. Any hint of an orgasm was quickly tossed to the side. I felt like a deflated balloon. I almost fell out of my chair. As I regained my composure and apologized to Derrick, I dressed in record time and abruptly ended the call. Damn. I was almost there. However, almost doesn't count.

lexie

Another two weeks came and went by at record speed. I was busy at work with a couple of new patients. Derrick was working different hours, a different shift, so we hadn't talked to each other on the phone since the first and only time. Besides, being busy was my perfect excuse for not talking with him again. To be honest, he scared me. I mean, if the man could take me that far with just his voice and imaginary fingers and mouth, well damn, what did the real thing hold? Imagine that. I had enjoyed numerous flashbacks to that conversation.

Even though we hadn't talked to each other again, we e-mailed back and forth whenever we could. And believe it or not, we discussed topics other than sex. I asked his opinion on numerous subjects, and Derrick was always open and straightforward with me. We talked about anything from politics to religion to the educational system to health care. My preconceived notions of him were rapidly dissipating into thin air.

Oh, don't get me wrong now. I know he thought he was play-ing me. Derrick is most definitely a roughneck, but he knows how to switch it off and on. I got the feeling that he could be whatever a woman wanted him to be. However, based on my experience and profession, that could only last for so long. Sometimes, he could do something so sweet, like forward me a poem or a photo of a setting sun that he thought I'd enjoy. Other times, he'd drop me a note to say hello and that he was thinking of me.

But . . . there were times when he'd send me the freakiest e-mail you can imagine describing exactly how he wanted to seduce me. And much to my disbelief, they turned me on. I'd read them two and three times before deleting them. Sometimes, he'd tell me about a weekend escapade he'd had, consisting of bedding some woman. I came to the conclusion that firemen didn't have any problems meeting women. Derrick met them everywhere. I guess there's something sexy about a man with a long hose, boots, and hat.

I had opened up with him enough that I'd told him a few things about myself. He knew that I lived in Atlanta and I shared with him a little about my family and friends. He had me dying over some of the stuff his baby's mama, Sheila, had tried to pull. Derrick hated her with a passion, but he had to try to get along with her for his son's sake. He joked, cursed, and laughed about her, but I sensed that just as much as he hated her now, at one point he had deeply loved her.

Around five-thirty Friday evening, I was getting ready to log out when something told me to check my e-mail one last time. There was an e-mail from Derrick. I smiled this big goofy smile that came out of nowhere. Sometimes his comments made my day, because outside of work, my family, and friends, I didn't have a life. I wasn't dating and didn't have anyone special. I had gotten to the point where dating just for the sake of dating was not an option anymore. It simply wasn't ap-pealing. I was about to hit thirty and casual dating was for women in their twenties. Now I chose dates as potential future husband material.

If I didn't feel you right off, I didn't waste my time or yours on even a first date. Sad, but true.

I clicked on Derrick's e-mail. It read:

E-mail: bigblackd@comcast.net

Message: Hey baby. I don't know if you'll get this before you leave for today; hopefully you will. Guess who'll be coming your way next weekend? Yours truly. You should see me. I have this big smile splattered all across my face. I have a friend who has moved to Atlanta, and I'm flying down to help him move into his new house. I'll be tied up most of next Friday, but I'll be free on Saturday. I'd love to see you, see your pretty face. 'Cause I know you're gorgeous. I know you are freaking out right about now. Yes, I know you (LOL). Calm down, baby, it's not that serious.

Think about my proposition over the weekend and let me know something on Monday. I'd love for your answer to be yes, but if you decide no, well, hey, life goes on. I'll respect your wishes.

Know this . . . I've always been up-front and straight with you, and I'm not about to change now. If we meet, I'm going to make love to you. I'm not good at maintaining a platonic relationship with a woman. If you're a woman and you're friends with me, I've probably fucked you, several times, in the past. The only women I'm platonic with are my two sisters, my aunts, and my moms. So . . . it's all good. I've laid it on the table. There's no reading between the lines. I wanna love you, touch you, taste you, have you spread out in front of me like a Chinese buffet. I wanna go inside you . . . !

Stay sweet. Think hard about what I'm saying and I'll chat with you on Monday.

Derrick was right! I instantly went into freak mode. Major freakout mode. My emotions were all over the place. Bouncing off the walls. I went from being excited to being nervous to being scared to being mad that he came right out and said he wanted to screw me. Just the thought of him being in Atlanta was terrifying. I could deal with him being in New York—my border hadn't been breached—but now he was going to be on my turf. In my backyard. In the South. Damn!

I admit, I was curious. I couldn't deny it. I did want to meet him and check out the man himself face-to-face. Yet I had to respect the fact that he stated it up-front and said don't waste his time if I didn't come prepared to drop the drawers. Tactless, but up-front nonetheless. Man. Decisions, decisions, decisions. What was a woman to do? After only a moment's hesitation, I picked up the phone and dialed Meshell's cell phone.

It rang three times. "Hello?" her distracted voice answered.

"Hey girl," I exclaimed in my happiest, upbeat tone.

"Oh hell no. Don't 'hey girl' me. I've been trying to catch up with your ass for almost two weeks."

"I know. I received your messages and the rest of the Crew's. It's just been so hectic around here lately."

"What's new? Hell, it's always busy around there; the same way it is always busy here. But I make the time, take a few precious moments to touch bases with my so-called friends."

"I know. You are so right and I'm so wrong. I'm sorry. Do you forgive me?" I asked in a sweet, babylike voice.

"Witch, stop. Don't even go there. You know I can't stay mad at you for over five minutes and yes, I forgive you," Meshell said, her irritation quickly faded.

"Good. Because you know you are my *bestest* friend in the entire world. I couldn't live another day knowing you're mad at me," I stated, still kidding around.

"Bestest? Is that even a word?"

"I don't know, but you are!"

"Whatever! Witch, what's going on? To what do I owe the pleasure of your call, since it took you two weeks to return mine?"

"Maybe I just wanted to hear your sweet, sarcastic voice. I've missed your crazy self. I needed a dose of Meshell."

"Yeah right. Tell me anything."

"By the way, what did you want?"

"Same thing. I needed a sympathetic ear or two to vent in. Lexie, the last couple of weeks have been hell around here. I've been assigned this horrific case: *State v. Owens*. I know you've heard about it on the news; it's been on every major network. Sad, sad situation. This father and his wife are accused of starving and beating his ten-year-old daughter to death. Had her hog-tied in the garage. The neighbors found her. This happened in a so-called quiet, upper-middle-class neighborhood.

"The neighbors were shocked. When they were interviewed, everybody had such wonderful things to say about the Owenses. How could a father murder his own daughter? And the child's stepmom helped? There are truly a lot of evil people in this world. It's like Tracee is always saying, with her New Age philosophy—the world is ninety percent darkness and ten percent light. I believe that."

"Yeah, I do remember hearing about that. Tragic. I hope y'all prosecute them to the fullest extent of the law. They don't deserve to live. Or better yet, let them spend the rest of their lives rotting in jail thinking about what they did to that child. Let the inmates dish out their own form of justice."

"If I could, I'd put them under the jail. What kind of monsters harm a helpless child?" she stated in a faraway voice.

"Meshell, I'm here now. Seriously, I'm sorry it took me so long to return your call. Being busy is no excuse. You know you got me whenever you need to vent and talk it out. I know it must be difficult to stay detached from these situations when they are right there, smack in your face. Stay strong."

"Yeah, I will. I'm cool. It's just so hard sometimes," Meshell said on the verge of tears. And Meshell rarely cried. She was one of the strongest women I knew.

"Yeah, I know what you mean. Listen, let's talk about something else before we both wind up depressed for the remainder of the evening. What's up with the rest of the Crew?"

"Tonya is out of town on some wine-buying trip. I swear, I don't think the girl truly has a job. How can flying all around the world and sampling wines be considered work? Oh, Lexie, before I forget, I knew there was something I wanted to tell you. I think Tonya may be sleeping with her boss," Meshell shared in a conspiratorial whisper.

"I know you are kidding. Right?"

"No, seriously. She let something slip a week ago," Meshell said.

"Her boss is potbellied, middle-aged, balding, and married with two kids."

"I may be wrong, but I don't think I am."

"What slipped?" I asked.

"Nothing major. Tonya just knows a bit too much personal info on the man and she slipped and called him by his first name."

"So?"

"But she used to call him by his last name. Why so casual now?"

"Damn! I hope you are wrong. She wouldn't want to risk damaging her thriving career. And what's going on with Tracee?"

"Tracee is in serious research mode again. She's working on a piece for publication in a major academic journal. Something about the life and lessons of author Zora Neale Hurston."

"Miss Academia herself. I think research gets her off," I said.

"Yeah, that and being an exhibitionist."

We both laughed.

"Oh, you'll never guess."

"What?" I asked.

"Tracee said she just *happened* to be jogging at that park about a week ago."

"What park?"

"You know, the one from her freak story."

"Just happened to be jogging? She doesn't even live on that side of town," I said.

"Tell me about it. My thoughts as well."

"What happened?"

"Well, she ran into the 'jack me off' jogger."

"You're kidding. What? She said she'd never go back to that park out of curiosity," I exclaimed.

"Okay! Get this. He didn't even recognize her and Tracee was actually pissed about it. I told her of course he didn't recognize her. Her pussy and ass weren't hanging out, and they were her identifying traits."

We laughed again as friends do. "What did she say?" I asked.

"Nothing. She hung up on me."

"I guess I'll catch up at the next Ladies' Night Out, which is right around the corner," I noted.

"Yeah, it sure is. This year is flying by. It'll be Thanksgiving and the end of the year before we know it."

"And speaking of Ladies' Night Out . . ."

"See, I knew you wanted something. Lexie, I know you. Spit it out."

"Oh, you make me sick. Your prosecutor nose can sniff out anything," I declared.

"Whatever. What's going on?"

"Well, I know this sounds silly, but I felt left out."

"Left out?"

"Yeah. Everybody had wonderful, exciting, and sexy stories to share. Me? Hell, y'all laughed at me," I cried out.

"Lexie, we didn't laugh at you. We explained that. We were laughing with you." I heard just a hint of laughter in Meshell's voice. Sounded like she wanted to burst out in giggles at any moment and was trying hard to hold it in.

"Well, I've thought long and hard and I realize I've never been that wild and free before, not a day in my entire life. I feel like I've missed out on something, like there is a void. I'm on the outside looking in. Like I haven't truly lived life to its fullest."

"Lexie, look at how you were raised. I mean, your parents are ministers at one of the largest African American churches in the country. You had an image to maintain."

I didn't say anything. Only sighed.

"Growing up, you probably thought God was watching your every move along with His host of heavenly angels. That's a hell of a lot of pressure to be under to be the perfect child while thousands of members of your parents' congregation watched. Some probably hoping you'd fail and end up pregnant, an unwed mother."

"It wasn't that bad."

"Lexie, girl. It's me you're talking to. I remember countless crying sessions where you felt like you were trapped in this life your parents had planned out for you. You didn't even choose your college. They did. They even tried to decide your major."

"And look at me now. A total disappointment to them. No man. No children. No prospects."

"Girl, you know your parents are proud of you. Your happy homemaker sister has enough babies for the both of you. You have plenty of time to give them grandbabies."

"You're right. But as I was saying, I still felt left out. Why do I always have to do the right thing? You, Tracee, and Tonya could have starred in your very own *Girls Gone Wild* video. So I set out to remedy my situation. Make up for lost time."

"What? Lexie, what did you do?"

"I met someone."

"Met someone?"

"Yeah, over the Internet," I explained.

"Please don't tell me you registered at one of those dating services? Blacksingles.com? Blackpeoplemeet.com?"

"No, nothing like that."

"Because there are a bunch of lunatics, crazies, and losers on those sites. They prey on women like you."

"Meshell, I didn't do that. Listen, I participated on this discussion board and met a man."

"A discussion board?"

"Yeah. It's where you discuss a particular subject at length with others who share a similar interest."

"And what was this similar interest?" Meshell asked.

I hesitated.

"Lexie? What was the similar interest?"

"Sex."

"Sex?"

"It's not as bad as it sounds. The discussions are tastefully done. Well, most of them anyway," I tried to explain.

"Lexie, dear. This is so unlike you. You are typically the by-the-book, straightlaced, responsible Alexis that we know and love."

"Exactly. And that's why this man—and this situation—are so exciting for me. He's everything I'm not."

"Hmph. Well, you do sound different. Excited. I guess as long as it's over the Internet and impersonal, it should be okay until you grow tired of the entire situation and him."

"That's the problem. It has already gotten personal."

"What do you mean?" Meshell asked hesitantly.

"Meshell, I've had phone sex with the man," I confessed in a whisper.

"Phone sex. Doesn't that involve a phone?"

"Yes, and before you go ballistic, I called *him*. He doesn't have my number."

"Still. Who is this man? What does he do for a living? Where does he live?" Meshell asked question after question.

"Meshell, he is the total opposite of any man I've ever been with. He's blue-collar, an NYC fireman, sort of a roughneck, can curse like a soldier, and can say some of the nastiest stuff to me—stuff that has me changing my panties after I log off my PC."

"Ummm. He got it like that?"

"Yet he can flip it and talk about politics or world issues."

"I can't even picture you with a bad boy. That's like picturing Tonya in a pair of Wal-Mart pants." Meshell laughed like she had told the funniest joke in the world.

"Well, it's true."

"How did you meet him?"

"Well, like I said, I posted a question on the discussion board pertaining to my lack of orgasms."

"You put that out there? I thought only you and I knew about that."

"Meshell, those people don't know me. To them I'm Mysterywoman; that's the beauty of the Internet."

"Mysterywoman, huh?"

"Yeah. It's kinda cool, isn't it?" I asked.

"If you say so."

"Anyway, Bigblackd . . . I mean, Derrick, answered my question and it spun off from there."

"And he can get you hot like that? From just his voice and words?"

"Yes! I can't believe it either," I exclaimed, actually blushing.

"Lexie, I didn't know you had it in you," Meshell laughed.

"I didn't either, but I have this other side I'd like to allow myself to explore. I was always too scared to be anything other than the 'good, wholesome girl.' "

"Lexie, being good isn't a bad thing. I love you just the way you are."

"I know, but I need to experience this because being 'bad' isn't a bad thing either."

"Well, there doesn't seem to be no shame to your game. I know you are responsible, careful, and discreet. Go for it. Get your groove on. Stella did. Well, on second thought, don't get your groove on exactly like Stella. Do! You! You'll bore with him soon enough because I'm sure you two have nothing in common. Sweetie, ain't nothing wrong with having a bad boy on the side. I personally know they can throw down in the bedroom. In your case, you'll have to enjoy the virtual bedroom, though. It can be our little secret."

"Maybe not."

"What do you mean? You're scaring me. Talk to me, Lexie."

"Well, Derrick's coming to Atlanta next weekend."

"How? Why did you invite——?"

"No, it's not like that. He's coming to help one of his buddies move," I said, interrupting Meshell.

"And?"

"He asked me to meet him at a hotel . . . for sex."

"And?"

"And, I'm thinking about it."

"Lexie, I don't know. You don't know this man. This could be dangerous. It's one thing to flirt over the Internet and another to meet in person."

"I've thought about all of that, but for some reason I trust him."

"I don't like it. Usually you are the one giving the sound, rational advice. This time the shoe is on the other foot."

"Scary, isn't it?" I laughed.

"Yeah, it is. I don't know what to say. So I'm going to go with my logical side. All I know is that you're grown and it's your business. Sometimes you have to trust your gut instinct."

"I can't explain it, but this is the first time that a man has brought out these extreme sexual feelings in me. I'm not searching for a love connection, just a lust one."

"Well, you know I'm behind you one hundred percent in whatever you do. If you do decide, let me know the name and room number of the hotel that you'll be in. And you call me when you get there and when you leave. Okay?" Meshell asked.

"Okay, mother dear."

"Witch, I'm serious. I see evil every day and you never know about people. Evil comes in nice bodies with sexy words, too. Better safe than sorry."

"True."

"Since you don't have time to have him take an AIDS test, make sure he wears a rubber."

"Of course. I haven't completely lost my mind," I said.

"One thing I do know. This needs to be a one-time deal. You need to hit it and quit it."

"That sounds so heartless."

"Call it what you want. Men do it all the time, Lexie."

"I know, but . . ."

"But, my ass. Lexie, you are an up-and-coming psychologist who's going places. You can't afford to get involved with this . . . man you met on a sex site. Be for real."

"You're right. Again."

"Like I said. Let him hit it and call it a night or maybe get a quickie next morning. If he's good, or actually great, then maybe you can get yearly checkups. Fly him in once a year to rock your world and then send him on his merry way."

"Meshell, you are too much with your nasty self."

"I bet he says worse."

"True."

"But I'm just being realistic. And you be careful—pick up some condoms and take some mace."

"You are acting like my mind is made up. I said I was thinking about meeting him. I haven't decided for sure."

"Lexie, I've known you a long time. If you are even talking about meeting him, then you will. And on top of all that, you're getting advice from me. Girl, you must be truly desperate—or seriously horny."

We both laughed at that. I was a little of both.

"Listen, as much as I love to talk to you, I gotta run. My evening is just beginning. I've got tons and tons of work on my desk to complete so that we can fry those bastards."

"Sure, but remember what I told you. Call me if you need me. I'm always here for you," I said sincerely.

"Same here. And you don't have to prove anything to the Crew. We love you just as you are. Fabulous."

"I know, but I need to do this for myself."

"I understand. Keep me posted."

"I will."

"Lexie, I just had a horrible thought."

"What?"

"What if Derrick weighs three hundred pounds, is bald-topped with that Bozo the Clown look, and has a two-inch dick?"

"Girl, you are too through. Bye."

"What if he is cross-eyed with bad breath?" Meshell asked.

"Enough! Bye."

"Okay. One more. What if he's like R. Kelly and likes to piss all over you after sex?"

"Gross! Let me let you get back to work."

"Okay. I'll talk to you soon."

I hung up with Meshell, knowing that I had made my decision. My weekend would be stress-free after I went to my weekly hair appointment and manicure and pedicure sessions. I'd just make sure to say some extra prayers at church on Sunday, because I was determined to get my freak story.

Monday morning came. I couldn't wait to get in to the office and e-mail Derrick, since my home PC was broken. He was going to be shocked over my quick decision. But then again, so was I. I was sick and tired of curling up with a trade journal or juicy novel over the weekends. I wanted a man in my bed. Preferably one who could make me feel good; I was sick and tired of faking it. Tired of my dates getting theirs and then turning over and going to sleep as if they had done something, while I lay there unsatisfied and still frustrated. Saturday, that was all going to end. My twenty-nine-year drought would cease. Would finally come to an end.

I logged on to my computer, went into my e-mail account, and typed out the following message:

E-mail: mysterywoman@msn.com

Message: Hi, Derrick. How's your morning going
so far? I have great news. I'd love to meet you
this weekend. Just tell me when and where. Don't
get me wrong, I don't usually meet strange men at
hotels, but there's something about you. I can't
put my finger on it.

I'm meeting you with the full knowledge that
we'll sleep together. Maybe we can solve my problem after all. I hope so anyway. There are a few
rules that have to be in place, that you have to
agree to, or I can't do this:
1. This is a one-time deal.
2. If I say stop or no, that means stop or no.
3. No buddies hiding in the closet, under the
   bed, or joining us later.
4. We won't share any personal info. I don't
   need to know and vice versa.
5. No rough sex, handcuffs, blindfolds, etc.
6. What happens at the hotel stays at the
   hotel.
7. Lastly, we will not have unprotected sex.

Chat back.

Within minutes I received an e-mail back from Derrick. It was as
though he had been sitting by his PC waiting for me to write. He wrote:

E-mail: bigblackd@comcast.net

Message: Mystery, you are a woman after my own
heart. You are a mess. Sure, I'll respect your
rules. Not a problem. As long as I get the chance
to hold you in my arms for one night, that is
enough for me. I can take that. Beggars can't be
choosers.

Believe me, I'd never do anything to hurt you
or harm you in any way. I know we come from different worlds, from what I've been able to piece
together about you. However, I can be a gentleman. If you don't want me to spank your ass, then
I won't (LOL).

I intend to live up to my initial promise.
I'm gonna have you squirming all over the place
(LOL). I can't wait to taste you over and over
again until I get my fill and suck your pretty
breasts and nipples. Man, my mouth is watering at
just the thought.
     About #3, No buddies hiding in the closet,
under the bed, or joining us later. Mystery, you
are a trip. I fuck solo. I don't need a copilot.
Believe that.
     Do you have any suggestions on what hotel I
should stay at?

After e-mailing Derrick back to give him a few hotel preferences, I focused on my patients for the day. I had a full plate, but I was pleased that I was making significant progress with some of them. It always brought me a great deal of pleasure, when I could see the light at the end of the tunnel. I have to admit that my mind wandered back to Derrick during some of my sessions. My concentration wasn't as focused as it should have been and Saturday couldn't come soon enough. I quickly dismissed the thought of a three-hundred-pound Derrick opening the door. I wasn't going to let Meshell's descriptions mess with me.

At lunchtime I had the opportunity to check my e-mail again, and I had several messages from Derrick. He stated that he had already made reservations at one of the hotels I recommended. He didn't waste any time. Plus, he was willing to come out of pocket because the hotels I suggested weren't cheap. By the end of the week, he'd let me know what time frame he intended to be there on Saturday. On the evening of our little rendezvous, we agreed that he'd e-mail me, using his friend's laptop, the room number. That way, I still wouldn't have to give him my phone number. I was trying to play it safe and use sound judgment just in case something went wrong. I made a mental note to pick up some mace, the kind you could place on a key chain.

The second message was very erotic. Derrick described in graphic detail exactly what he intended to do to me. From my head down to my toes. I don't think I had ever had a man suck my toes. I read it over and over again, at least three times. If he did what he stated in the e-mail, I couldn't wait. I prayed that I wasn't going to be disappointed. It would be a damn shame if he turned out to be all talk and little action. The third and final e-mail of the day was about his newest baby mama drama. He claimed "the bitch from hell" got him drunk over the weekend and seduced him. Derrick said it was like a scene straight out of *The Best Man* when he awoke on Saturday morning to find himself naked in bed with Sheila. He said he looked over at her, screamed, and scrambled for his clothes. He couldn't take enough hot showers and had been having horrible nightmares ever since.

I realized I was going to miss this man. Meshell was right, though. I couldn't continue this sort of relationship with him. I couldn't do the undercover thug lover with the baby mama drama who lived out of state and thought his sexual conquests made him a good man scenario. And it wasn't fair to Derrick either. Don't get me wrong, he wasn't whispering any promises in my ear either. For him, it was all about the conquest.

This was all about sex. Pure and simple. Yeah, he was helping me out, but he was getting some new and fresh coochie in the process. I wasn't a fool, and I didn't take him for one either.

Much to my surprise, the rest of the week zoomed by at ninety miles per hour like cars on Interstate 75. I didn't have the opportunity to second-guess my decision, chicken out, or become nervous about my tryst. My patients kept my mind distracted with their many problems and dilemmas. I didn't have time to worry about myself. Good. My problems appeared trivial to some of theirs. So, before I knew it, it was the night I was to meet Derrick, a.k.a. Bigblackd. Which brings us up to date.

I had sat in the parking deck of the hotel for over twenty minutes, debating back and forth with myself. In his e-mail, Derrick had stated that he looked forward to meeting me and he hoped I didn't disappoint him by not showing up. If so, he would understand. I thought that was quite noble.

If my parents knew what I was about to do, they'd probably disown me or check me into a mental ward. As it was, I wondered if I would be able to face them the next day at church without looking guilty. I couldn't believe I was going this far myself; it was still surreal. As I often told my patients, mature adults realize that, at some point, you have to stop worrying about what other people think of you and live for yourself. Life is too short.

That's what I was going to do. Start living for myself. Right then and there. Right that very minute. Before I lost my nerve, I jumped out of my Benz, turned on my security system with a click of my key, and headed to the up escalator from the parking garage and then to the bank of elevators off of the main lobby. To my delight, with each floor I took to the next level, my confidence increased. I had the feeling that tonight was going to be a very special one, a night I would never forget for as long as I lived. Each floor that blinked past me on the button panel elevated me closer to my personal revelations. In no time at all, I had made it to the fourth floor.

As I made my way down the hallway, I was confident that I was looking and smelling good. My hair was tight; I had gotten it retouched just that morning. I had it in a wavy, textured style that stopped just above my shoulders. I had indulged in my usual manicure and pedicure, so my nails and toenails were hooked up. I even survived my first bikini wax. My body was soft and silky from my body lotion. Lastly, I had spritzed on my favorite perfume. I even treated myself to a fancy bra and panty set from Victoria's Secret. I wanted to present my 34Bs in a pretty, sexy way since Derrick is a breast man.

It was now or never. I stood directly in front of room 457. I tried to press my ear to the door to hear what was going on inside. Nothing. I took three quick breaths and knocked on the door. It seemed like my knocks echoed off the surrounding wallpapered walls. I held my breath.

I heard a sound and then a familiar deep voice ask, "Who is it?"

I swallowed and stood up taller, straighter. "Mystery."

The door quickly opened to a gorgeous specimen of a man with a beautiful smile. Derrick didn't disappoint in physical appearance. Damn! The man was divine. I think in his e-mails he had played down his looks. He was very attractive in a rugged sort of way. In his Timberland boots, black jeans, and black sweater, he had it going on. I saw in his eyes that he liked what he saw in my appearance as well. As his eyes took in my face and body, I was pleased and felt sexy and free. Wickedly free.

I stepped in and Derrick closed and locked the door behind us. I looked behind me at the door and back to him. Our eyes met. For a brief second, I panicked. Then Derrick gave me a smile that simply melted my insides. It was showtime. Lights, camera, action.

"Hi, Mystery. It's so good to finally meet you," he said sincerely, pulling me into his arms for a strong hug. My breasts pressed up against him. I wanted to stay there forever and a day. He smelled manly. Earthy and strong.

"You too," I murmured against his chest as I breathed in his aroma. Masculine. I thought, *He is the ideal height. I fit perfectly in his arms.*

"You are a very beautiful woman; not at all like what I expected."

I stared at him. Couldn't take my eyes off him for other reasons as well. I was lost.

"Wait, that didn't come out right," he apologized. Whatcha doing to me, Mystery?" Derrick smiled a crooked smile.

We laughed and in that instant my tension left. Drifted out of the room, right along with my inhibitions.

"Don't try to explain. I know what you mean. We are both a little nervous."

We stood in the middle of the room for a few awkward seconds. I quickly checked it out, in the corner of my eye. I didn't see any dark shadows lurking or anything out of order. Everything was neat and clean and to my satisfaction.

"Excuse my manners. My moms raised me better than this. Have a seat." He gestured with his hands.

I chose to sit on the edge of the queen-size bed. Derrick pulled up a chair in front of me and just stared like he couldn't believe I was real. I smiled sweetly and shyly. We were within inches of one another. I could feel the heat rising from his body.

He moved his hand and I jumped. Derrick leaned in closer and rubbed his big hands up and down my arms. "Are you cold?"

"A little."

"Come here. Don't be nervous. I won't hurt you. There's something I've been wanting to do for the longest," he said, gently reaching for me, gripping my chin, and pulling me into a passionate kiss.

I resisted for only a second. Derrick was an excellent kisser. I loved the way he teased me with his tongue. Bit on my bottom lip. Lovingly caressed the side of my face. After he had explored the depths of my mouth, he pulled away and stared at me again. Made me nervous.

"That was nice." He smiled. Derrick had such lovely white teeth. "Why are you trembling? Just relax."

I shook my head. Tried to shake off the effect he was having on me. Already I saw lust light up in his soft eyes and my heartbeat sped up.

Out of the blue, Derrick got up and walked over to the head of the bed and reclined against several of the plush pillows. "Mystery, undress for me. Slowly."

"What?" *Where did that come from?*

"You heard me. Undress for me. We both know why we're here."

"I thought we could talk for a while."

"We can talk later. We have all night," Derrick stated, his eyes never leaving mine.

Realizing how silly I was acting, I smiled shyly and slowly started to unbutton the tiny buttons on my black dress. Taking my time. I had decided to dress very feminine in a simple button-down dress that showed off a bit of cleavage and legs. My dress dropped silently to the floor in a crumpled heap. Derrick took me in, inch by inch, with appreciative eyes. When he got a glimpse of my bra, I saw his eyes linger on my breasts.

"Show me your breasts."

I slowly removed my fancy, expensive black bra and threw it to the floor on top of my dress and covered my breasts with my hands.

"Show me."

I slowly lowered my hands.

"Oooh yeah, thick, dark nipples," he stated, licking his lips. "Touch yourself for me. Rub your hands across your breasts."

I hesitated for only a moment. I did as I was told.

"Now, I want you to very slowly pull down your panties, step out of them, and play with yourself."

His eyes didn't leave my face. I did everything he asked me to with no shame. I was hot, horny, and willing.

"Come here, baby. You want me to taste you and make you feel real good?" he asked, reaching for me. I was still trembling. I nodded my head.

"I can't hear you. Listen, tonight that shy persona is out the door. Okay? You're going to talk to me and tell me what you want. Communication is the key. Now, you want me to taste your pussy?"

"Yes."

"Well, tell me," he stated from behind half-closed eyelids. "I wanna hear you say it with that cute southern accent."

"I . . . want . . . you to taste . . . my . . . pussy."

Derrick made himself comfortable, shifted around. "You are so sweet."

As he reached out his hand, I walked the short distance to him. I didn't hesitate. I didn't have second thoughts. I realized tonight would change my life. And if anyone could take me over the top, it would be Derrick with his smothering eyes and skillful touch. I definitely intended to find out in as many ways as possible.

"Open your legs," Derrick said, while expertly massaging my breasts.

As I stood before him and he inserted two fingers to check my wetness, my legs opened wider and he lowered his head. I moaned so loud that I scared myself. I didn't know where to put my hands, so I placed them on top of his head.

He looked up one time and said, "Oh, you taste so sweet, girl. Like a Georgia peach." Then he lowered his head again and reached up with his right hand to squeeze my nipple. My legs started to tremble . . . and I knew it was on! The night had just begun. . . .

I hadn't decided if I would share this experience with the Crew at another Ladies' Night Out. For now, it was enough for me that I accomplished my mission and enjoyed it immensely. I didn't have to have them all up in my business. Let them keep thinking I was a goody two-shoes. What they didn't know wouldn't hurt them. A girl has to have some secrets!

meshell

As I tapped my recently pedicured foot beneath the rectangular wooden table, I checked my gold Rolex watch, trimmed in diamonds, for the second or third time that evening. I let out a loud, exasperated sigh. Patience was not one of my virtues. *Where are those witches?* I silently asked myself, glancing yet again at the grand entrance to one of the finest restaurants in Buckhead. Damnit! Reservations at five thirty meant five thirty. Not five forty-five or six o'clock. I was a stickler for promptness; I didn't run on CPT—colored people time. Working for the district attorney's office guaranteed that.

My right foot was doing a serious jig, to its own beat, underneath the table, and my fingers were dancing to a different drummer on top of the table. Five more minutes passed, according to my watch and the dwindling ounce of patience that I had on reserve. I looked to the elegantly gold-trimmed glass door yet again. Finally! Hallelujah! I saw Alexis, decked out from head to toe, looking gorgeous, headed my way with a big smile on her face that instantly squashed my displeasure. As I pointed at my watch I frowned, but then smiled back because I couldn't help myself. Alexis made her way over in swift, full strides.

"Sorry I'm late. The traffic was horrific, but this is Atlanta," she squealed, standing in front of my table with outstretched arms. "Give me a hug, show me some love, and put that pout away."

"Happy birthday, Lexie!" I shouted, planting a kiss on each cheek and giving her a big, genuine hug in return. It was hard to stay mad at her.

"Thank you, I guess," she said, seating herself directly across from me.

"What is that supposed to mean? 'Thank you, I guess'?"

"Meshell, I'm thirty. The big 3-0. I'm getting old. By some, I'm no longer considered young and fertile."

"Oh, please! I turned thirty three months ago and you don't see me crying and freaking out. Age is just a number. I know I'm not getting old, just better—like a fine wine."

"If you say so. It's hard to believe you didn't feel slightly anxious," she stated, checking out the menu.

"I'm serious. Haven't you heard, thirty is the new twenty? Embrace it, girl. Or as Tracee would say, listen to your inner spirit and come into your own. Life is just beginning."

We laughed and reveled in each other's company. Due to conflicting schedules, we hadn't talked much in the last few months. At least not like we were used to. There were a few five- to ten-minute conversations that ended too soon. I missed my friend.

"By the way, your dinner is on me today."

Lexie picked the gold and black menu back up. "Well, in that case, let me check out the lobster again."

"Be my guest. Whatever you want, birthday girl."

This particular evening, Lexie had her hair down, long, loose, and flowing with a few spiral curls that framed her pretty brown face.

Most of the time, her appearance was very professional loo[k]
French twist pinned at the nape of her neck.

"You look very pretty this evening. New outfit?" I a[sk]
ing Lexie's dark green suit, which I knew was a designer [...]
designer price tag to match.

"No, just something I found in the back of my closet[...]
a few moments to take in her surroundings. "I had totally [...]
about it; still had the price tag on it and everything."

Earlier, I had noticed there were several couples dining [...]
Over in the far corner, I think I even spotted Faith Evans wit[h...]
tourage. I hadn't noticed any lone eligible bachelors. Believe m[e...]
looked and looked some more.

"Well, that color looks great on you."

"Thanks, lady. You're not looking too shabby yourself in that h[ot...]
red suit and matching three-inch heels."

I smiled.

"How do you walk in those shoes?"

"With practice," I laughed and winked.

"Well, that's too much work for me."

"Is that a new diamond tennis bracelet? It's gorgeous," I told her,
fingering it.

"Yes. My parents brought this by early this morning, unannounced,
wrapped up in a pretty gold box with a gold ribbon." She rolled it
around and around her tiny wrist; Lexie was a petite little thing. The
overhead restaurant lighting reflected off the diamonds and cut across
the room with a brilliance of color.

"I've told Mother about spending all this money on me. This was
definitely too much, too expensive. She always goes overboard . . .
with everything. But as always, my words go in one ear and out the
other."

"Please, send her my way. She can spoil me anytime, any way she
wants to. Okay?" I said with a wave of my wrist.

"And then, to make matters worse, Mother had the nerve to be

ouldn't spend the remainder of my day with her and the

ou and your mother are still, after all these years, going at
vious that you both love each other. And your father gets
middle of your mini war. Maybe you and she need to go
nd get to the root of your troubles."

er would die first. She wouldn't be caught dead seeing a
when she has God in her corner," she quipped.

ll, enough of parents. Today is all about you," I stated, chang-
subject.

You know what? You are absolutely right. Today is all about me.
once, I'm going to be selfish."

"That's right and you deserve it."

"Where's the rest of the crew?" Lexie asked. "I'm ready to get my
birthday celebration started. Tracee and Tonya had better come on
before we start without them."

"I know that's right. I couldn't pay you guys to be on time. Y'all
wouldn't be on time if your lives depended upon it. You will probably
be late to your own funerals."

"Heyyyy, it's my birthday; I can be fashionably late. I'm the birthday girl, remember?"

"Okay, I'll excuse you this one time. I know old age is catching
up with you and you move a little slower at thirty," I teased. "But those
other witches . . ."

"Speaking of which, here they come," Lexie announced, looking
back over her shoulder.

I followed Lexie's eyes and glanced toward the front of the restaurant and sure enough Tonya and Tracee were making a grand entrance
like true divas. A few heads turned. I saw a middle-aged woman give
her man the evil eye and kick him underneath the table. He winced
and sneaked one last look. The last two members of the Crew spotted
us, waved, and strolled over. Tonya couldn't possibly put any more sway
into her walk and Tracee's dreads were all shiny, pretty, and bouncy.

"Why do they always have to be the center of attention?" I asked Lexie, not expecting an answer.

"Some things never change. One day I'm going to have to analyze them, especially Tonya, and see where her illusions of grandeur come from." We laughed because we knew the results would be a trip.

I relaxed a little and was relieved the Crew was finally together because I had put a lot of time and special effort into planning this evening's Ladies' Night Out event in honor of Alexis's thirtieth birthday. We were doing a leisurely dinner and then attending Tyler Perry's play, with front row seats, over at the Fox Theater. I wanted everything to run smoothly and efficiently and on time.

For my thirtieth, we had patronized a popular strip club that had some of the sexiest chocolate brothers I had seen in a long time. Mmm, they were delicious . . . tight muscles, tight asses, and big, black dicks, especially Chocolate Thunder. He was irresistible. Unbeknownst to my girls, I had discreetly slipped away for a few minutes to sample his goods. I couldn't help myself; sometimes I had these wild impulses and I just acted on them. It's funny, I can't remember what lie I told them in order to sneak away, but whatever it was, it worked. They were probably too buzzed to care where I went.

I slowly walked down a long corridor, a bit buzzed, holding on to the wall to steady myself, trying to remain cool, calm, and collected, and going into this cold air-conditioned room that was vacant except for a long conference table and a few mismatched office chairs. Chocolate Thunder was standing in the corner, in the shadows, patiently waiting for me with his sexy ass. He couldn't have been any older than twenty-four, twenty-five. Young stud.

He strutted over and started to speak, but I placed my index finger over his thick lips, slipped it into his mouth, and he gently sucked on it as I pulled it in and out. I didn't want conversation or dialogue; I only wanted one thing . . . for him to satisfy the savage heat between my legs. Other than the adventure I had told the Crew about at the last get-together, they didn't know about this other side of me. The side that even I couldn't understand or control at times.

I climbed unsteadily up on the table, but not before stripping off my red silk panties and tossing them to the floor in a slow, dramatic manner. Chocolate Thunder walked back over to the wall to watch and enjoy the show. In no time at all, the hem of my dress was up against my waist and the top portion pulled down under my heaving, swollen breasts. I leaned back on my elbows, laughed, and watched Chocolate Thunder appreciatively admire the parts of me that made me a woman. I slowly opened my legs and played with my budding flower. By now, my wetness was easing its way down my inner thighs. Combined with my previous drinks and the excitement the dancers had aroused in me, staring at this fine specimen had me trembling with desire.

I spoke one sentence during the entire episode. "Let me see what you're working with, but make me come with just your fingers." Chocolate Thunder wasted no time in unzipping his pants and releasing his manhood. I moistened my lips a few times and took him in with my eyes.

I called him over closer with my index finger; a seductive cat-and-mouse game was in progress. I could tell he was an arrogant son of a bitch; too many women had blown up his head with compliments of excellence and prowess in the bedroom. He strutted over with dick in hand as he rubbed it up and down, teasing me. A tiny drop of wetness glistened on the very tip.

I simply reached for the back of his head and pulled him toward my swollen breasts. For a moment, he looked into my eyes and smiled another cocky grin. As he swiftly pulled me forward on the table, the tip of his tool rubbed against my stomach. He wanted to prolong my agony. Within seconds, Chocolate Thunder quenched my fire with wonderful sensations every time he licked or sucked my brown nipple; I had always been hypersensitive there. I moaned with no shame and raised my body up to meet his greedy mouth and tongue. At the same time, I reached for his huge hand and placed it between my parted thighs.

This boy learned fast. He knew what my body needed. In no time at all, his fingers were working my clit over and thrusting in and out of my throbbing womanhood with the others. I was on fire and Chocolate Thunder was doing a great job extinguishing the flames.

At one point, he pulled up one of those chairs, leaned me back on the table, and just had a field day with my pussy. He had me wide open. That man rubbed me up and down, sideways and under, right and left with no mercy. He served me up right . . . and then that wonderful feeling embraced me like a cocoon. That cocky smile reappeared. Totally sated, I rose up, straightened and pulled my dress down, put my panties back on, and rejoined the celebration without missing a beat and no one the wiser.

"It's your birthday, it's your birthday . . . Happy birthday, happy birthday, Miss Goody Two-shoes," Tonya and Tracee screamed in unison as they bestowed hugs and kisses upon Lexie. Girlfriend simply beamed; in fact, she was glowing. I noticed a few people look our way because of all the noise and commotion we were making; we didn't care.

"Look at you. You look lovely, Lexie," Tracee stated. She had on a sharp pantsuit that showed off her fabulous figure, which she maintained with much work.

Before Lexie could say a single word, I cut her off. "It's about time you witches got here. My personal invitation did not say five forty-five. It clearly stated five thirty. And I know we all can read."

"Diva, don't go there. *Do not* get your panties in a bunch this evening. We are only fifteen minutes late and, after all, this is Atlanta, where the traffic and a little rain always make you late," Tonya calmly responded. "It's expected."

"Well, next time, leave early since you know that."

"Don't talk to me like that. I'll knock you into the middle of next week, Meshell."

"And I'll kick your ass on Thursday."

"Whatever," Tonya stated. "You are not going to work my last nerve today; I'm looking too cute." She was right. She was looking rather grown and sexy.

As usual, when we were together, we got caught up in our own little world. Others around us ceased to exist unless we wanted them to. Lexie and I were seated opposite each other. To my right was Tracee, seated across from Tonya.

Once we were settled, our stately and patient waiter made his way over, efficiently took our dinner orders, and went off to retrieve our requested champagne. The ambiance of the restaurant was cozy and intimate; it reeked of fine dining and money. This particular restaurant was known for hosting celebrities when they visited Atlanta. So there was no telling who might walk up in the place before the evening was over.

"It is so good to see everyone," Lexie stated, looking around and taking in each of us. "I truly missed not getting together last month for our monthly ritual. There was a void."

"I know, I was disappointed too, but lately we've all been so busy with work and other commitments," Tracee chimed in. "Where is that waiter with our champagne?" she asked, looking around for him. "I'm ready to unwind; I've been waiting all day to meet up with you guys."

We nodded and I thought, same old Tracee. That girl could live solely off of a bottle of liquor. In college, I'd seen her drink fraternity boys under the table. It was such a contradiction to everything else about her. She swore up and down that we were sellouts since we processed our hair or wore weaves. Tracee was working her way toward becoming a vegan. She swore by herbs, received a psychic reading once a month, got a colonic once a quarter, and swore that yoga and meditation were the best things since white bread. Her home was an eclectic mixture of candles, incense, and color. Yet, her one vice was alcohol. A mixed drink, a glass of wine, a beer . . . or two or three or four.

"After playing phone tag with y'all the last week, I'm simply exhausted." Tonya laughed heartily.

"Tell me about it. I know I must have left at least two messages for each of you. So, what's been going on with everybody?" Lexie asked, picking up her water goblet and taking a long sip.

Something was different about my friend. At the moment, I just couldn't place my finger on it, but she was simply glowing. I intended to solve this mystery before the night was over.

"Let's play catch-up like we always do." This was one of the unofficial rules of our ritual; we caught up on each other's lives before we did anything else.

"Divas, let me tell you about this get-together I went to the other weekend over at my sister Pam's house. You know she recently moved in with her boyfriend, Stan, which I personally think is a huge mistake. But hey, she's a grown-ass woman and if she hasn't learned by now, she won't. Anyway, there was a guy there, her boyfriend's best friend, I think his name was Darold, David, something like that, and he was a flat-out, certified fool. I didn't know they still bred them like him in Georgia," Tonya stated in her usual manner, with her hands and arms flaying through the air with a couple of tosses of her mane thrown in for good measure.

Tonya paused. At that moment, our waiter, crisply dressed from head to toe in black and white, brought our chilled Cristal over. Minutes later, we held our champagne flutes in the air as we toasted to our girl.

"Lexie, here's hoping you have many, many more birthday celebrations. We love you and couldn't live without you in our lives. We wish you nothing but peace and blessings," I said.

The Crew clicked glasses and shouted, "Cheers." Lexie was beaming.

Looking at the Crew, my girls, I didn't know what I'd do without any of them. I admit, Lexie and I were probably the closest, but I couldn't imagine life without Tracee teaching me how to meditate and to listen to my inner voice or Tonya teaching me to embrace my femininity and true diva-ness. And Lexie, she was my confidante. We all complemented each other in so many different ways. Me, I guess I was the unofficial leader. I was the gel that kept us together over the years.

"Hmm, this is good," Tracee stated, taking another big gulp. We nodded in agreement.

"Getting back to my story. This guy David, he was actually kind of cute. You know the type: clean-cut, bald-headed, goateed, sexy in an understated way, with smoldering bedroom eyes, average height and weight, brown skin, conservative but tasteful clothes. I was seriously thinking about giving him a minute of my time and seeing where his head was. Like I said, he was attractive until he opened his big mouth. Big mistake."

"Please, I'm sure you have met worse," I shared.

"No, Daniel had them all beat."

"I thought you said his name was David," I questioned.

"David, Danny, whatever," Tonya said. "Does it matter?"

"What was the event?" Lexie asked.

"Nothing special. Pam invited a few friends over for food, wine, and interesting conversation. Of course, I supplied the wine. There were about five single women, a few couples, Pam's boyfriend, his cousin, and this Dexter character. When I first arrived in my cute little capri pants and top, showing a bit of cleavage, I saw him sitting there and my first thought was that he was quiet and laid-back. Not."

We laughed, refilled our glasses, and leaned back. We knew from experience not to rush Tonya and to let her tell her adventures her way. With lots of drama and flair. She always kept us in stitches.

"Divas, it all started when someone brought up this book they were reading, I forgot the title and the author had a weird-ass name. Essentially, the book was about a young woman who found herself caught up in an abusive relationship and how she turned to her abuser's best friend for support. And get this, the best friend wanted more than friendship."

"Damn, that sounds like a winner," I stated. "Drama and scandal and sex. I see it every day. Sometimes real life is stranger than fiction."

After selecting a roll, I passed the bread basket around.

"So, Mr. David explains how he had read parts of the book, and he felt the woman, the main character, got exactly what she deserved. Supposedly, this woman ventured into a relationship knowing what her man expected of her, and she thought she could change him and his ways."

"What? No, he didn't!" Tracee questioned in between sips.

"Yes, diva. Don essentially said that this woman deserved to be beat down by her man because she knew before she married him that he wanted one, two, and the other from her and she didn't live up to his expectations."

"Oh, no. I couldn't have been there," Tracee said. "What were the other guests saying?"

"Believe it or not, some of them, a few of the women, were agreeing. Furthermore, this David went on to say that he'd hit a woman if she didn't behave. Not a problem for him. His woman had to respect him, let him be the man, perform her womanly duties, and essentially obey him and he'd take care of everything else. There was to be no arguing, questioning him, or whining. Just do what he said and all would be good in paradise."

"Oh now, he's a character. Obey him. He's living in the wrong century," I stated, biting into my buttered roll.

"Oh no, get this. That's not all. He gave examples of how he has sent women on their way in the past—an ex-wife."

"Yeah, and that's why she is what she is . . . an ex," Lexie stated. We nodded in mutual agreement. "She probably couldn't wait to get the heck out of Dodge."

"Dexter said he didn't have time for arguing, discussing, talking, et cetera. Just do what he said, know your place, and everybody would be fine in the relationship."

"Well, personally, I don't know where he will find a woman like that. I don't know any of them and wouldn't want to," Tracee interjected between swallows of champagne.

"Exactly, me either," I agreed.

"Maybe he should go down to the backwaters of Mississippi or Alabama and find himself a woman or slave or trained dog," Tracee continued. "Or perhaps send away for a mail-order bride."

"I admit some of his points were valid," I interjected.

"What? You've got to be kidding! Which ones?" Tonya asked, leaning in closer with raised eyebrows for my response.

"Okay, for one, I agree if men would step up to the plate and be the men in relationships, then we wouldn't have to be superwomen. Two, I agree that we all have roles that we play in any type of relationships, even friendships. Three, we can't change people. In the words of Maya Angelou, 'When people show you who they are, believe them.' "

Tracee jumped in. "Okay, I can get with all that, but this guy has some other deep-rooted issues with women that are a bit twisted. To take the stance that he won't compromise, he's God in his household— please. All that is pure bullshit with a capital B," Tracee stated. "Sounds like he's the perfect candidate for some therapy."

"From a psychologist's point of view, I think David has been hurt, hurt terribly in a past relationship, and this is his defense mechanism. He doesn't want anyone to get too close for fear of experiencing that loss again. So he comes up with all these rules to protect his heart," Lexie said, sounding every bit the excellent therapist that she is.

"Divas, then he started talking about his sexual prowess in the bedroom," Tonya continued.

"What? Oh no! If you got to talk about it, then it must not be all that. Actions speak louder than words in my book," I shouted, high-fiving Tonya. "Show me. Show me the dick."

"Diva, he almost pulled me in, though, when he started talking about what he could do with his tongue. You know that's my weakness. He kept sticking it out, making that poking, swirling motion. Had me hypnotized and mesmerized."

We howled.

"You are a mess," Tracee said, twisting a lock of hair around and around her finger.

"David said he could slap it, smack it, and rub it down."

"Isn't that a line from an old BBD song?" I asked.

"I don't know. But I was secretly thinking, he can slap my butt a couple of times if he got it going on like that. Slap me, baby," Tonya exclaimed.

"Too funny," Lexie laughed, leaning against Tonya.

"But what disappointed me the most were the women. Of course the men were going to agree with him, the whole macho, dominance crap, but some of the women were nodding their heads too. Of course the women who disagreed, in Dante's opinion, were lesbians. I wanted to tell him that's why he is alone, with a cat, in his big house on the hill. Black women don't put up with that shit, not even the desperate ones. You don't put your hands on me, you treat me as your equal, and I don't obey any damn rules. We ain't playing kindergarten," Tonya said, visibly irritated.

"Amen, amen, amen."

"Next time that fool comes through, just call us on over to Pam's house, we'll ride through. He can't handle us, not these divas. We'll give him some intervention," I laughed, feeling good.

By the time our waiter came back with platters and plates filled with hot, delicious-smelling entrees and dishes, we were ready for another bottle of champagne. We had ordered four different entrees. We had everything from seafood to beef to pork to veggie platters. The evening was still young, there was more catching up to do, and our night was just beginning. The Crew was in the house.

meshell

"Hello?"

"Good morning, girl. I was just calling to see if you recovered from last night," I joked to a groggy Lexie.

Stifling a yawn, she replied, "I don't know if I've recovered yet, but I did have a wonderful time."

"Good. The crew wanted your thirtieth birthday to be memorable."

"Well, it was. Thank you guys, again."

"The play last night was hilarious; I'm still laughing at some of those scenes," I said.

"I know. Tyler Perry is too funny."

"And too rich."

"So, what are your plans for this lovely Sunday morning?" I asked, opening the door to my bedroom closet and pulling out my large suitcase. The one I carried with me on all my business trips.

"Oh, I don't know. I haven't thought that far yet. I still have on my pajamas and haven't even brushed my teeth yet."

I laughed. "Get up, sleepyhead. You're wasting a beautiful day."

"I have some psych journals I need to catch up on reading."

"Huh, that sounds like tons of fun," I stated sarcastically. "What a way to spend a Sunday afternoon. Buried under articles talking about crazy people."

Lexie chuckled and yawned again.

"So what exciting plans do you have?" she asked.

"I'm not much better; I'm packing for my DC trip."

"Oh yeah, you did mention that somewhere between my second and third glass of champagne last night."

"Yeah, I'm leaving bright and early tomorrow morning. Seven a.m."

"Do you need a ride to the airport?"

"No, I'm cool. My neighbor is driving me because she works out that way."

"How long are you staying?"

"Not long, just three days. I'll be back Thursday."

"Well, be safe and be careful."

"Always," I said.

"About a week ago, I saw this show about how dangerous it is for women to travel alone in this country and internationally. You should have heard some of the horrific stories."

"No, thanks. They will only scare me and make me anxious. Since 9/11, you know sometimes I still have to take a sleeping pill before boarding a plane."

"Okay. I'll tell you about it another time."

"Thank you."

"I understand this is a business trip and all, but are you planning on hooking up with your friend?" Lexie asked.

"Who? What friend?"

"Okay, whose old age is catching up with them now? Meshell, you know who I'm talking about."

"Oh. You mean Charles?"

"Duh!"

"I might call him up; I'll play it by ear," I responded nonchalantly. I didn't dare let Lexie know that Charles's cell phone number and business number were among the first things I placed for safekeeping in my BlackBerry. With my prior hectic schedule and a big trial just ending, which had gone on for weeks and weeks, I needed someone who knew how to relax me and lay it down in the bedroom. Charles definitely came to mind.

My body was screaming for some loving because my sexual healings, lately, had been few and far between. I didn't know what the deal was. I know I'm attractive, better than average even, I'm intelligent, but I don't get asked out on many dates. Don't get me wrong, men look and admire from afar, but an actual date is not a routine occurrence.

Lexie's voice pulled me out of my reverie. "Yeah, you do that." I heard her smile through the phone. "I don't know who you think you're fooling."

I continued to cross back and forth from my big walk-in closet to my king-size bed. I had over a dozen outfits laid out. I was the type of person who packed everything but the kitchen sink. I never knew what to take, so I usually ended up bringing a bit of everything. Just in case.

"Oh, I remember what I meant to ask you," I stated, stopping in my trek to the closet. I balanced my phone on my ear and held up an eggshell-hued silk blouse.

"What? I'm listening."

"I know thirty is a milestone and all, but last night you were simply glowing."

"And?"

"So, what's up?"

"Now, why do you think that simply because my skin is healthy that something is up?" Lexie teased.

"Friends sense things, and I know you. I know you aren't pregnant, so it's not coming from that. Spill the beans, Lexie."

"I hate to disappoint you, but there is no big secret to share other than Mary Kay cleanser and moisturizer #2," she laughed.

"Okay, witch. What's the deal with the Internet dude?"

There was a brief moment of silence that didn't escape me. I was paid, and paid well, to observe and interpret nonverbal cues.

"Derrick?"

"If that's the Internet guy," I stated.

"Nothing. We chat from time to time."

"Really, now?"

"Yeah."

"And you aren't doing more than chatting?"

"Girl, please . . ."

" 'Girl, please,' my foot. I know we had a conversation not too long ago when you were thinking about hooking up with Internet dude and handling some business."

"His name is Derrick," she said defensively.

"Okay, Derrick. Don't get so testy."

"Like I told you, that moment in time passed and my rational self came back to reality. You caught me in a rare moment of weakness. I never agreed to meet him."

"Mm-hmm. Tell me anything."

"I didn't."

"Well, we all have them. Our moments. Where our desires overtake our sense of rationality. We all answer the call of inner freak at some point or another. Whether they want to believe it or not, all women are capable of it. Remember that," I suggested.

I vaguely noticed Lexie didn't comment one way or the other. I heard a couple of quick beeps on my line.

"Hold on a minute, Lexie. I have a call on my other line."

"Whatever you do, don't keep me holding long."

I clicked over and heard a sugary voice say, "Good morning, diva."

"Hey, Tonya. You mean, for once you are actually up before noon on a Sunday?"

"Yeah, I can't believe it either. Every now and then I surprise even myself."

"Hold on. I have Lexie on the other line. I'll click us back over."

Without hanging up, I somehow managed to get the three of us connected. Sometimes technology didn't agree with me, so I wasn't sure.

"Hey, Lexie," Tonya screeched in Lexie's and my ears.

"Good morning, sunshine," Lexie shouted.

"What are you divas gossiping about so early this morning?" Tonya inquired.

"It's not really that early; it's almost noon," I said. "Anyway, who said we were gossiping?"

"I was talking about what a wonderful time I had last night," Lexie interjected.

"It was fun, wasn't it?" Tonya stated.

"Yeah, once y'all finally showed up."

"Meshell, let's not get started on that again."

"Well, be on time the next time," I said.

"Whatever. I'm not going to let you steal my joy this morning."

"Ladies, ladies, be civil," Lexie piped in.

"She started it," Tonya screamed back in retaliation.

"And finished it too," I shouted in defense.

"Ladies, be good," Lexie stated. "You act like small children."

"Guess who has a lunch date?" Tonya asked.

"Who? You?" I asked.

"Yes, with this gentleman I met at the play last night."

"Now, how did you manage to snag a date in the midst of a play?" Lexie inquired. "Leave it to Tonya."

"Skills, diva. Skills. Watch and learn."

"And who is the lucky fellow?" I asked.

"Do y'all remember that attractive older gentlemen who was sitting one row up from us, on the left side?" Tonya asked.

"No," we chimed in. I was trying hard to remember.

"Well, he had on the black Armani suit and was wearing a Presidential Rolex. He was sitting by a pretty, slim woman with freckles."

"No," we stated again.

"Y'all are the most unobservant divas I know. No wonder you never get dates—you don't keep your eyes and ears open for potentials. Anyway, he invited me out to a late lunch."

"When? How?" I asked.

"During that one intermission when I went to the restroom to freshen up my makeup, he came up behind me, near the phones, and slipped me his cell number on his business card."

"Didn't you say he was there with a date?" I asked.

"Yes, but I didn't see a wedding ring."

"I know, you couldn't get past the expensive watch," Lexie joked.

"Don't hate me because I have expensive tastes," Tonya said indignantly.

"These men are scandalous, just scandalous," Lexie stated.

"No more so than the women. I've seen some pretty grand schemes that women get away with. With the man none the wiser," I said.

"Speaking of scandalous, listen to this. You know Tracee rode with me last night, so when I dropped her off, you'll never guess who was waiting for her," Tonya shared in a conspirational tone.

"Who? It was almost three o'clock when everyone left my place after deciding not to spend the night," Lexie asked.

"That professor. He was waiting in his Mercedes and got out as soon as we pulled up."

"What? The boring one? What's his name—William?" Lexie asked, fully awake now.

"Yes. You know my nosy ass waited. And he did go in with Tracee and the lights never came on upstairs."

"Damn, y'all act like y'all have never had or made a booty call late at night," I said.

"I haven't," Lexie volunteered.

"I'll plead the fifth," Tonya laughed.

"As long as you take it for what it is, ain't nothing wrong with that," I said.

"I thought the professor was a cold fish in the bedroom," Lexie stated.

"Well, I guess a little something-something is better than nothing, ladies," I said. "Besides, maybe she opened the curtains so the neighbors could watch."

"Girl, you wrong for that," Lexie laughed. Then we all laughed at my little joke.

"I don't know. I think I'd prefer to go without if a man isn't experienced enough to bring me to orgasm. What's the point?" Tracee asked. "I might as well leave him out of the equation and get my own self off."

"You are too much. Sometimes it's not about the act itself, it's about the intimacy and warmth that you share," Lexie stated.

"Lexie, you been reading too many romance novels. Sometimes I want my man to simply rock my world. Plain and simple. Fuck me and fuck me good. Give me a Calgon moment and take me away."

We laughed again. I had finally selected my outfits. I pulled out and packed three outfits that I considered my hoochie gear. They were usually in the back, far back portion of my closet. My girls would never believe I'd wear such raunchy numbers. I love having close friends, friends as tight as sisters, but we all have our secrets. I moved over to my mahogany underwear drawer next.

I heard Lexie and Tonya giggling like schoolgirls. "What's so funny?"

"Well, if you had kept up, you would have heard," Tonya said.

"Tonya mentioned how she was so buzzed last night that she started to ring up David and invite him over," Lexie volunteered.

"Knowing you, you probably did," I said. "Probably wore that man out and had him following your rules."

"Well, divas, I'm shocked that you think that lowly of me," Tonya mocked. "Believe me, if I did Dexter, you would have been the first to know. However, as much as I love talking to you, I have to go. Have to call Tracee and find out what was up last night."

"Nosy witch," I said.

"Oh, you know you want details too. Don't even go there."

"You're right. Call me when you hang up."

"Me too," Lexie said.

"Okay, bye, divas. I'm off to play detective. Smooches." And she was gone.

"Bye," Lexie and I said in unison. I hung up with a smile on my face. My friends had lifted my spirits, and I was ready for my DC trip and Charles. Maybe I'd splurge and throw in his friend KeVon as an extra bonus.

tonya

"Hello?" I asked.

"Hello?"

"Tracee?"

"Yes, this is she. Who is this? Tonya?"

"Diva, that was strange. I didn't even hear the phone ring on your end."

"I know. Me either. I guess I was calling you at the same time you were dialing me up. See, we are psychically linked," Tracee said.

"It's too early for all that mumbo jumbo. What's going on, diva?"

"Not much, I just finished my yoga and brunch."

"What did you have for brunch?"

"A veggie platter with fat-free dip," she replied.

"Yuck. I don't know how you survive off that mess."

"Don't knock it until you've tried it. So, what are you into?"

"Nothing. I just got off the phone with Lexie and Meshell."

"What are they up to?"

"Same ole, same ole. Meshell is packing for her business trip to DC and Lexie is chilling," I explained.

"Meshell's been flying up to DC a lot lately."

"This is only the second time this year that I'm aware of," I stated.

"You may be right. I can't keep track. It seems like you and Meshell are always hopping on a plane to somewhere or another."

"It's one of the great perks of my job as a wine buyer that I truly adore."

"I heard that. My profession keeps my head buried in books, articles, and research libraries. Not exactly the glamorous life."

"How's your paper on Zora Neale Hurston coming along?"

"I can't complain; I'm on schedule. I plan to make a pilgrimage down to Florida to visit her gravesite. Do you want to join me?"

"Not unless you are going to South Beach in Miami after."

"I guess you won't be going, then. I didn't realize what a truly fascinating woman she was. For her literary legacy—"

"Enough of that academic shit. I wanna know why the nutty professor was waiting on your doorstep last night when I dropped you off."

"He wasn't waiting on my doorstep, drama queen. You are always exaggerating everything," Tracee declared matter-of-factly.

"Well, close enough. He was waiting in his car."

"If you must know, I text-messaged him at Lexie's and asked him to come by."

"Can you say, 'booty call, booty call'?" I asked.

"The last I checked. Uh, I am a grown woman. Grown and sexy."

"True. You got me there. Well, how was he? I'm shocked because you said he was boring as watching paint dry in bed."

"Not much has changed. William is set in his ways; I thought that maybe I could show him what I liked sexually and he would learn how to satisfy me. Didn't happen."

"What did we say last night: you can't change someone? You weren't paying attention," I said.

"Well, this is different. I'm not trying to change his thinking or personality, just his sexual skills."

"Well, good luck. Keep trying. You're a better woman than me. I'd have to set him free, diva! Give him his emancipation papers."

"No, there won't be another time. I give up. The man is one of the most intellectually fascinating and brilliant men I know, but that is where the attraction ends. He has book sense and that's about all."

"Did you set the mood? Maybe he needs stimuli to lead up to the lovemaking," I suggested.

"Yes. I thought about all that. Tonya, I lit candles, had on soft romantic music, the lights were softly dimmed. I took a quick shower and changed into something really sexy and seductive. I tried out one of my new oils for the first time, so I was smelling good. I even brought out the chilled wine and cheese and crackers."

"What happened?"

"We danced and held each other, stole sweet kisses, danced some more, and then William led me to my bedroom with lust-filled eyes. I knew he wanted me because I could feel the outline of his hardness through his pants. Lighted candles were flickering on the nightstand and dresser of my bedroom, casting a romantic and alluring mood as they created shadows across the wall over my bed. While I undressed him, in between kisses, William slowly pulled down the straps of my negligee and let it drop to the floor. He gently laid me back on the bed, and climbed on top of me, moved up and down about three or four times, squeezed my nipples and breasts, let out a few high-pitched moans . . . and then he came in one big shudder, rolled off of me, and fell asleep within five minutes."

"Damn, Tracee! That's pretty awful. Pathetic, actually."

"That's what I said. So much for making love into the wee morning hours and watching the sunrise. I couldn't wait until his ass left this morning. He was talking about spending the day together and checking out some antique flea markets; I just wanted him out before I told him what he could do with his fun-filled day and four-inch dick."

"Funny. Well, that was messed up, big time. I presume you're still horny as hell."

"What do you think? Give that lady a cookie. You got it—horny as all get-out."

"Poor baby."

"It's not funny, Tonya. You know when you hit thirty your sex drive increases."

"Well, go mix up one of your energy drinks to take the edge off."

"I don't think that will help me at the moment."

"Well, you usually have a cure for everything. Take this herb, drink this mixed with that, rub this on your face. You're our resident voodoo lady," I laughed.

"Unfortunately, this time, I don't have any potions for my condition."

"Well, last night I went home, climbed into bed between my one hundred percent pure silk sheets, and was out for the count. While you and the kooky professor were rolling around for your three minutes of bliss, I was already in sleep mode." I didn't dare tell Tracee that I got some and made up for both of us. That was my little secret, for now. I don't think my friends would understand my choice of bedmate. So, hush, hush was the word of the day.

"Don't get me wrong. My night wasn't a total waste. Something sorta weird happened."

"What? The professor got a second wind and turned into Superman with a mighty dick that slew your dragon?" I chuckled at the thought.

"No, I wish," she laughed. "I said something weird happened, not miraculous."

"What are you talking about?"

"Afterwards, I was still feeling antsy and hyper; unlike William, I wasn't sleepy. So I tiptoed into the living room and left William asleep in my bed. I poured myself another glass of white wine and unwound. I could feel my stress and disappointment floating away into the stillness of the night. My apartment was dead quiet. It was that eerie time before daybreak. My candles were burning down low and it was peaceful and serene. At some point, I walked out onto my patio to get some fresh air."

"Okay? I'm with you."

"You've been in my new apartment and you know how my patio faces the open courtyard below. When I walked outside, I noticed that in the other four units that face mine, at different angles, all the lights were out. I assumed everybody was safe and sound, tucked away in dreamland. After all, by now, it's maybe four, four thirty in the morning. Suddenly, I had the crazy desire to disrobe and literally feel the light breeze that was stirring in the distance. Get back to nature."

"You are crazy—you and your exhibitionist self. All the lights were out, right, because I see where this is going and I hope that I'm wrong."

"Yes, they were, but once I had discarded my gown, I noticed someone, a dark, male figure, standing behind one of the windows, the one that faces me directly."

"And what did you do, Tracee? I hope you got your buck-naked ass dressed and went in."

"I don't know what came over me. Just the thought of someone watching me sent chills up and down, all over my arms."

"Tell me you didn't!" I exclaimed with utter disbelief etched across my face.

"I vaguely remembered the tall, dark brother who had moved in there a little over a week ago. I had totally forgotten someone was living in that apartment."

"Sure you had."

"Seriously," she stated.

"Okay, if you say so."

"Anyway, I could feel his dark eyes on me, pulling me in. Drinking in my body, little by little. I stared back into the darkness and slowly started to touch myself, my breasts, my womanhood. I slowly cupped and caressed my breasts, squeezed them, pulled on my nipples until they were erect and budding. I felt free. I slowly trailed my hands down my stomach and met the warmth that radiated outward."

"You nasty thing."

"Tonya, I was so turned on, I can't explain it. I saw movement behind his curtain. My breathing had sped up and I was in a zone. My own personal zone."

"I can't believe you. You were out there essentially masturbating for the world to see."

"No, just the dark chocolate brother next door," Tracee said nonchalantly.

"What if William had woken up?"

"So?"

"Why do I have such crazy friends? Why? Are you serious?"

"Listen. There's more."

"It's not enough that you prance around there in your birthday suit with the windows wide open, but now you are getting off in public."

"Listen. I started easing my fingers in and out in a frantic pace. I had even lifted one foot up on the patio rail. My neighbor ventured out on his patio, took a seat, with a beer in one hand, and watched the show."

"No. And you a respectable professor. What would your students think?"

"People who live in glass houses shouldn't preach?"

"What is that supposed to mean?" I asked.

"Never mind. Anyway, that man doesn't know me from Eve, and I don't intend to get to know him."

"I hope not on both points."

"I glanced across the way at him from time to time to make sure I had his undivided attention. And I did. He hadn't—couldn't have—taken his eyes off me."

"I'm sure he didn't. You were putting on a free show that he couldn't get at the gentlemen's club. He was front row and center."

"In fact, girl, the dude had gotten a pair of black binoculars and was looking through those. Oh, I put on a real show for him. I had at least four delicious orgasms—I lost count—and when it was over, I walked calmly into my apartment, closed the blinds, locked the sliding glass door, and crawled into bed with William and snuggled. And he was snoring, out for the count, and none the wiser."

"Scandalous. Now, what if you see this dude on the street?"

"I'll just see him. He doesn't know me; it was dark."

"Duh . . . Are you sure you're a professor? He could walk over to your apartment. Dude knows what apartment building you live in."

"I doubt it. He wouldn't be that bold."

"I hope not, but you don't know. Tracee, these are dangerous games you are playing. First the dude in the park and now this. This is too close to home. Get a grip."

"I'm a big girl."

"If you say so. Big girls can get burnt. You are never too big to fall."

"Okay, okay. Now you are starting to sound like Lexie. Give me a break."

"Well, hussy, be careful—not stupid. Now, let me let you go."

"Why? So you can run back and tell Meshell and Lexie what you found out?"

"What?"

"Don't act all hurt. I know your M.O."

"I love you too."

"Yeah. Whatever," she said.

"If you must know, I have to get ready for my lunch date."

"With who?"

"A guy I met at last night's play."

"Oh yeah. I meant to tell you, I saw that move. Calling me scandalous. Go look in the mirror. The man's girlfriend was inches away."

"Like I told Lexie and Meshell, I didn't see a wedding band."

"Whatever, you better watch that karma. It can come back around in powerful ways. Karma doesn't play. Anyway, it's only a little after twelve. Why the rush?"

"Diva, perfection takes time."

"Bye, girl."

"Bye. Talk to you soon," I said, hanging up the phone, shaking my head.

I couldn't wait to call Lexie and Meshell.

meshell

"*Please place your tray tables and seats in an upright position, fasten your seat belts, and prepare for landing. We will be arriving at Washington, DC's Ronald Reagan National Airport in approximately ten minutes.*"

Waking from my light nap, I pulled my seat into an upright position as requested, looked out the window to the skyline below, stretched, and checked my watch. We were only ten minutes behind our scheduled landing time of ten a.m. Cool. I quickly checked my hair, securing a few stray strands back in place, and placed my lipstick back in the small compact from my purse. With my head against the headrest, I leaned back. I couldn't wait to check into my hotel room in the historic district, take a leisurely hot shower, eat a quick bite from room service, and then call Charles. Yes, Charles would be my dessert. I couldn't wait to serve him up with a cherry on top. Whipped cream would be nice too. Maybe some chocolate syrup.

So far, so good. Luckily, I didn't have anyone seated next to me who talked me to death during the entire hour-and-a-half flight, so I was able to nap and read a little from the O magazine I'd purchased. I didn't even have to take a sleeping pill. *Is DC home? Are you flying in for business or pleasure? How long are you staying? What do you do?* Those types of questions from complete strangers drove me crazy. I wanted to scream *nonna*—none of your damn business. And Lord help me if I replied I worked for the district attorney's office in Fulton County; then the questions continued at a rapid-fire pace. *What was your most high profile case? What made you decide to go into law? Have you ever thought about being a defense attorney? What are your views on the O. J. Simpson trial?*

Nor was I held captive by a young child behind me, directly across from me, in front of me, or seated next to me, who cried or screamed or kicked the back of my seat during the entire duration of the flight. Of course, the parent or parents conveniently turned a blind eye or deaf ear to the little monster that insisted upon messing with me. I had come to the conclusion that I was a baby magnet.

I still felt terrible that I had to lie to my friends. As far as they knew, I was on a business trip with intentions of attending a conference. The less they knew the better. They thought of me as the strong one, the leader of our group; the person who was always in control, the gel that held our friendships together. How could I confide in them that lately I was seriously losing it? Rationally, on a certain level, I knew that that's what friends are for, but I didn't want to shatter my image. Call it pride or whatever, but it was the truth.

I'd recently ended a long, drawn-out trial that sapped every ounce of energy out of everyone involved. Long nights, skipped lunches, and working weekends were the norm. I was burnt out emotionally, mentally, and physically. My career choice was making me more and more cynical of the human race each additional year that I invested into it. In the past, when people would ask me why I became a prosecutor, I'd answer because I thought it was my duty, my calling to serve and protect the citizens of my county. Besides, someone had to do it. Why not me?

On a day-to-day basis I saw the worst that mankind had to offer—scum of the earth. I had come face-to-face with true evil many times over. Don't let anyone tell you that it doesn't exist because they'd be wrong, dead wrong. And naïve. I've placed a face with it, felt its hot breath upon me, and put a name on it. Evil does exist . . . and it does vile and despicable things, ruins human life, tears families apart—and it will never change because its very existence strives on chaos and despair.

Evil is our quiet next-door neighbor. The pastor of our church, the Boy Scout leader, the PTA mom, the choir director. Yeah, it existed and everyone that we placed behind bars for the rest of their natural life or gave a death sentence to . . . it was a victory. A small one, but a victory nevertheless. But sometimes, late at night, it seemed like it simply wasn't enough.

Many nights, I tossed and turned in bed because I couldn't get the horrific crime photos I'd seen or the sobful, heartfelt stories I'd heard the day before out of my mind. Images flicked over constantly, like a movie projector racing through my soul. Evil was spreading too, corrupting our teenagers now; it didn't discriminate. Bottom line, I needed a break. Needed to get away.

Recently, I had found myself regressing, much to my displeasure, back to past patterns that I hadn't practiced since my law school years. This scared me because I didn't want to go back to those days and times. Those were not my proudest moments, but were definitely my darkest days. I discovered this pattern was how I reacted when I was under severe stress and turmoil.

As Tracee had taught me, I breathed in slowly and prepared for landing. This mini trip would do me a world of good. As I massaged my forehead, I could feel the tension slipping away already. Oh, before I forgot, I reached into my purse and did one last thing—double-checked my BlackBerry for Charles' phone number.

"Thank you, madam! Enjoy your stay," the jovial bellhop stated as he backed into the hallway and closed my hotel door with a generous tip in hand.

"Thank you. I intend to."

Placing my purse on the bed, I walked around and surveyed my room. Perfect. When I traveled I preferred to stay in first-class accommodations. I believed in being as comfortable as possible when I was away from home and had no qualms about paying for it. The additional dollars were worth the extra amenities I typically received, and I felt I deserved it.

I sat down on the edge of my plush, king-size bed and attempted to make a local call. After finding the appropriate phone number, I dialed and listened to several rings before a deep voice came on, delivering a professional-sounding voice-mail message. After listening to the typical corporate greetings, I left a quick message.

"Hey, Charles, it's Meshell. Surprise! Surprise! Listen, I'm in town for a couple of days, staying over at the Ritz-Carlton. I know this is last minute, but I'd love to hang out. Preferably tonight. Call me back at 555-1212 or hit me up on my cell. Room 203. Talk soon." I hung up the phone.

I lay back on the bed and thought of how it was a damn shame for a brother to be as sexy, intelligent, handsome, and good in bed as Charles. Then I started laughing as I thought of Tracee's minuteman. After what Tonya told us, I had to talk to that crazy-ass girl when I got back in town. It was okay to get your groove on, but not with your neighbor watching a few feet away. Tracee was a free spirit, but that was a bit too free. Back in our college days, Tracee was overweight, but you'd never know it now. Through a strenuous regimen, she had lost all that weight and truly blossomed.

Now, with my phone call out of the way, my growling stomach signaled it must be lunchtime. I wasn't a big breakfast person, but I had to eat lunch, which was usually my first meal of the day. Initially, I was going to take a quick shower and then order room service, but I had a sudden change of plans. I decided to go out for lunch. It would do me good to get some fresh air and venture out into the city. I figured I wouldn't hear back from Charles until the evening. He was probably somewhere wheeling and dealing, making money for his bank, and wouldn't retrieve my message until much later.

Two hours from the time I ventured out, after picking up the local newspaper and grabbing a cup of coffee and blueberry muffin from Starbucks, I was back in my room. To my surprise, the red light on the phone was blinking, indicating I had a message.

I played it and heard: "Hey, Meshell, it's Charles. You know I'd love to hang out with my favorite southern belle tonight, but you're right, you didn't give me much prior notice. I already have plans. I promised my girl that I'd spend time with her tonight, take her out to dinner, but we can hang out tomorrow. Not a problem. If you can handle it, I want to take you to my special place. I'll drop by around eight and pick you up. Later."

"Damn! I was looking forward to going out tonight," I stated out loud, slamming the receiver back on the base and plopping down on the bed.

"Now, what am I going to do? Oh well, tomorrow is another day. What is his special place?" I wondered out loud.

For the remainder of the afternoon, I pampered myself by taking a leisurely bath in the Jacuzzi tub, with lots and lots of bubbles. Then I lay down for a bit, took a long nap, and finally went downstairs and received a full-body massage and facial. Heaven. I had already gotten my hair, nails, and feet done before I left Atlanta. I came back to my room several hours later, refreshed and relaxed. I spent the remainder of the night in, ordering room service and relaxing and watching TV (*Sex and the City* reruns) in my fluffy, hotel-issued bathrobe.

For the life of me, I couldn't figure out what Charles's special place could be. My curiosity was getting the best of me because I was not one who loved surprises. I'd soon find out.

The next day, day two, I slept late, but arose refreshed with a bundle of energy. I was doing good. Since I'd landed in DC, I'd thought only once or twice of the things I'd seen and heard during the trial. After showering and dressing, I decided to go out. It was officially fall and it was nice and crisp out. My black sweater was just right; a coat would have been too much. I walked a couple of blocks over from the hotel, window-shopping and taking my time. I saw a few art galleries I wanted to check out before I left the city; I made a mental note on how to get back to them. Finally, I slipped into a small café that looked cozy and inviting from the outside. It wasn't as crowded as some of the other more trendy spots I had passed during my sightseeing expedition. Today, I didn't want to deal with a bustling crowd of impatient lunchgoers.

When I strolled in, a chime sounded. I seated myself at a corner table, near a big picture window, and looked over the menu. The selections were few, but pricey. After deciding on a baked chicken Caesar salad and a Diet Coke, I sat back, sipped on my water, which had a lemon slice in it, and stared out the window at the various black professionals that walked by looking crisp, confident, and powerful. Washington, DC, was nicknamed Chocolate City for good reason.

The chime on the front door of the café rang out, and I instinctively turned to glance at whoever had walked in. I was met with an admiring stare and smile from an attractive middle-aged white man. He was a dead ringer for a younger version of the actor Richard Gere, gray hair and all. He held my eyes for a few moments until I quickly turned away and looked back out the window. Being hit on or flirted with by white men was nothing new for me; however, this one reminded me of someone from my past. One I chose to forget. Like a time travel machine, my mind swiftly slid back in time, to an incident that I had tried to purge from my system over the years.

The early morning sunlight gently nudged and pulled me awake. I had a raging headache. As I halfway opened one eye and then squinted out of the other, I checked out my unfamiliar surroundings. I was in a bedroom with masculine features. Burgundy wallpaper. Forest green curtains. For the life of me, I couldn't remember or place where I was. The pain behind my right eye was distracting and I couldn't focus. The room reeked of sex and weed. An intoxicating mixture. And why was I lying naked with a white sheet tangled around my waist and stickiness between my legs?

Before I could mentally answer that question, in walked a familiar, smiling white face carrying a bamboo breakfast tray. It took a few seconds for my brain to comprehend who was standing before me.

"Good morning, Meshell."

"Professor Steiner?" I questioned in disbelief, attempting to cover my nakedness with the thin sheet. I could have slithered through the floor.

"Please, please call me Steve. Let's not be so formal, especially after the good time we shared last night." He laughed a knowing dirty chuckle. I cringed.

Professor Steiner closed the short distance between the door and the bed and placed the tray, which held a raisin bagel, cream cheese, and orange juice, on the nightstand. I tensed, unsure of what to do. I closed my eyes, hoping when I opened them this would all be a terrible dream. Unfortunately, I had no such luck.

"Juice?"

Shaking my head and sitting up, I said, "No. No, thank you. Really, I've got to go."

He sat on the edge of the bed. "Don't rush off, Meshell. It's a lovely Saturday morning. Relax. Eat your breakfast."

I leaned back, still in disbelief, and he handed me a glass of orange juice. I took a couple of sips and it did taste good and it quenched my thirst. I licked my dry, chapped lips. I silently willed myself to think. Think. Think.

Professor Steiner sat patiently on the edge of his bed and stared at me like I was some rare, exotic creature that he had discovered, captured, and caged.

"You are so beautiful, Meshell. The first time you walked into my classroom I was captured by your radiance."

I had heard the stories around campus of him messing around with his law students. Before, I had always dismissed them as lies. Never believed them until now.

I nodded. I didn't know what to say to my law professor whom I had, based on the evidence, slept with and smoked an illegal substance with.

"Here, pull this down. You are all tangled up in the sheets." Steiner then proceeded to pull the cotton sheet down to expose my bare breasts. When the coolness of the room connected with my body, my nipples stood at attention for him.

"Lovely."

He leaned over to kiss me, but I beat him to the punch and pulled the juice glass to my lips again. He smiled knowingly. He wasn't in a rush. I took a few more sips.

"You know, Meshell, you are one of my most brilliant students. The sky's the limit. You're going to make a great attorney one day." Suddenly, his fingers were kneading my breasts and panic set in for me.

"Don't," was all I murmured. On the outside I appeared calm. The inside was a different story. I was in total emotional turmoil.

Professor Steiner continued to talk and feel on me as if he hadn't heard me speak. "I could be a wonderful ally to have in your corner. With you being an African American female, let's be real, it will be harder for you to break through the good-ole-boy network. I, however, have contacts at some of the top firms." As his left hand gently took the juice glass from my right hand, his moist mouth found a nipple. And suckled. He reached for the strawberry cream cheese and proceeded to smear it across my nipples and lick it off.

I gasped in horror and said quietly, "No. Stop." I didn't raise my voice. It came out in a whisper.

He didn't. Stop. One breast was in his mouth and with his free hand he caressed my other one.

It was all so surreal. "Does that feel good?"

I didn't respond.

"Maybe this does," he stated, squeezing a little too hard.

His hand reached to pull the sheet completely off; he had to pry it away from my fingers. "When I saw you last evening at the Honor Students Meet and Greet, I was again captivated by your dark beauty and presence."

"I have to go," I stated, trying to swing my wobbly legs off the bed.

"As I was saying, you scratch my back and I'll scratch yours. I'll take care of you." As I attempted unsuccessfully to press my legs together, his fingers sought out the inner warmth of my thighs. I held back a desire to scream as loud and as hard as I could. I wanted to pummel him with my fists until his face was a bloody mess. But I didn't.

"Open your legs, Meshell." His fingers were inside me now, stroking. "So wet. You know I won't hurt you," he said almost in a whisper. I had to strain to hear.

We had a staring contest for a few seconds that seemed like eternity.

"Open your legs. Wider," he repeated. Slowly I did as he requested.

"You enjoyed the pleasure I brought you last night. Don't you remember, you came back with me after the gathering, we drank some more, smoked a blunt, and then made love?"

That was the problem. I couldn't recall much of the previous evening. I remembered drinking a bit too much and feeling stressed and anxious and wanting to make a good impression on the faculty members present. Now, I wondered if Professor Steiner put something in my drink, a date rape pill.

My eyes were huge as saucers. "You know," he continued, "I've always been attracted to black women. There's just something amazing about you beautiful creatures." He bent down and gently bit and kissed my neck. Now he was pulling down his pajamas and releasing his pale manhood that dismissed the myth of size.

"Touch it."

I refused and he laughed again. "You weren't shy last night." He kissed me, hard, and rammed his tongue halfway down my throat. "Come here," he ordered, pulling me over to him. "One for the road and then you can go. I promise."

"I don't know. I don't feel well. Give me a minute to think about it." I was trying to buy some more time.

"I know my A student doesn't have to think this through," he suggested, pulling on my nipples and palming the back of my ass. "Come over here, Meshell. Please."

As he touched my most intimate spot, I scooted to the edge of the bed, with his fingers still in me, and opened my mouth to receive him. What felt like a lifetime later, he finished. My cheeks were sore and bruised.

"Climb up on the bed and spread those pretty black cheeks for me." I did as I was told and the nasty-ass started licking my butt crack. I was totally numb.

Two hours later, after he had had his way with me in almost every possible way, he dismissed me. And I learned a valuable lesson: My actions can have dire consequences.

When I looked back up toward the registers, the Richard Gere look-alike was walking out the door with a couple of bags in his hand and a large container of hot coffee. He glanced back at me one last time and smiled; I looked away. I knew his type. My breathing subsided and shortly afterwards, the waiter brought over my food and soda. I didn't realize the portion would be so huge. I had salad and chicken for days. I could have easily fed another person.

My mind drifted again. The only other person I ever shared that story with was Lexie. The day it occurred, I calmly recapped to her the rape. Never shed a tear. She encouraged me to report it, but I couldn't. Too much was at stake—my future. I finished Professor Steiner's course, which was one of the hardest things I ever had to do, tolerated him lusting after me, received the A that I deserved, and went on with my life as if that night had never occurred. In my reality it didn't.

The ring tone of my cell phone snatched me back from my dark reverie. I fumbled around in my purse to find it, pulled it out by its slim antenna, and checked out the phone number that was displayed. It had a DC area code.

"Hello."

"Hey, sexy."

"Well, hello to you. What a pleasant surprise. I didn't expect to hear from you until later this evening."

"Now you know I had to check up on my favorite girl."

"Your favorite girl?" I laughed. Charles knew how to pour on the charm.

"What's so funny? You are my favorite girl."

"Whatever, Charles. Remember, this is Meshell you are talking to."

He chuckled. "What are you up to?"

"Not much. I just finished lunch, and I'm on my way to check out a couple of art galleries I passed earlier. What about yourself?"

"Working hard. Always."

"I remember back in the day, you were the man when it came to math and finances. Among other things."

"Back in the day, I remember you wouldn't even give me the time of day. You hung around with this group of stuck-up girls and wouldn't glance my way."

"Stuck-up?" I questioned.

"Yes. You heard me. Stuck-up."

"Well, I recall a rainy night you drove me home from the infamous frat party that everyone talked about for days."

"Yeah, your hooptie had broken down, wouldn't crank, and for once you weren't with your crew, and I volunteered to drive you back to your dorm."

"My girls had gone home for the weekend. But, hey, don't you talk about my car; I loved that little red Cavalier."

"Well, it was a hooptie. Admit it. I call them as I see them."

"Okay, okay, you got me. I admit it; it was a hooptie, but it was all mine," I laughed, recalling that car.

"And before the night was over, we made love and you never gave me the time of day again. I'd see you on campus, at the library, with your head buried in a book, and I'd wonder if I imagined the entire rendezvous."

"Correction: And before the night was over, you had fucked me, forgotten my name by the next day, and went back to your whoring ways."

"Whoring ways? I was into my books."

"That wasn't all you were into."

As I paused in front of the first gallery and peeked through the window, Charles and I laughed heartily. "I'm glad you're laughing because our recollections of events are not on the same page. I seem to recall you being surrounded by a collage of women, twenty-four/seven. You didn't need me. You were such a contradiction: bookworm during the week and a party girl on the weekends. It was like there were two Meshells. I could never figure you out."

He chuckled again. I didn't comment. As an overachiever, I had to let off some stress during the weekends.

"As for me, I was young, dumb, and full of come. I was on a college campus bursting with beautiful black women; I thought I had died and gone to heaven. You couldn't tell me anything. Those were the best times of my life."

"Well, we are adults now. The party is officially over."

"It doesn't have to be. I know you aren't getting cynical at thirty!"

"No, but what I'd give to be young, carefree, and have no major responsibilities again."

"I hear you. Listen, I just wanted to let you know I look forward to seeing you tonight."

"Me too. What did you tell your girlfriend?"

"Don't worry about all that. You just be ready for me."

"Be ready for you?"

"Yes, you heard me right. I hope your back can handle what I'm coming with."

"You're crazy. Eight o'clock?"

"No, let's change the time; I can't wait that long. Why don't I pick you up at six o'clock and take you out for a nice dinner?"

"Sounds good."

"If it's okay with you, we can go to the restaurant in your hotel before we go to my special place."

"Sure, not a problem. But you are killing me with this special place. What is it? Where is it?"

"You'll see soon enough."

"Charles, I don't like and don't do surprises."

"Let's just say it's a setting where you have to check your inhibitions at the door."

"What? So, now you're talking in riddles?" I heard voices in the background.

"Listen, I have to run to a meeting, but I'll see you at six, love."

"Okay, see you then. Take care."

"Peace." His line went dead. I clicked off. *Leave your inhibitions at the door. What is Charles talking about? Oh well, I guess I'll find out at six.*

I opened the door to the first gallery, walked in, and was immediately assaulted by bold colors and designs. As my footsteps echoed on the concrete floor, I spent the next couple of hours lazily lost in observation as I checked out very unique pieces of paintings and sculptures. For the life of me, I could never fathom how something that looked like a first grader drew it during art class could sell for thousands of dollars. Some of the pieces scattered throughout the gallery looked like someone simply threw some paint against a canvas, called it art, and attached a steep price tag.

Surprisingly, the remainder of my day went by rather swiftly. I took a yellow taxicab over to one of the museums and walked around in there for a while. When I traveled to new cities, I loved to explore the history and usually I checked out the local museums. Before I knew it, it was time to return to my hotel room to prepare myself for my night out. I adored getting in the mood for an evening out. Setting the mood was just as enjoyable as the actual outing.

I started out by tuning the radio to a smooth R&B station and retrieving a miniature wine from the bar. Then I ran myself a long, hot bath and laid out what I was going to wear. Charles had mentioned dinner downstairs, so I figured I'd wear a black skirt with a sexy, low-cut, sky blue blouse. I didn't want to be too dressy or underdressed. My hoochie gear would be a bit too revealing for the downstairs restaurant and crowd.

At six on the dot, a sturdy knock came at my door; I smiled as I walked over to open it. I took one last glimpse in the mirror and was pleased at how stunning I looked. I glanced out the peephole, sucked in my breath, and opened the door.

"Hi."

"Hi yourself. You look lovely," Charles stated, kissing me lightly on the cheek.

"Come on in." I opened the door wider and moved to the side.

He stepped in and I inhaled his manliness. Charles was simply breathtaking. He was the total package, with an arrogance to match. I loved aggressive men; weak men did nothing for me. They didn't even begin to ignite my flame.

"Are you enjoying your stay so far?"

"I am. I needed to get away from Atlanta and get some rest, relaxation, and clear my mind for a minute."

"I feel you. I just hope I can help you with the clearing-your-mind part." He displayed a seductive smile. "However, I can't guarantee you're going to be able to get any rest with me, as sexy as you look and as good as you feel," he told me, copping a quick feel.

"I'm sure you can handle it."

"Are you ready for dinner?"

"I am. I'm starving. In more ways than one."

"That's what I love, a lady with an appetite."

I think I blushed.

Dinner and conversation were nice and stimulating as far as that goes. I kept pulling myself out of daydreams of Charles and me between the sheets doing the dance of love. Or at least the dance of lust. Charles and I flirted with each other relentlessly, talked business, and caught up. It was obvious he was doing well for himself. I didn't miss the bling on his wrist. He admitted that his girlfriend, Tara, who was from one of the more affluent DC families, was pressuring him about marriage.

I added my two cents. "Well, the way I see it is when you are ready you are ready. You can't let anyone force you. I think a forced or rushed marriage would be a huge mistake. Resentment would settle in at some point."

"What about you?"

"What about me?" I asked.

"I don't see any ring, engagement or otherwise, on your finger?"

"No. My career is my man."

"I know you are a big baller, Miss Assistant District Attorney and all, but is that enough?"

"For now it is."

"Does your career make you come?" Charles asked.

"Excuse me?"

"You hear me? Is your career satisfying you in bed?"

"Explain to me why a woman can't be into her career, but men can," I challenged him, with attitude.

"Calm down, lady. I was just messing with you."

"You better be."

"Honestly, though, I did think, when women got close to a certain age, all you could think about was wedding bells and babies and the big house on the hill."

"Not all of us."

"Well, I wish Tara were more like you. I wish she were more independent and career-minded. Her biggest worry is what china pattern to choose."

"Do you really?" I asked, leaning back in my chair and fixing him with a stare.

"Yes."

"I don't believe you. I think you like the hold you have on her. You can tell her anything and she'll believe you, like tonight. And that way you can continue to have your cake and eat it too," I stated, caressing his leg with my foot underneath the table.

"When did you become a man and get balls?"

"I have a brother; I know how men think. My brother has a lovely wife who adores him, yet he continues to be a dog when the cat's away."

"You're a trip. You think you have men all figured out."

"Not all, just the majority. Do you love her?"

As if thinking it through, Charles paused. "I do. In my own way. But the thought of settling down, having babies, and being with the same woman for the rest of my life scares the shit out of me."

"Bottom line: you can't fathom not having new pussy for the rest of your life?" I whispered.

"You are crazy, but if you want to break it down like a dude, yes.

"So, Meshell, you admit you are married to your career. That's clear. However, you still never answered my question: Doesn't your bed get cold and lonely?"

"It does . . . at times. Oh, I have my maintenance men who keep everything running properly and smoothly. Regardless of the pressure and stress, I really do love my job and for now, that's my focus and passion."

"Me too. I love the power and the ability to start off with one dollar amount and amass thousands, millions more. It's thrilling," he said, staring off into the distance. Like he could picture the dollar bills stacking up.

I laughed. "Look at us. Can't get away from talking business."

"I know; it's a damn shame. By the way, how's your food?"

"Good. Yours?" I asked.

"My steak is a little overdone, but it's okay."

I nodded and took a few more bites of my shrimp linguini. "I can't take it anymore—what's this special place you mentioned?"

"I'm not going to tell you. Gonna make you wait," he stated, gently caressing my hand on the tabletop.

"Come on."

"If I tell you, what you gonna do for me?"

I licked my lips. "Anything you want."

"You're good."

"I am and I can back it up," I said sassily.

"I believe you."

"Well? What's the spot?"

"It's a place I check out from time to time."

"Really. From time to time."

"Yeah, it's a different scene. You have to have an open mind. Sexually."

"Okay. I think I fit that bill. I'm definitely not a prude."

"After that night with me and KeVon, I know you would have no qualms about this scene. Girl, you were insatiable."

I smiled and blushed at the memory.

"Where is KeVon? I'd love to see him."

"I'm not sure. Believe it or not, we haven't talked in a while. He has this new job that keeps him pretty busy."

"Stop changing the subject. Where's the spot?"

"Do you know what a swingers club is?"

"Yes, of course I do. I don't exactly live in the boonies."

Charles paused and continued. "Well, I belong to one outside the city."

"You're kidding!" I said, placing my fork down to give him my undivided attention.

"No, I'm serious. It's by invitation only, but members can bring guests through."

"Do you mean couples are actually switching partners and having sex in front of each other and other people?"

He laughed and leaned back in his chair. "Something like that. It was pretty wild the first time I hit the spot. I had never seen anything like it in my life. People were fucking in every nook and cranny, in every possible way."

"Wow!"

"Meshell, you are funny."

"Does your Miss Tara know about your antics?"

"What do you think? Hell no. Tara is a good, Christian girl."

"Sounds like my friend Lexie. The very concept of a swingers club would blow her mind."

"Lexie, that name sounds familiar."

"Yeah, she was one of the girls I hung out with, still do. Her real name is Alexis Miller."

"I remember her. Cute, petite, and straightlaced," he recalled cutting into his steak.

"You pegged her. But if Tara is such a good, Christian girl, how does she satisfy you in bed?"

"She does one thing that drives me wild; I've trained her in that area."

"And what is that?" I paused in midbite.

"She gives exceptional head; she prides herself on it. Thinks it will keep me in her bed and her bed only. I can be watching a football game and she'll walk up, pull it out, and get busy until halftime."

"Damn. Sounds like a freak to me. If she likes to suck on dick that much, you'd better watch her ass." I laughed. Charles didn't.

"One of my sorors loved to perform fellatio. She had this little pink

journal that she kept beneath her mattress that listed in detail all the
sizes, descriptions, and identifying marks of the dicks of the men she
had been with. She even had drawings."

"Stop. Get out of here," he said with wide-open eyes.

"You were probably in there, Charles," I kidded.

"What was her name?"

"I'll never tell."

"Well, if she was with me, she had a mouthful."

"You are so arrogant." I lightly kicked him underneath the table.

"Anyway, getting back to the club, are you game?"

I hesitated for only a moment. "Let me ask you a question first."

"Sure. Go ahead."

"Do I have to participate? Can I just watch? I need to make sure
I'm feeling this first."

"Not a problem. They have separate rooms for the spectators."

"Spectators?" I questioned.

"Yeah, the people who just get off watching others."

"Okay, alrighty then. I'll try anything once."

"Let's finish up here and get this show on the road."

"Cool," I said, as butterflies fluttered in my stomach. I had no idea
what I was getting myself into. Charles was bringing me right back
into a lifestyle I had tried for years to escape.

Charles and I finished up our meals in record speed. Just the
thought of what we were about to do excited both of us immensely.
For the remainder of dinner, we flirted even more and everything had
a sexual connotation to it. We had our own private jokes that we
giggled at like two kids. Forty minutes later, we were stepping off the
elevator and unlocking my hotel door with the scan card. Charles had
suggested I change into something more suitable for our little adventure. He was dressed pretty casually in a dark pinstriped button-down
shirt and khaki pants with expensive loafers.

"Come on in and close the door. What should I wear?" I asked,
tossing my purse on the bed and making a beeline for the tiny closet.

"Something sexy and daring. I want all the men to be drooling at the mouth because they see something they want and can't have."

"That's right, they can't touch."

"You're safe with me. Don't worry about that," Charles reassured me.

I walked over to the closet, opened it, and pulled out several pieces of my hoochie wear. Charles looked them over, and we finally agreed on a short black dress that had a plunging neckline and frilly long sleeves. I had ankle-high black boots that matched.

"That's the one," Charles stated.

"You sure?"

"Baby, trust me. I can't wait to see you in it."

I walked into the restroom to change, brush my teeth, and reapply my lipstick. Charles helped himself to the minibar and patiently waited. Then we were ready. Just as we were walking out the door, Charles had a special request.

"Stop. Hold up."

"What now?"

"Pull off your panties."

"No, I wouldn't feel right."

"Come on. Be adventurous. You may never do anything like this ever again. That will be super sexy. Knowing you are bare-assed underneath that dress would give me an instant hard-on."

With a slight hesitation, I honored his wish.

"Only for you," I stated, holding on to his shoulders as I stepped out of them and tossed them on the floor near the TV stand. "Only for you."

We rode the elevator down like two excited teenagers and walked arm in arm to Charles's car. I couldn't resist the urge to stop pulling on my dress. Charles pretended he was going to snatch it up, so I kept hitting his hand away.

I still couldn't believe I was doing this. I actually agreed to go to a swingers club. It definitely wasn't my everyday scene, but I admit I was a bit curious. I'd heard of these places, but never personally knew of anyone who had ever gone to one, or at least, admitted to it. I had wondered if they really existed. I couldn't picture a place where every-day people coupled up, and in some cases tripled up, and performed all types of sexual acts in front of each other with no inhibitions. No one judged anyone and all had a good time, willingly. That completely blew my mind.

Charles promised that we'd drop by this club, stay no longer than an hour or two, have a few drinks, observe, and leave. He wouldn't let anyone touch me nor would he touch anyone. He promised. We'd simply check out the scene, see if I could get into it, and then leave. It sounded safe enough with those parameters in place.

As we drove over, Charles informed me that his business associate, Ford, had invited him to join months ago. This Ford guy was a pro-fessional in midlevel management for the same financial firm Charles worked for. He was gaining a reputation as a financial whiz too. So, his future glowed bright. If you saw him, according to Charles, you'd think he was the most conservative, geeklike person alive. He made Bill Gates look like a party animal. He wore stereotypical pinstriped suits, bow ties, and thick glasses that did nothing to complement his facial features. He talked very, very properly and enunciated every syllable. Ford came across as shy and unsure with the ladies, especially the black women. Yet at his parties, he let it all hang out. Literally. I had already learned that you never really know people.

Ford's rules for his sex parties were simple: attendance was by invi-tation only or you had to know someone who knew someone. Any-thing went as long as the participants were game. What happened at the house stayed at the house. Respect the owner's property because Ford wasn't always in attendance to monitor his guests. And, finally, only professionals could attend. The parties were held twice in a week, once during the weekday and once during the weekend, usually a Sat-urday night, once a month. This was a business where membership fees were charged to your credit card account.

As Charles's right hand made its way underneath the fabric of my dress, we drove through the streets of DC. I opened my legs for easier access and just as I was on the brink of losing my mind from his skillful fingers, we were there.

"Well, this is it."

"Okay," I stated, looking around at my surroundings. It was around nine o'clock and Charles and I had pulled up into the secluded circular driveway of a three-story house in an exclusive residential neighborhood.

"Remember, I'm going to be right by your side. Don't be afraid," Charles stated, walking around to open my car door.

"I know," I replied, feeling myself get nervous and unsure.

"By the way, if I haven't told you enough already, you look sexy as hell tonight."

"Thanks." We kissed passionately before getting out of the car and afterwards I didn't feel so tense.

Charles and I held hands like we were simply going to visit a friend. We were in the neighborhood so we thought we'd drop by. Parked in the driveway were Mercedeses, Lexuses, Hummers, and BMWs. Charles rang the doorbell. Within seconds, the door opened.

"What's up, man? Haven't seen you in a while," asked a young man dressed in all black with a clean-cut appearance.

"Been busy," Charles replied.

"I see. It's all good," he stated, looking me up and down with hungry eyes, licking his lips in an LL Cool J sort of way. I looked away. I didn't like feeling like a piece of meat on the auction block. I adored aggressive men, but not ghetto ones.

"Well, the party's already in full force. It's getting hot in there. Man, there's some wild shit going on tonight."

They both chuckled knowingly. I smiled and gripped Charles's hand even tighter. He squeezed back and guided me in with his arm around my waist. I tugged on my little black dress, the one that seemed even smaller right about now.

"You ready?" Charles asked, looking at me.

"Sure. As ready as I'll ever be."

We walked further into the foyer of the beautiful home. You could tell that great care had been taken in decorating and furnishing it. In what I assumed was the living room, I could see couples sprawled on the sofas, chairs, and thickly carpeted floor. A good time was being had by all. Even from the foyer, the scents and sounds of sex were in the air. The lights were dimmed and candles were lit throughout the house. Moans filtered from all corners, through the walls.

As we made our way through various rooms and inched by couples, I noticed Charles nodded here and there at a few men and women. He was very familiar with the layout of the house and knew many of the participants. Charles was not a stranger here. He held my hand and led me through. I blindly followed. I noticed a few women giving me the once-over. Looking me up from head to toe. I was like a kid gliding through a scene from *Alice in Wonderland*. I couldn't believe my eyes. People were making out all over the place. There could be two people carrying on a conversation and right next to them, a couple having sex. Men and women were boldly walking around naked, with no shame to their game. Liquor and the smell of weed were heavy in the air, too. I noticed a jar of brightly colored pills of all shapes and sizes sitting in the middle of a coffee table.

"Are you okay? You're too quiet."

"Yeah, I'm alright. Just observing. I've never seen anything like this before. I can't believe it," I responded, looking left and right like a kid in a candy store.

"These people are sexually liberated and know that sex is as natural as breathing. There is nothing to be ashamed or embarrassed of."

"I'm not."

"Well, what do you think?"

"I'm still taking it all in. These look like everyday people."

Charles laughed. "Meshell, they are. What did you expect? A house of three-eyed people with five arms?"

We made it to the kitchen and Charles grabbed a few beers from a huge cooler. I needed something after what I had witnessed. Even in the kitchen, up against the wall, there were two women locked in a passionate kiss. Their shirts were off and they were caressing each other's breasts, totally oblivious to us. I felt hot. Their moans followed us out of the kitchen and down a hallway.

Charles led me down some narrow stairs and we found ourselves in another dimly lit room. It took a few moments for my eyes to adjust to the lighting and layout. However, the sensual moans assaulted my ears instantly. *Aaah! Aaah! Aaah! Ooh! Ooh!*

"Let's try to find a seat over in the corner," Charles said, reaching for my hand again. I was shaking uncontrollably and moistness was creeping between my legs.

"What is this? Why are all these people just sitting around drinking and smoking?"

"This is the one room where you can watch couples having sex. No one will approach you in here unless you want them to."

"Is this safe?" I asked, holding back. "I know some of it isn't legal."

"Come on, Meshell. We've discussed this. You know I won't let anything happen to you," he stated, pressing up behind me. I noticed that he already had an erection. His right hand grazed against my left nipple and I shuddered.

"I know you won't."

We finally found a corner spot that was somewhat secluded. I sat down on an ottoman between Charles's legs. Everyone else was cluttered around the bar. Yes, there was a bartender. I gulped a few swallows of my beer, and looked around some more in awe. It was a total circus. There were about twenty people in the room who were seated, drinking, conversing, and watching. There were all ages, sexes, and races congregated in the room.

The center of attraction was four couples in the middle of the room, on an expensive-looking oriental rug, who were in various acts of fornication. There was one thirty-something couple who were just starting to undress each other. The attractive woman with short twists had just unzipped the muscular man's pants and pulled out his erect penis. She wasted no time taking him into her eager mouth while he fondled her huge breasts, which he had freed from her sweater.

A second couple, an older man and younger girl, were going at it. Frantically. She, down on all fours, was screaming out in ecstasy or pain every time he entered her from behind. The older man had a tight grasp on her ass cheeks and was drilling her as if his life depended on it. He was telling her, "That's right. Take all this dick."

An interracial couple, a clean-cut white guy and a chick with long braids, were not as aggressive. She was serenely lying on her back, supported by multicolored throw pillows, with her legs spread wide, while the dude ate her out. He was taking his time, enjoying her. You'd never know that he had twenty people watching his tongue action. Evidently he was doing a wonderful job, based on her sensual moans and the wetness seeping from her pussy. I felt my own convulse.

Last but not least was a threesome of sorts. A twenty-something female had a tall thin female and a shorter, balding man servicing her every need. Fingers, tongues, and other body parts were all over the place. Based on the expression on her face, I don't even think she realized where she was. Girlfriend was definitely feeling no pain. She was in her sexual zone.

I hadn't realized I'd finished my first bottle of beer until Charles handed me another one. I took a few more gulps. This was unbelievable. I wasn't sure what or where my feelings were. I was torn between a mixture of excitement and disgust.

I turned to find Charles staring at me with a strange look on his face. "Is this turning you on?" he whispered seductively, licking my earlobe. He laughed loudly. "Don't even answer. I know your pussy is throbbing."

"Dude over there is tearing her shit up. He's all up in that," Charles stated, pressing against me as I sat in between his open legs.

"I see. It looks like he's hurting her."

"Some women like that rough sex. They like to get their asses spanked and roughed up," Charles explained, taking another swallow of his beer and placing his hand on my knee. "I dated this one chick that enjoyed being slapped around before I screwed her. She said it turned her on."

"You actually hit her?"

"Not hard. I would push her around, be rough like she liked it. Slap her a couple of times."

"That's sick."

"Don't trash it until you've tried it."

I didn't comment; I just glanced back at him like he was crazy. Again, you never knew people.

This tall, very attractive, well-dressed guy stopped by. It was obvious he had money and he looked familiar. I couldn't place the face; possibly a sports personality. He made brief eye contact with me and his eyes traveled over my body within seconds. He didn't care that I noticed. He and Charles exchanged a few whispered words and Charles grabbed two more beers from him and handed me one. Out of the corner of my eye, I watched him approach a chocolate sister who sported a small natural hairstyle. He simply went up to her, backed her into a corner, and started kissing on her neck, then he pulled up her short dress, slowly turned her to the wall, and entered her from behind in one thrust, with her thong pushed to the side. She let out a small scream, but didn't resist. When he smiled, licked his lips, and nodded at me, I quickly looked away.

"Check out the white dude over there. He's eating her stuff up. Look at how wet she is."

Charles was right. She was dripping wet. He had pulled his fingers out of her and she tasted herself when he inserted his fingers into her mouth.

I could feel my buzz coming on strong. Yet I continued to drink beer out of nervousness and the sexual excitement I was experiencing.

The female of the threesome who was being serviced let out a loud orgasmic moan. The entire time, the other female never stopped lapping at her. I saw the trembles start from her chest and flow down to her legs. She came hard and strong.

I felt myself getting even wetter and I shifted around in my seat.

"Is this making you horny?"

"A little," I lied.

"How about a lot?" Charles whispered into my ear. "It's alright to admit that your little pussy is throbbing. I bet it's seeping wet and purring for me. Why are your legs shaking?"

I hunched my shoulders in response.

"Let me see," Charles stated, trying to reach under my short dress.

"Stop!" I shouted, playfully knocking his hand away.

"Nobody is paying us any attention. Let me touch you."

"No. Stop!"

"Turn around, baby. Just give me a kiss then."

"Maybe."

"One little kiss. Quit playing hard to get. I'm supposed to be your man tonight," he teased.

When he saw that I was giving in, Charles pulled me into his lap, with me facing him.

"That's my girl. Just relax. I just want a kiss. That's all," he stated, gently rubbing my back over and over in a firm circular motion.

Charles cupped my chin, kissed me slowly and sensually. He took his time exploring my mouth and then savoring my tongue. I felt so uninhibited. Charles felt so good and I sensed my body giving in to his touch and forgetting where I was. The beer helped, along with the erotic moans filling the room.

"Hmm, you taste sooo good. I can never get enough of you. Never. You need to come to DC at least once a month."

"I think I'm a little light-headed." I really wasn't a drinker. With the Crew, Tracee had us all beat in that department. I was only a social drinker.

"You'll be alright; you're here with me. Relax."

Charles started feeling my breasts. Caressing them through my dress. He rubbed my nipples through the fabric in slow circular motions and then pulled. I moaned. My moan soon blended in with the others in the room.

Charles started to pull down the top portion of my dress.

"No! Wait! What are you doing? Are you crazy?"

"Damn, baby, nobody's watching us. They're into their own groove. I want to touch you, your bare skin."

He kissed me again and took my breath away. I was lost in the moment. Next thing I knew, the top portion of my dress was pulled down. The cool air made my nipples erect and hard. My head was still floating.

He continued to suck and stroke my breasts, which were exposed for all the room to see. Amazingly, no one was really watching us. Charles was sucking them just right, just like I like it. I moaned again and closed my eyes, embracing the sensation of his skillful tongue. Between the beer and the sucking, I was feeling no pain. I was actually forgetting where I was.

"You feel how hard my dick is?" Charles asked, placing my hand between his legs.

I nodded my head. "Yeah, it wants some." I giggled and closed my eyes again.

"I bet you are dripping. Let me check."

Charles kissed my neck and fondled me some more. Then he took his free hand and stuck it underneath my dress. When his finger entered me, a huge shudder went through my entire body. He pulled it out and stuck it back in. My legs involuntarily opened further apart.

"Oh yeah, you are good and moist. You ready for some dick. I knew this shit was turning you on."

"Hmmm," I chanted, moving up and down to push his now two fingers deeper inside me.

"Yeah, go with it. That's my girl. Get yours." I kept my eyes closed tightly.

"Hmmm," I moaned as I licked my dry lips several times.

"Hell yeah! I know how to make you feel good, don't I? I know what you need."

"Yessss," I cried. With my eyes clamped shut, I had totally forgotten where I was. All I was focusing on was Charles's breath in my ear, what he was whispering to me, and his fingers working me over. All my senses were heightened tenfold; it was really weird.

"You want to suck my dick?"

"Nooo," I slurred.

"Yes, you do."

"Maybe. We'll see."

"My fingers are cramped. Pull your dress up some then."

"Nooo, don't stop!" I screamed as he stopped abruptly.

"You want me to keep going?"

"Yesss!"

"Pull up your dress."

I did what Charles said because I didn't care anymore and all my inhibitions were drifting swiftly away. They were almost completely out the door, and walking up the sidewalk. Charles got his rhythm back within seconds. My eyes were closed again, my head thrown back, and it felt sooooo gooood that I was biting down on my finger.

"You want me to stop?"

"No. Don't stop."

"You sure?" Charles whispered as he touched my spot and went back to kissing my neck. Suddenly I knew something was wrong, different somehow. Something didn't feel the same or smell right. A different, unfamiliar scent assaulted my nose and space. The hands touching and the mouth sucking my breasts so deliciously felt alien. I slowly opened my eyes and looked up. A strange man, the attractive guy who had stopped by earlier with the beers, was fondling and sucking my breasts as Charles continued to touch me. The moment froze in time and I recognized him for the sports figure he was. Hell, I'd watched him on TV the other night. A decision had to be made. My inner good girl and bad girl fought back and forth. In the end, let's just say my bad side won out.

The next day, I arose late once again. Spent, tired, but satisfied. I reached over to answer the phone when I noticed the blinking red light. The message stated: "You have a delivery at the front desk. The hotel will deliver at your convenience."

After dragging myself into the hottest shower I could muster and staying in there until I was a prune, I dressed in a jogging suit and walked downstairs to find a beautiful bouquet of flowers waiting. The attached note simply read: *Thanks for a most memorable night. Damn, girl! Have a safe trip home. Charles.*

With my flowers in tow, I smiled all the way back up on the elevator. The rest of the day was spent shopping, shopping, and more shopping, eating ice cream, and taking in a movie at the mall. As I entered my room later that afternoon, I ran to pick up the ringing phone. I figured it was someone from the front desk.

Tossing all my bags on the bed, I snatched the receiver up in one swift swoosh. I thought, the workout room was definitely calling my name. My DC trip had totally thrown my usual eating patterns out of sync. I didn't diet, but I ate certain foods and at certain times. The last few days, I'd been all over the place.

"Hello?" I asked while making myself comfortable on the bed.

"May I speak with Meshell?" a deep, unfamiliar voice asked.

"This is she. Who's calling?"

"This is KeVon, Charles's friend. We met last year. During another one of your visits to the city."

"Oh yeah. KeVon." I blushed. "I definitely remember you."

He chuckled at that last statement.

"I bumped into Charles this morning, and he mentioned you were in town and had asked about me."

"Yeah, I did. He said he hadn't seen you in a while, though."

"True, true. I've switched jobs and have to get up pretty early every morning, so I don't hang out as much."

"I see," I said as I fiddled with the phone cord, twisting it around my fingers.

"But I'd make an exception for you. How'd you like to hang out with me this evening?"

I hesitated for only a moment. "Sure, what do you have in mind?" I asked, turning onto my back and looking up at the ceiling.

"I'm sure if we put our heads together we can come up with something," he stated. "I want you to have a good time."

"Count me in."

"Why don't I pick you up at, say, seven thirty in the lobby, and we can decide then. We can go somewhere and get drinks or something. We'll play it by ear. Unfortunately, we'll have to call it an early night."

"Sounds good and that's cool with me."

"Cool, it's a date. See you at seven thirty."

I hung up the phone with a huge grin on my face. "Yes!" I screamed, pumping my fists, two times, in the air. "I didn't even expect getting two for one."

Checking out the clock, I realized I had more than enough time to take a nap before tackling the task of packing my suitcase and getting that out of the way, and then getting dressed for my outing. I didn't know if I could handle another night, but I was definitely willing to try. The previous night had been wild!

I stepped off the elevator and walked into the lobby of my hotel at seven thirty on the dot. There he was. Just as I remembered. A chocolate god. He hadn't seen me yet, but he must have sensed my thoughts. KeVon stood, his face lit up like Christmas lights as he smiled and came my way.

Kissing me on the cheek, he stated, "We meet again."

"That we do."

"I had forgotten how beautiful you are, Miss ADA."

"Thank you. You too."

"Huh?" he questioned.

"You're beautiful."

"I don't think I've ever had a woman tell me that."

"Well, you are. You remind me of that male model Tyson."

"Thank you. That's quite a compliment coming from you."

KeVon was dressed casually, stone-washed blue jeans and a pullover sweater. Even through the thick sweater, I could see the outline of tight, taut muscles. I remembered when he was moving inside of me and how his muscles rippled up and down. I could watch all day. I was pleased I hadn't dressed up and had chosen to go casual as well in my black jeans, black T-shirt, midriff sweater that tied below my breasts, and black boots.

Linking his arm through mine, he asked, "Are you ready?"

"Let's roll."

We strolled out to the circular drive. KeVon opened the car door for me and walked around to the driver's side. He got in next to me, looked over, and smiled as if he couldn't believe I was there. "Are you comfortable?"

"Yes. Very."

KeVon turned the key in the ignition and we were off. He had his radio station tuned to some hip-hop station and it was blasting.

"Do you like hip-hop?"

"Yes. Some of it. I don't like the songs that downgrade women or call us names."

"I figured you for R&B or pop music."

"Well, see what you get for figuring?" I laughed. "If I could ask one favor, though, could you turn the volume down some?"

"Not a problem. Sometimes I forget that everyone doesn't like their music blaring as loud as I do."

I nodded my head.

"Where do you want to go tonight?"

"This is your town. You choose; I'm with you."

"Well, seeing as how you're so open-minded, I had a place in mind."

"Cool. Let's check it out. I trust your judgment," I stated.

We rode for another fifteen, twenty minutes or so before turning into the parking lot of what was a very colorful building on the outside. It was painted bright blue and yellow and the parking lot was packed.

"What is this?" I asked, looking around.

"You'll see," he said in a very secretive way.

KeVon came around and opened my car door, and I stepped out cautiously.

Grabbing my arm, he said, "Come on. I won't steer you wrong. Trust me."

"Okay. Lead the way."

We walked up a ramp and entered a side door. Once my eyes adjusted to the darkness, I realized we were in a gentlemen's club, except this one had men and women dancers letting it all hang loose. I also noticed there were just as many women patrons in attendance as there were men. There was a front stage that had two runways; one veered off to the right and the other to the left. At the moment, I counted six or seven strippers shaking what their mama gave them to a hot hip-hop beat. This club consisted of a mixed atmosphere with black and white strippers, male and female.

KeVon pointed. "Let's grab that table over there." Holding my elbow, he led the way.

A few minutes later, we were seated over to the side, with a good view of the stage and a few beers to get us started. I sat back and relaxed and observed. This was very tame compared to what I had witnessed and done the night before. One of the male strippers was giving special attention to one of the women near center stage. She was screaming, stuffing one-dollar bills down his thong, and copping a few feels on his ample butt.

I caught KeVon staring at me as he sipped his beer.

"What?"

"You know I haven't met many women like you."

"Really? Like what?"

He leaned back in his chair and took another swig of his beer. "Oh,

I don't know. One who is secure in her sexuality. If I had attempted to bring another woman up in here, she would have cursed me out and slapped me across the face."

"I work hard and play even harder. Why should you men have all the fun?" I asked, clicking my beer bottle with his.

"There are not a lot of sistahs who would be willing to, uh, experiment the way you do."

"To each his own. You gotta do what works for you. Do. You!"

KeVon lifted his beer bottle to toast me. "True. To each his own." We clicked bottles again. "Do. You!"

"Seriously, as long as I'm comfortable with what I'm doing, I'm in control. I'm not hurting anyone and I'm happy in the process, so I don't see a problem. I enjoy sex."

"When Charles first mentioned you were an assistant district attorney, I thought you'd be all stuck-up."

"Stuck-up? For what reason?"

"Oh, come on now. You must be banking some serious dollar bills back in Atlanta, and me, I'm totally blue collar, trying to get by. Paycheck to paycheck."

"Well, my grandmother didn't raise me to think I'm better than anybody else." My mother was another story.

"Your grandmother raised you?"

"Not literally. I didn't live with her, but my mom wasn't always around. Work called."

KeVon didn't say anything, as if expecting me to continue.

"Long story."

"And one you don't care to talk about."

"Right," I simply stated.

"You are one mysterious woman."

"Not really. Most men don't bother to find out about me."

There was a comfortable silence.

"How do you and Charles know each other?" I asked.

"Charles and I basically grew up together. We were best of friends from middle school through high school. Then Charles went off to college and I joined the army. He was always the brain and I guess I was the brawn. Charles is cool. We've had a lot of fun together. Believe me when I say we have many tales to tell our future sons one day."

"Did he tell you where he took me last night?"

"Yeah. What did you think of it?" KeVon asked, checking for my answer.

"Like I said, to each his own. The sexual energy was definitely in the house. Let's just say I saw freaky shit."

KeVon laughed. "I bet you did."

About that time, one of the female strippers danced her way over. I couldn't tell if she was dancing for me or for KeVon's attention; she flirted with both of us. I watched in fascination the way she moved her tiny body to the music; she was an excellent dancer. I watched KeVon slip her a few dollars. In thanks, she jiggled her breasts in his face and moved on shortly afterwards.

KeVon and I talked and drank, drank and talked. I had a wonderful time observing people and checking out the strippers. I wondered what each of their stories was. Personally, I could have gone with a bit more chocolate in the house, but I was cool.

"You want me to call that one over for you? You keep checking him out." KeVon pointed to a tall, brown-skinned brother with a clean-cut appeal.

"No, I don't."

"Yes, you do. I've seen you look at him over three times in the last five minutes."

KeVon held up some dollar bills and Mandingo strutted his stuff over. "Hey, man, dance for my lady. She's feeling you tonight."

Mandingo produced a brilliant, Crest commercial smile. "Hey, pretty lady."

"And if you make her real happy, I'll tip you an extra ten dollars."

Mandingo put on quite a performance. He danced his butt off, and what a nice one it was, and I enjoyed every second of it. After peeping under the trunks, I understood the reason for his name. I think I loved seeing the reaction on KeVon's face more than the actual performance. I could tell that him seeing another man turn me on turned him on. The entire time Mandingo danced for me, KeVon didn't take his eyes off me. In fact, he touched my hands and intertwined his fingers in mine.

I knew Mandingo had ignited some fires when I had to pull off my sweater because it was suddenly hot in the building. KeVon's eyes almost popped out of his head when he spotted my nipples poking through my thin T-shirt; I had decided against wearing a bra.

After his lap dance, we quickly paid Mandingo for his services, left the building, and drove back to the hotel. I invited KeVon up, but he declined, to my dismay. I was very disappointed, but I understood he had an early morning ahead of him. KeVon said he knew if he came up with me, we'd end up sexing each other into the wee hours of the morning. He had that right.

So I settled for messing around in his car for a few minutes. It took me back to my high school days and petting in the back seat after the game. KeVon and I kissed, touched, and stroked and it was fabulous. He pulled my T-shirt up and stroked and sucked my breasts while I moaned mercilessly. I managed to pull my jeans down around my ankles, and he played down there as I stroked him. We moved to the back seat. Somehow, don't ask me how, KeVon managed to position himself between my legs and his tongue and mouth went to work. Ten minutes later, I was holding on to his head like it was my personal life vest. Five minutes after that, I was getting on the elevator to go upstairs to my hotel room with a smile on my face.

Just as I entered the room, the phone rang.

Now who could that be? I snatched it up. "Hello?"

"Have sweet dreams, beautiful."

"I will," I stated as I slowly hung up the phone.

When I left the following morning for the airport, I had accomplished my goal: I was relaxed and focused again.

tonya

I sluggishly walked into the tiny kitchen and plopped down in a chair at the raggedy, dull, dented kitchen table that we had pulled in from the curb, where someone had discarded it as trash. My mix-and-matched chair wobbled and I caught my balance. Mama was busy putting the finishing touches on some meat loaf, a can of beans, and corn bread. Man, I hated meat loaf; we had it all the time.

I sighed and my ten-year-old chest heaved up and down.

"What's wrong, Tonya?" Mama asked, turning around from the stove to peer at me.

"Nothing," I stated as pitifully as possible.

"Where are your sisters? It's too quiet."

"They're watching cartoons." I sighed again.

Mama stopped mixing the corn bread batter and focused her full attention on me.

"Come here, sweetie," she told me, holding out her arms. "What's wrong? You can tell me."

I walked over and buried my face in her apron. I couldn't hold the pain and embarrassment in any longer. I was bursting at the seams to release it.

"Tell Mama what's wrong."

"At school, some of the girls make fun of me."

"Who? Who's messing with my baby?"

"Jasmine, Blair, and Marsha."

"What do they say? Fast asses."

"They make fun of the way I dress. They laugh and point, call me names, and say my clothes are always old and too big or too small."

I instantly saw the agony appear in my mama's eyes. Like a curtain being opened.

"Don't you worry about them, sweetie. You may not have the newest clothes, but your clothes are clean and lovingly cared for. That's all that matters."

"That still doesn't make it better," I whispered under my breath.

"Sweetie, I try so hard to provide for you and your sisters. That's why I work these two jobs. But sometimes, most times, I can't get ends to meet. I do the best I can with what I have."

"I know, Mama. I know."

"You just wait. All my hopes are on you. When you grow up, you won't live like this. You'll have the best of everything. I can picture it now. New clothes, expensive shoes, big house, fancy cars, maybe even your own personal maid. Just wait. My baby is going to have it all. Nobody will make fun of my baby ever again."

"And I'll take care of you, Mama, and you won't have to work cleaning up other people's houses. I'll hire someone to clean up your house."

"I know you will. I know you will, sweetie."

"You just wait and see."

The ringing phone, lying on top of my stomach, jerked me wide-awake.

"Hello."

"Hey, baby."

"Where are you, Brad? You should have been here over an hour ago," I screamed, looking at my watch.

"I know, sweetie. That's why I'm calling."

"Don't you dare say it! Don't you cancel on me! This will be the third time this month."

"I know, but I can't help it. I'll make it up to you."

"I don't want you to make it up to me. I want you here. Now!"

"Well, I'm sorry, Tonya. That's not going to happen tonight. My wife is—"

"Your wife. It's always your wife, Brad. When are you getting your divorce? When?"

"Tonya, please let's not start again. I give you diamonds, pearls, designer clothes, you name it, and you still complain. I can never satisfy you."

"Sometimes it isn't enough. I'm not *all* about material things. I do need attention and affection."

"You could have fooled me," he whispered.

"What? What did you say?"

"Nothing. Besides, I showed you plenty of affection last weekend."

"For once."

"I have to walk back in the house before she comes out. I told her that I was coming out to the car to get some important papers out of my briefcase."

"Whatever!"

"Don't be like this, Tonya. I'll make it up to you. I promise."

"Don't bother."

"You don't mean that. You've hung in here for four months— don't give up on us now."

I didn't comment.

"Tonya?"

"I'm here. You promised me that you were getting a divorce. I'm not one of those stupid women you can string along for years with false hopes of being with you."

"I didn't say you were, sweetie."

"I'll walk."

"Let's talk about this Friday."

"No. Let's talk now," I demanded.

"I'm coming by your office to have a meeting with some of the salespeople."

"So?"

"Can I take you out to lunch?" Brad asked.

"No."

"Come on, sweetie, don't act like this."

"Don't treat me like this then."

"I hate this more than you do. I'd give anything to be there with you tonight."

Silence.

"Holding you, touching you."

"Well, you are not here. You are there with her."

"Can we do lunch? We can talk. Really talk."

"I don't know, Brad. I'm sick of this whole situation."

"It was going to be a surprise, but I purchased that Tiffany bracelet you were admiring a couple of weeks ago."

"Really?" My anger released its hold on me temporarily.

"Yes, and it has your name written all over it."

"Okay, Brad, fine. We can go to lunch. But you are not going to continue to treat me like a second-class citizen. You need to decide and soon."

"That's my girl."

"You said you wanted to marry me, have babies with me."

"I do. Just be a little more patient with me. You've never been married; you don't understand the dynamics that exist."

"I'll try, but I can't promise that for much longer."

"I promise, we are going to be together, and I'll give you everything you've hoped and longed for. What you deserve."

"Yeah, right," I said with a smart-aleck tone.

"Sweetie, I hate when you have that smart-mouthed attitude."

"Well, don't give me a reason to, Brad."

"Why don't you make reservations over at the hotel for around one o'clock Friday and we'll take a long lunch?"

"Maybe I don't want to go to the hotel," I declared.

"Who are you fooling? Certainly not me. I may not be the most attractive man alive, but I have two things you simply love."

"And what is that?"

"Money and a magic tongue."

"Whatever, Brad."

"Yeah, I got your whatever. You don't say that shit when my head is buried between your thighs."

In the background, I heard a feminine voice. I couldn't understand what she said, though. "I gotta go. Make the reservation." Then all I heard was a dial tone.

Shit! Shit! Shit! I was tired of Brad and his lies and cancellations and more lies. I couldn't believe I was caught up in being the mistress on the side, the other woman. I never in a million years would have thought I'd be in this situation. Not me, not the diva.

But here I am. Sitting at home on Friday nights, lying to my friends. Hell, I didn't have brunch with that man I met at the play the other weekend. He did give me his number, but I never called. That was just what I told the Crew. Actually I drove over to our spot and spent a leisurely few hours in bed with Brad.

Brad, my boss. Brad, married with two teenage kids. Brad, bringing in a high six-figure salary. Brad, who can go *downtown* with the best of them. *What is a diva to do? What is a diva to do?*

Do I love the man? Hell to the no. Do I love his money and the lifestyle he can provide? Hell yes. I could marry for money, no problem. Brad is not much to look at, but he is very generous with his money and favors. I grew up watching my mama work two jobs, raise three girls, clean up other folks' houses, bring home their throw-outs and hand-me-downs. I decided early on that that wasn't going to be me. I realized I was meant to be treated like a princess, a diva. I was meant for bigger and better things, and I deserved the best that life has to offer. I work hard, I have good friends, I love my family, and I'm kind to people; I deserve to be placed on a pedestal. And Brad can afford to do that. Love isn't the end-all.

Do I feel guilty? Hell to the no! Brad and his wife are hanging on, but barely. They are two people who should never have married. To put it simply, they make each other miserable. They come and go like strangers in that big old house that could hold three families easily. (Unbeknownst to Brad, yeah, I drove by and checked it out.) If it weren't for his children, Brad said he would have been long gone. He even thinks *she* may be seeing someone on the side. There have been a few too many phone hang-ups in the middle of the night.

How did all this get started? Well, let me tell you.

Approximately four months ago, my employer had a weekend retreat at Spa Chateau. For those of you who don't know, Spa Chateau is exquisite. Customers are treated like royalty, with complete spa packages and pure relaxation in a back-to-nature, woodsy setting. It was the company's way of thanking us for hard work and going above and beyond our sales quotas. Don't get me wrong, it was a working weekend, but we had lots of free time to do whatever we wanted to do. I took advantage of everything.

Brad was there since he's regional sales manager for the Southeast and Midwest. Before the retreat, I hadn't had a lot of dealings with him because I reported to a direct manager who is over the buyers. My dealings with Brad were very limited, and I thought of him as my overweight, middle-aged, average-looking, but very well paid superior. I'm not sure what happened that weekend. I don't know if it was the wine that was readily available or the romantic, scenic setting or just Brad being very flirtatious with me. I learned the man can be very charming and goes after what he wants with a mission. Money and power can be quite an aphrodisiac.

That weekend Brad wanted me. He charmed me, complimented me, went out of his way to be around me. Brad even invited me to a special breakfast that was usually reserved for the bigwigs. I sat to his right, like the first lady. Later, we chatted late into the night and he listened and gave me advice as a mentor would do. He seemed genuinely interested in my career, family, and friends and he shared with me that he was in an unhappy marriage, had been for many years.

As the weekend wore on, I started to see him in a different light. He wasn't *that* overweight, his dimple was very flattering to his plain face, and his bank account was very handsome. The Crew, myself included, would never, ever in a million years date a married man. That's why to this day, they don't know about Brad's and my relationship. We laughed at women who waited around year after year, wasting their best years, for men like Brad. Hoping and praying that one day they'd leave their wives for them. Hoping their big payday would arrive. However, I learned to never say never. That's one life lesson I've learned.

It was no surprise to me when, on the last night of the retreat, Brad showed up at my room, with my gold shawl in hand. We had had a semiformal farewell dinner and, knowing it would be cool, I had worn my shawl.

Opening the door, I said, "Oh, hi, Mr. Benson."

"Brad, please."

"Brad."

"You left this in the dining room," he said, holding it up.

"Oh, silly me. Thank you," I said, reaching for it. In the next few seconds, his hand lingered on mine a bit too long.

My door was open and Mr. Benson was standing in the hallway, peeking into the darkness of my room. The only illumination came from the TV screen and a few candles I had lit.

"I hope I'm not disturbing you," he stated, not attempting to leave anytime soon.

"Oh, no, I was relaxing and hating that we have to leave tomorrow.

I simply adore this place. They've spoiled me. But I'm a true night person, so I'll be up for a while."

"Well, you know I have a membership here. You can come back on me anytime you'd like."

"No, thanks. I couldn't do that."

"Really, you're welcome," he volunteered.

"No, thanks anyway."

"Well, if you change your mind let me know."

"I will."

There was an unsettling silence. I didn't know what to do or say, for once in my life. "Uh, would you care to come in for a nightcap?"

To my surprise, he said, "Sure. I'd love to." And proceeded to walk boldly in and close my door.

With his presence there, it seemed like my room instantly got smaller. I pulled my robe closer. Tighter. "I had changed into my gown, but I can change into something more appropriate."

"Don't be silly."

"I wouldn't want anyone to get the wrong idea."

"How so?"

"Well, you are my boss, in my hotel room," I blabbered on and on.

Brad smiled because he knew he was making me nervous. There was a power, a presence, about him. When he walked into a room, people paused and took notice and thought he was somebody.

"Are you happy with your room?" he asked, walking around my space as though he owned it.

"Yes. It's lovely."

"Good. I want only the best for my employees. First-class accommodations."

"Yes, this has been a wonderful trip. I think it was very productive and everyone had the opportunity to get to know each other better and reinforce that we are working toward a common goal."

"Spoken like a true spokesperson for the company."

By now, he was sitting in my one recliner and staring intensely at me.

I cleared my throat and pulled on my robe some more.

"You look very beautiful tonight. You're simply glowing."

"Thank you."

There was an awkward silence and I looked away.

"Your boyfriend is a lucky man."

"Boyfriend?"

"I assumed a lovely lady such as yourself would be dating."

"Dating? What's that?"

He laughed. "You have a wonderful sense of humor. Please, sit down. Make yourself comfortable."

I sat on the edge of my bed. The only sound was the TV. I had turned it to some movie on HBO. At the moment, a couple was in bed making love.

I quickly looked away.

"Looks like they are having fun," he said, winking at me.

I nodded.

"What if I told you I was very attracted to you?"

I swallowed a couple of times. "I'd say I was very flattered."

"Well, I am. You are a very beautiful woman. I'm sure you're told that all the time."

"Thank you, again."

"I'm sure you date or are approached by men that are younger, more fit, or more attractive than I am, but I bet they can't give you too much financially."

I listened carefully, took it all in, and didn't utter a word.

"Tonya, you appear to be a woman who likes the finer things in life. I can tell, you like to be pampered and placed on a pedestal. You love being seen and appreciated. Adored even."

I nodded. I couldn't speak because my voice had left me.

"I believe in getting straight to the point. I can provide that and much more. More than you can ever imagine or even wish for."

By now, Brad had stood up and was standing directly in front of me. My eyes hadn't left his since he started talking.

"May I kiss you?"

I thought to myself, a simple kiss wouldn't hurt anything. I nodded my head because I didn't trust my voice.

Brad pulled me up to a standing position and gave me the most delicious, sensual kiss I think I've ever experienced. When he released me, somehow my robe came open. Underneath it, I was wearing one of my sexy, see-through negligees, with no panties. That was one of my quirks; I didn't wear underwear to bed.

"Beautiful," Brad stated as his eyes roamed hungrily up and down my body. I should have covered myself up, but I didn't. I pushed my chest out. I let him take me in. Let him appreciate what I brought to the table besides my intelligence. However, at the moment, I don't think he was interested in my mind.

Brad sat me back down and caressed my arms with his thick hands. I was shivering. His mouth met mine again; he teased me with his tongue. Then he lowered his mouth to my shoulders, where he planted small, wet kisses. As he kissed my ears, my cheek, my neck, his hands roamed and pulled the spaghetti straps down. I heard him take in his breath as my swollen breasts were freed.

"I want you. I need you now."

"Your wife."

"My wife is seventy miles from here and will be none the wiser. At the moment, she is the last thing on my mind."

"But she's on mine."

"Don't you worry your pretty head about my problems. I want you."

Before I could say nay or yea, Brad had my gown wrapped around my waist, and his thick fingers inside me as he feasted on my chest. In no time at all, Brad was between my spread legs, and I immediately realized he was very talented. Very gifted indeed. What he lacked in physical attractiveness, he made up for with his oral skills. We had sex that night for the first time and he discreetly left before sunrise.

When I saw him in the lobby just before checkout, he was as gracious as ever. No one thought or saw that anything was different between us. When I arrived home, I had a lovely pair of diamond stud earrings awaiting me via the UPS man. Compliments of Brad. That became our pattern. Sex and gifts. Lies and broken promises. More sex, more gifts. Now I was caught up.

tracee

"Hey, lady," I said.

"Hello to you too, stranger."

"How was your DC trip?" I asked as I fumbled with one of my dreadlocks and juggled the phone between my ear and shoulder. I had just finished up a meeting with one of my students, Cherylyn, who wanted to become a professor eventually. I think she looked to me as a mentor, which was cool with me. I am always about giving back. *To whom much is given, much is required.*

"Witch, that trip was over a week ago and you're just now asking about it?"

"I can't help it if your ass is never available. I get sick of talking to your voice mail and leaving messages. Messages that you never return, by the way," I exclaimed.

"I heard that and I apologize. It's been crazy around here. But, my trip was business as usual; thanks for asking."

There was a pause. I expected Meshell to go on and on about the boring meetings or the people she met, but surprisingly she didn't.

"Tracee, I'm glad you did call, though; I've been meaning to talk to you."

"About what?" I asked, leaning back in my swivel chair and looking out the window to the landscape below.

"Witch, I'm not going to beat around the bush. What's up with that twat show you put on for your next-door neighbor?"

"I should have known Tonya wouldn't be able to keep her big mouth shut!" I gushed.

"And you should have known not to tell her your business if you didn't want us to find out. Anyway, Tonya was just worried about you. We all are."

"Don't be. Like I told Tonya, I'm a big girl. I can take care of myself."

"Tracee, you don't—"

"Meshell, stop the preaching. Damn! You are not exactly Miss Sunday School Teacher yourself. People in glass houses shouldn't throw stones."

"Yeah, I've done my dirt. And I don't pretend to be nothing I'm not, but I also don't do things that put me at risk."

"I don't either. I was safe and secure in my own space. Besides, I didn't tell my neighbor to watch."

"Duh, think, Tracee. Don't you think that dude knows where you live now?"

"So? What if he does? I know where he lives too."

"Forget it, Tracee. You are in la-la land or maybe your dreads are too tight, and I didn't call to fuss with you. Just remember, sooner or later, everybody's bill comes due."

"What is that supposed to mean?"

"You figure it out. You didn't tell him to watch? You are hilarious. Any warm-blooded male is going to watch and enjoy when a twat is stuck in his face."

"Enough. Okay?"

"Fine. Don't say I didn't—"

"Hmp," I shouted, throwing up my hand.

"I'm done."

"Good. What are you up to?" I asked, changing the subject.

"Same ole, same ole. Work."

"Me too. Between teaching and doing my research, when I get home all I want to do is crash. As it is, I'm surviving off of four hours of sleep per night."

"Well, our office was just assigned a new case."

"Really?"

"You've probably heard about it on TV."

"Which one? There are so many."

"The man accused of molesting and killing his own daughter."

"Oh yeah. That's so sad. Breaks my heart," I said.

"Tell me about it. I'm about to get up close and personal with it."

"I don't know how you do it, day in and day out."

"Someone has to."

"I know I've never told you this, Meshell, but I truly admire your dedication and devotion to your job."

"Well, thank you, sis. I appreciate that. What's on your plate for the remainder of the day?"

"I'm supposed to be meeting Lexie for lunch in another hour and a half."

"Where are y'all going?"

"I told her to meet me at this spot in Midtown; they have the best down-home soul food."

"No! You are going to splurge and put some greasy, fatty foods into your precious body? Not you!"

"No. Hell no! Actually, they have veggie platters and a vegetarian menu as well."

"I should have known. Well, you ladies have fun. Wish I was there, but work calls. See, I can appreciate a good meal, but you'll probably count every calorie and ask the waitress what's in everything."

I laughed because it was true. "I'm seriously thinking about becoming a vegan. What do you think?"

"Tracee, you are asking the wrong sistah, because I don't know anything about that lifestyle. I just know I couldn't live without eating any meat."

"I think it provides for a healthier lifestyle, leaving out all animal products from your diet."

"More power to you."

I laughed. Meshell loved herself some steak and potatoes. She'd die before she'd give that up.

"I admire how you've managed to keep your weight down all these years. You look great, have a body to die for, and you'd never know . . ."

"Say it. A few years ago, I was overweight, approaching obesity?"

"Well, yes."

"It's all about diet, self control, and desiring a healthier lifestyle. In fact, later today, I'm supposed to be talking with this group of overweight teens at Spelman."

"Good for you. I remember seeing those old family photos of you, and I couldn't believe you were the same person."

"Me either."

"As much as I love you and enjoy talking with you, work calls," Meshell said.

"What about lunch? Aren't you stopping to eat?"

"Witch, please. Lunch is a bad word around here. I'll grab something later."

"Yeah, when you walk out of there at nine o'clock tonight?"

Meshell didn't comment one way or the other. So I figured I had hit a nerve.

"See, I'm worried about you. You give so much to your job that you forget to take care of yourself. You mentioned before that your hair is shedding excessively. That's stress, girl. I'm going to drop by this concoction I use on my hair. It'll make it healthier."

"Cool. The Crew needs to take a tropical vacation for about a week; I think we are all working too much. Lately, I can't believe we go days without speaking with one another. That's not like us."

"I know what you mean. But let me go, so you can get back to work and I can get ready to meet Lexie for lunch."

"Okay, love you."

"Love you too," I said sincerely.

"Think about what I said."

"I will. Take care." Yeah, I'd think about it. Done. I thought about it.

An hour and a half later, I was backing my silver BMW into the only vacant space in the restaurant parking lot. I had spotted Lexie's Mercedes when I drove in, and I wondered how long she had been waiting. I was one of those people who belonged to the "can never be on time" club. As much as I tried, something or someone always made me late. It drove Meshell crazy because she was the exact opposite; she strived for promptness. She called Tonya and me "the CPT sisters."

I remember laughing out loud when I read somewhere that there was a book club in the Atlanta area called We're on Our Way Book Club. They were named that because they were always running late and calling each other on their cells phones, saying, "I'm on my way." I thought that was cute. Real cute.

After reapplying my M-A-C lipstick in the rearview mirror, I got out and approached the line that was already forming at the entrance to the restaurant. It wasn't much to look at from the outside, but it served some of the best soul food in Midtown.

When I walked in and glanced around, I was pleased to see Lexie was already seated at a table near the wall. Looking up from her Black-Berry, she spotted me and waved me over.

"Hey, you been waiting long?" I asked, giving her a hug and kiss on both cheeks.

"No, I got here about ten minutes ago. Before this lunch-hour-crowd madness began."

"Good. If this had been Meshell waiting, she would be having a hissy fit right about now," I said.

We laughed at the visual image of it as I sat down and placed my purse in the empty chair to my left.

"Since you suggested we meet here, what do you recommend?" Lexie asked, looking every bit the psychologist in her slim, black, fitted skirt, white blouse, jacket, hair pulled back in a bun, and thin, gold wire-framed glasses. She made simple look chic.

"Anything and everything. You can't go wrong."

"What are you getting?"

"Veggies," I said.

"How did I know? I might get some collards and black-eyed peas with a breast of chicken and fresh-squeezed lemonade."

"A wise choice."

"Is it fresh-squeezed?"

"Of course. They don't do any concentrate here. It's the real deal."

Just as I finished selecting my three vegetables, our waitress walked over with pen and pad in hand. After the overly friendly and talkative waitress left with our lunch orders, Lexie turned to me with a curious look on her face.

"So, how are things?"

I immediately became defensive because of her tone and body language. "What things are you referring to?" I questioned.

"Work, family, life in general."

"Fine."

"That's good," Lexie said, looking directly into my eyes, as though she thought I was lying. "Anything interesting happen lately?"

"Lexie, you are about as subtle as a gay pride parade marching down Peachtree Street."

She shifted uncomfortably. Lexie was all about keeping the peace. She didn't like confrontations.

"I know Tonya told you guys my business."

"Well, you should know by now that Tonya can't keep anything to herself. She thrives on gossip; the juicier the better. So telling Tonya was your silent plea for help."

"Whatever. But, if you must know, Meshell has already talked to me, before I left to meet you. If you and she think I need some type of intervention, you are sadly mistaken. I'm grown."

Lexie leaned back in her chair and pushed her glasses up on her forehead. "Tracee, you have to admit you are displaying some pretty strange, irrational behavior characteristics, even for you."

I had to laugh at that one. I thought about how these women, my friends, had some dirt on me if we ever became enemies.

"What's strange for you isn't necessarily strange for me," I suggested.

Our waitress took that moment to return with our entrees. They looked and smelled delicious. There's nothing like fresh, homegrown foods. I grew up in the country, so I knew the difference. I noticed Lexie took a moment to bow her head and give thanks. I dug in.

"Tracee, I'm not trying to attack you. I want you to stop, take a moment to look at your actions, and think about why you are behaving this way. I can help you."

"First of all, don't come at me with that psychobabble. I'm not one of your patients. I'm a grown-ass woman and can do whatever the heck I please."

"I'm sorry, Tracee; I don't mean to upset you. Please lower your voice, people are staring."

"I don't care what people are doing. Let them look. That's your problem—you always worry about what everybody else will think. Live your life for yourself. Quit worrying about other people's perceptions of you, including your mom."

That stopped her. Lexie dropped her fork and glared at me with this indescribable look on her face. I immediately felt bad.

"Tracee, you didn't have to go there. I'm working on my relationship with my mother; I realize there is a problem with her being overprotective and overbearing at times. But you, dear, need to realize that showing your ass to every Tom, Dick, and Harry is only a temporary fix in making you feel sexy, desirable, and beautiful."

"What are you talking about?"

"Tracee, it's classic. Even though you are gorgeous and have a lovely body, great career, beautiful home, great friends, you still look back on those years when you were overweight and didn't feel worthy or deserving. So, to experience those feelings of self-worth, you get off on showcasing your body to complete strangers. Their reactions lift your self-esteem, temporarily, and make you feel alive."

"Bullshit. Bullshit. I smell bullshit. Lexie, like I said before, I'm not one of your patients. So I'd appreciate it if you didn't try to analyze me. If I ever decide I need therapy, you'll be the first to know."

"Okay, fine."

"Fine, then."

"Fine."

"I said fine."

"Tracee, we care about you. We don't want to see anything bad happen to you. There are a lot of crazies in the world; they may take your antics the wrong way. You don't want to send out the wrong message to the wrong man. Don't invite trouble. We don't care if you walk around buck-ass naked in the privacy of your own home, but when you start being an exhibitionist, well, that's another story."

"Yes, it is. My story. And I write the beginning, middle, and end."

Lexie shrugged her shoulders.

"Let's just agree to disagree," she said.

"Fine."

"Stubborn ass," she whispered under her breath.

"Meddling ass," I whispered back.

"Freak."

"Anal-retentive," I volunteered.

The waitress walked over and placed her hand on my shoulder. "Is everything okay, ladies?"

"Yes," we stated and smiled sweetly. She nodded and left.

"How is your food?" I asked lovingly, as if the last few moments didn't just happen.

"It's good. This chicken is so tender and moist. It almost falls off the bone."

"See, I told you this was the place. Reminds me of my mama's cooking." I took a bite of my veggies. "What's been going on with you lately?"

"Working."

"Aren't we all?"

"I've taken on a few new patients, so my plate is pretty full."

"Good for you. I'm putting the finishing touches to my research project."

"I read somewhere that Oprah Winfrey was producing a made-for-TV movie based on one of Zora's books," Lexie said.

"Oh, really? That's interesting. Which one?"

"I think it's *Their Eyes Were Watching God*."

"If anyone can bring it to network TV, Oprah can. That is one powerful lady. And she has such a wonderful, giving spirit that radiates from within," I declared.

"I know. I can honestly say she inspires me to be the best I can be."

"Speaking of radiating, I meant to mention it to you before: you've simply been glowing the last few times I've seen you. What's the deal? If I didn't know any better, I'd say you were in love."

"Please. With who?" Lexie asked.

"You tell me." I leaned in, observing her closer.

"Let's just say I discovered some personal truths about myself that were my 'aha' moments."

"Well, maybe I need to discover some, if it would make me as radiant and glowing as you are."

We talked, we laughed, and we enjoyed the bonds of friendship. A little over an hour later, arms linked, we walked out the front door, stuffed. Out of the corner of my eye, I saw movement coming our way. We were interrupted by a homeless man, pushing a beat-up shopping cart, who stumbled by begging for change, twenty-five cents. What could twenty-five cents possibly buy? Lexie and I both dug in our pockets for dollar bills and gave them to him. He mumbled his thank-yous and went off in search of another sympathetic person and probably a cheap bottle of wine.

"You know, I heard that they were trying to pass legislation to make panhandling illegal in certain parts of downtown."

"I'm not surprised," Lexie stated.

"Well, that's a damn shame that they'd sacrifice human life over tourist dollars."

"Welcome to America."

We had made it to Lexie's car. I gave her another warm hug and she searched deep in her shoulder bag for her keys.

"I've told you a million times about always having your keys out before you reach your car. That's a proven safety tip."

"Look who's talking about safety," she quipped.

As she pushed her keypad to unlock her door, I rolled my eyes at her back.

"I'll talk to you later."

"Okay, drive safely," I said.

"You too."

"Love you."

"Love you back."

"By the way, that pantsuit looks great on you," Lexie shouted as she backed out.

"Thanks, girl."

As I drove away a few minutes later, I thought, that's what I loved about the Crew. We could disagree without any major drama and no judgments were dished out. Bottom line, we loved each other regardless, flaws and all. How many people can say that about their friends?

I sat quietly in the back of the small room and looked around in awe at the number of young girls who were in attendance. The young ladies ranged in age from thirteen to eighteen and all shared one common characteristic: they were all overweight. From what I had learned from the facilitator, they either lived in the community, were children of associates at the Atlanta University Center, or were sent via referrals through various governmental agencies. Tonight was their weekly support group, and I was an invited guest speaker because I constantly shared my success story of major weight loss.

Presently, a young lady named Sarah, with pretty, long braids, was relaying events of her week. It was hard to understand Sarah at times because she was so emotional, and it was difficult for her to talk without interrupting her story with loud sobs.

"My mama's boyfriend was having dinner with us and he . . . he started teasing me . . . like he always does. He said he was going to buy a heavy padlock and put it on the refrigerator. I laughed it off, but his comments really hurt my feelings. He looked at my mom, then back at me, and said I looked like I had gained more weight. I told him I hadn't. Ron went on and on about how he was an ex-Marine, and how he was going to put me on an exercise regimen and work this fat off. He said all I needed was just some good old-fashioned discipline. My little brother giggled and laughed. I wanted to shrink and slide under the dinner table. Later on, when I tried to get another pork chop smothered in gravy, because that's one of my favorite foods, Ron swatted my hand away. The saddest part . . . was . . . that . . . the entire time my mom didn't say one word."

Murmurs of "Sarah, you aren't alone; we got your back" went out across the room.

My heart reached out to Sarah, and I wanted to give her a big hug and protect her from the people who made snide remarks at her as if she didn't have feelings or was invisible. I had already sat through a couple of other gripping stories. Nothing had changed. Any one of these girls could have been me fifteen years ago. To put it simply, society was not kind to big girls. Images of slim, beautiful women dominated the airways and magazines every day. Fashions were designed with slim women in mind. Americans are obsessed with weight and have a love affair with slim, fit women and men.

The facilitator walked to the front of the room. "Next, we'll hear from Professor Tracee Hinton, who is an English literature professor here at Spelman College. Girls, please give her a warm welcome and round of applause."

"Good evening, ladies," I stated as I reached the podium and smiled brightly, trying to make quick eye contact with each and every one of them. Most looked down or away.

"I said good evening."

"Good evening," some said quietly.

"Oh, come on. Y'all can do better than that."

"Good evening!" they shouted.

"That's better. Much better," I stated, looking around. "Before I go any further, I'd like to say, you are all beautiful and don't let anyone—your friends, your peers, your teachers, your family members—tell you any different."

Some smiled, others looked down at the floor.

"Peering out into your sea of pretty faces, I realize, there go I fifteen years ago." I paused for effect. "There go I."

With that said, all eyes focused on me. I saw I finally had their undivided attention. I could sense that they never expected me to have a fat story to share.

"I was overweight as a teenager. I was teased, picked on, sometimes made invisible by others. At times, I wanted to disappear. I didn't have any dates, was constantly told by family members and friends that I needed to lose weight. Food was my crutch when I was unhappy or stressed. And I must say, your teenage years are some of the most stressful years you'll ever survive. And you will survive them. So, I was stressed all the time. And I ate all the time."

I received a few chuckles and head nods.

Pointing at a few of the girls, I nodded. "See, things haven't changed, huh?

"I found myself caught up in a vicious cycle. I was unhappy because I was overweight, and when I was unhappy I . . ."

"Ate!" they all screamed in unison.

"This went on for the duration of my high school years. My social
life consisted of talking on the phone. I didn't attend many parties or
go to any of the football or basketball games. Sadly, I didn't even attend
my junior or senior prom; no one wanted to take the fat girl. And I
heard all the lines: But you have a cute face. It's good you're smart. If
you'd just stop eating."

More head nods.

"It didn't matter how cruel the comments were or what was done
to me. My eating habits didn't change; I barely exercised other than to
walk to the refrigerator to get something else to eat. And I hated dressing out in gym class. That was the worst. I was quickly on my way to
becoming obese, and then the summer before I was to go off to college,
someone changed all that."

I saw anticipation in their eyes. I stared out at the sea of faces and
smiled again. I wanted to give them time to digest what I had just said.

"My mama took me for a physical and my doctor, Dr. Choo, informed us that if my weight continued to rise I'd soon be at serious
health risk levels. I'd be at risk for a heart attack, diabetes, and a host of
other complications and diseases. I didn't want that. I didn't want to die
early in life. At that moment, it was like a lightbulb went off—I realized
I did care about myself, about my life.

"That was my wake-up call. That summer I set out to change all
my bad eating habits. Once I made the decision to do it for myself,
and not anyone else, there was no turning back. I exercised by walking
every single day, rain or shine. At first I could barely make it around
our block, but with consistency I built up my stamina. I drastically
changed my diet too. But most of all, I changed my attitude."

Pointing at each girl, I said, "Each one of you has to experience a
wake-up call too. Some of you may have already. But, most importantly,
you've got to want it for yourself."

I saw them glancing out of the corners of their eyes at those around them.

"If you young ladies don't take anything else away today, I want you to take away this: You are powerful! You are powerful in your own right! Whatever you set your mind to do, you can achieve it. The mind is powerful; if you believe it, you can achieve it. Don't ever underestimate the power of having a strong mindset, envisioning yourself as you see yourself, and having a positive attitude to achieve it. I'm a walking witness to that."

I noticed the facilitator, in the back of the room, smiling and nodding her head up and down.

"Now, if you really want to lose weight . . . First of all, quit feeling sorry for yourself. The world doesn't care. Get up and do something about it. I'm not saying it's going to be easy or even fun. Most things worth having take effort. I challenge each of you to determine a weight goal, develop a timeline, and put a positive attitude in place. *You can do this!* I know you can and I have faith in each and every one of you.

"I'm a firm believer that everything happens for a reason. And I believe I was meant to be here tonight and you were meant to hear my story.

"In closing, I'd like to share with you a portion of one of my favorite quotes: 'Our deepest fear is not that we are inadequate. Our deepest fear is that we are powerful beyond measure. It is our light, not our darkness, that most frightens us. We ask ourselves, Who am I to be brilliant, gorgeous, talented, fabulous? Actually, who are you not to be?'

"Think about that. Now, are there any questions?"

About a dozen hands instantly shot up. For the next thirty minutes, I was bombarded with question after question. Before leaving, I noticed Sarah was smiling as she walked over to the door and gave me a hug. I exited the building with tears in my eyes and love in my heart, just knowing I had inspired someone.

lexie

Another week had come and gone in a murky river of patients, sessions, tedious notes on yellow legal pads transferred to tape, and skipped lunches. In between, I performed my daughterly duties and, over at the church one evening, hung out with the woman who birthed me. Chatted with my girlfriends.

However, I left work each and every day tired but fully satisfied. There was no question about it. I adored my job. I loved helping people and making them emotionally healthy again; no one should go through life unhappy. I sincerely felt psychology was my calling or ministry, as Mother would say.

I was taking a break because I didn't see another patient for another two hours. Earlier, Mrs. Johnson, one of my new patients, had called and canceled. I used the unexpected free time to catch up on my e-mails and talk on the phone with Tonya.

"You never told me, how was your lunch date?"

"Lunch date? What lunch date?" Tonya asked.

"Uh, the date you had with the guy you met at the Tyler Perry play."

"Oh, him. Diva, he wasn't all that. I let him loose after the first date. When I realized it wasn't going to work out between us, I told him to get to stepping."

"Why?"

"He wasn't willing to give me his full devotion and undivided attention. Evidently, he thought I was into man sharing and evidently he thought wrong."

I laughed. "You are too much."

"I know this is the A-T-L and all, and men can have their share of beautiful women, but I'm not going to knowingly date a man who is dating several other women."

"I hear you." I laughed. "And you shouldn't have to. None of us should. Men only get away with what we allow them to."

"But, diva, I admit, he was sexy. . . ."

I didn't hear another word of what Tonya was saying. Her words became a distracting muffle of sounds and syllables. My eyes were glued to the e-mail that had popped up on my screen and taunted me. I immediately recognized the e-mail address: bigblackd@com cast.net.

It mocked me. Daring me to open it. I stared at my screen for a few seconds, frozen like a deer caught in the headlights of an oncoming car. That was how I felt. This was definitely a surprise, a shock to my system. I hadn't heard from Derrick since our night together; that was our agreement. No contact. Now he had broken rule number one.

"Diva, he had on a platinum link bracelet that probably cost him over a grand. And his suit was easily . . ."

"Tonya."

"Eight hundred or more."

"Listen, Tonya, I have to go. Something has come up. It's urgent."

My heartbeat had sped up and butterflies assaulted my stomach from all angles. I gripped the corner of my desk to steady myself.

"Okay, just call me back later."

"Sure. Bye," I said in a daze.

"Ciao."

I leaned back in my chair, took a deep breath, let it out, and bit down on my lower lip. I heard a little voice say: *Open the damn thing, girl. It's not going to bite you; quit being a scaredy-cat.* With nervous hands, I clicked my mouse to open the e-mail. It read:

```
E-mail: bigblackd@comcast.net

Message: What's up, pretty lady? Knowing you, you
are freaking out right about now because I've con-
tacted you. I know, I know, I broke your number
one rule (LOL). You and your rules. I just wanted
to say hello and see how you were. As crazy as this
may sound, I can't seem to get you out of my head.
I know we went into this with one goal in mind,
which we accomplished, but somewhere along the
way, you've gotten under my skin. I miss you.
Derrick
```

I clicked my nails over and over on my desktop. The clickity clack mirrored my racing mind. What to do? What to do? I wanted to say hello to Derrick, because if I was real honest with myself, I missed him too. Missed our heated debates, lively conversations, and strong sexual vibe. It wouldn't hurt to just say hello.

```
E-mail: mysterywoman@msn.com

Message: Hi, Derrick. I hope all is well . . . My,
this is a surprise. I didn't think I'd ever hear
from you again—after all, that was the agreement.
How have you been?
```

Within seconds, I received a response. He must have been watching the screen, waiting for me to respond.

E-mail: bigblackd@comcast.net

Message: Come on now, Mystery. You can do better
than that. You can drop the formal act. We've been
intimate, remember? You can't even bring yourself
to say that you've missed me?

E-mail: mysterywoman@msn.com

Message: I see you haven't changed one bit. Arrogant as ever. How do you know I've missed you?
Has it ever crossed your mind that maybe, maybe I
didn't? And you don't have to remind me that we've
been intimate.

E-mail: bigblackd@comcast.net

Message: Mystery, you are one of the few women
I know who can get me hot under the collar in a
matter of a few seconds. Don't consider that an
honor.

E-mail: mysterywoman@msn.com

Message: Hmm, maybe it has something to do with
the fact that I don't fall down at your feet and
worship you.

E-mail: bigblackd@comcast.net

Message: As I recall, you fell down at my feet and
did much more than that. Lady, you are a trip. I
take the chance of e-mailing you and sharing my
feelings, and you act like you are talking with
one of your lowly employees.

E-mail: mysterywoman@msn.com

Message: Is sex the only thing that is ever on
your mind? I don't know what you want from me.
Enlighten me, please. I refuse to change the way I
think and speak to please you and boost your ego.
Talk to me with intelligence and leave the sexual

machismo in New York. Maybe your woman enjoys it, but it doesn't agree with me.

E-mail: bigblackd@comcast.net

Message: How soon you high and mighty, proper women forget. Do I have to break it down for you? You know I can get gutter. You asked me to fuck you and make you come for the first time. You did that. You allowed me to have phone sex with you, talk dirty as hell to you, and eat you out until you begged me to stop. You did that. You, Miss Mystery, sucked my dick like you were licking a lollipop, rode it like a professional rodeo cowboy, stripped for me with no shame, and allowed me to do whatever the fuck I wanted to with you. I know every nook, cranny, and crevice of your body, and you have the audacity to ask me if sex is the only thing on my mind.

E-mail: mysterywoman@msn.com

Message: You are sick! How dare you say all that dirty stuff to me?

E-mail: bigblackd@comcast.net

Message: I've said much worse and it only turned you on more. See, I know you and oddly enough I understand your reluctance. Since birth, it has probably been brainwashed into that pretty head of yours that I'm the type of man you stay away from. I scare you!

E-mail: mysterywoman@msn.com

Message: You don't know me! And you definitely don't scare me!

E-mail: bigblackd@comcast.net

Message: Mystery, let me tell you something. Your innocent act doesn't work with me anymore. You

and I both enjoyed everything that went down that
night. YOU LOVED IT! I saw it in your eyes, the way
your body reacted to my touch, the way you kissed
me back, touched me. YOU ABSOLUTELY LOVED IT! And
you have probably thought about that night and fan-
tasized about that night dozens of times since.

If I was in Atlanta, I could walk in your office right now, lock your door, and take you bent
over your desk. YOU'D LOVE IT!

E-mail: mysterywoman@msn.com

Message: You're right, your ego isn't inflated.

E-mail: bigblackd@comcast.net

Message: I know you are trying to be a smart-
ass, but you're right, it isn't inflated. I speak
the truth. Tell me you didn't enjoy everything
I did to you that night. Mystery, you had your
first orgasm at almost thirty years old. You relaxed, you trusted me, and it was beautiful. I
wish I could have taken a picture, frozen it in
time, or you could have seen the expression on
your face when you came that first time. It was
priceless. You went from disbelief and surprise
to embracing it and rolling with the pleasure
waves. I held you as you shuddered, calmed down,
and your breathing returned to normal. And my
eyes never once left your face. Never once. You
were glowing.

E-mail: mysterywoman@msn.com

Message: Okay, Derrick. What do you want me to
say? Give you your props. Okay. YOU MADE ME COME
FOR THE FIRST TIME IN MY LIFE. There! Are you happy
now? You are the best I've ever been with. No one
has ever made me feel the way you did. I have woken
up in a sweat, dreaming of you touching me again.

E-mail: bigblackd@comcast.net

Message: I bet you are wet now.

E-mail: mysterywoman@msn.com

Message: Nasty ass.

E-mail: bigblackd@comcast.net

Message: (I'm clapping) Did that kill you, baby
girl? To admit those feelings to me? But, actually, what I really want to know is, do you miss
me? Miss me not from what I can do to your body,
how I can make you feel, but do you miss me?

E-mail: mysterywoman@msn.com

Message: Why does it matter?

E-mail: bigblackd@comcast.net

Message: Because I'd like to think I wasn't just
a good time for you. I know that's what you think
you were to me. I admit, you started out that way,
but now I don't know. So, have you missed me?

E-mail: mysterywoman@msn.com

Message: YES!

E-mail: bigblackd@comcast.net

Message: That's all I wanted or needed to hear.
That you missed me. Even though it was like pulling teeth, thank you, Mystery. One day, maybe
you'll feel comfortable enough to at least tell
me your first name.

I didn't respond because I wasn't about to tell him my real name.
No way.

E-mail: bigblackd@comcast.net

Message: Complete silence. Just like I thought.

Miss Mystery, enjoy the rest of your day! I won't
take up any more of your time.

E-mail: mysterywoman@msn.com

Message: You too!

And just like that Derrick was gone. Disappeared into the black
hole of the Internet. I waited over fifteen minutes for him to chat some
more, but he had logged off. I was left with a sense of anticipation and
desire that I had never experienced with anyone other than Derrick.
When I was with him or talked to him, he brought out this other side
that I didn't even know existed. He forced feelings to erupt to the sur-
face of my being. Derrick was dangerous, and I was determined not to
speak with him again. I was glad he had logged off. He brought out too
many personal truths. Good riddance, Derrick.

tonya

"Oh hell, no! Brad, you may have told wifey that you were going out with the fellows to watch the game, but I *know* you aren't going to actually watch it!" I challenged him, standing in front of the TV in a sexy, provocative pose with my hands on my hips.

"Baby, baby, get out from in front of the set. You are making me miss the play," Brad said calmly and patiently, reclining on the sofa in our spot, our favorite hotel. Sometimes I felt Brad thought he was dealing with a child. I was known to throw tantrums with him.

Fondling my breasts, I said, "You are going to let all this go to waste over a damn game?" I had on a wicked leopard-print lingerie set that so far, Brad hadn't given a second look. To say the least, it displayed my assets in a major way.

"No. When half time comes around I'm going to show you what's what."

"Oh, are you now, big daddy? You know how I like for you to ravage me," I seductively said as I sucked on my index finger.

"I promise I'm going to set you straight as soon as halftime rolls around. Bring me another beer, sweetie," he said, setting an empty can on the floor. Brad was reclining on the sofa like he was king of the castle with his khaki pants and preppy, button-down shirt on. Although he knew how I hated cigar smoke, he was puffing on one.

"Get it yourself. I'm not your damn wife."

Brad turned to glare at me, opened his mouth to say something, and then activity happened on the football field. He was quickly pulled back into the Falcons game. I absolutely hated football, and any sport for that matter.

I poured another tall glass of wine for myself and sipped on it, savoring the smooth flavor. With Brad, it was always the best; that's what I adored about him. First class all the way. Earlier, we had a nice meal delivered from the restaurant downstairs. I even ordered dessert, which was something I typically didn't do. I considered picking up the scattered dirty plates and dishes, but then I thought that's what the maids are for. On second thought, after remembering how hard Mama had worked for her money as a maid, I piled all our dishes into a nice, sturdy, neat stack and set them outside the door.

With wineglass in hand, I strolled over to the window to check out the view below. As usual, the street was full of cars and pedestrians. I looked back to find Brad staring at me.

"What?"

"You look so cute when you pout."

"Well, you should know—you get to see it enough."

"Don't be like that."

"I thought this was our time, not game time."

"Come sit on Daddy's lap," he said with an apologetic smile as he patted his thigh.

With my hand on my hip and the other holding my wine, I walked over. I stopped five feet from him.

"What?"

"Come here," he stated, taking another puff on the pungent cigar and patting his lap again. "Sit."

"What do you want?" I felt my defenses coming down.

"I want you," he whispered seductively.

"Why don't you put out that cigar? You know how I hate that smell. That smoke gets in my clothes and doesn't come out without dry cleaning. It gets in my hair."

"Anything for my sweetie," he declared, crushing it on the top of the beer can. "Is that better?"

I walked closer and Brad pulled me onto his lap, facing him. "Have I told you how sexy you look?"

I shook my head no with pouty lips.

"Well, you are extremely sexy and smell so good. Did my money buy this little number?" he asked, fingering the flimsy material.

"No, mine did. I work."

"Well, I love it. I love you," he said, kissing all over my neck and breasts.

"Do you?" I asked.

"Why the attitude today? Huh?"

"Since we don't spend much time together, when we are together, I want your undivided attention."

"My selfish little Tonya," he said, nibbling on my neck.

"Yes, I am selfish. I admit it. If you'd take care of your little problem, we wouldn't have to worry about our time together. We wouldn't have to sneak around, baby."

"I'm working on it."

"Are you? That's what you always say."

"I promise. I give you my word."

"What's that?" I asked, bouncing up and down on his lap.

"I'm going to show you what that is in a few minutes." Brad ground against me.

"Naughty boy."

Pulling the straps of my gown down, he said, "Feed me your nipple."

"Take what's yours, Daddy. Ravage me."

He smiled mischievously. "Oh, you want to play rough today? I'm game. Want me to tie you up again?" His mouth sought out my taut nipple.

"Ohh, that feels good," I cooed.

"I got something else that feels better."

"Do you now?"

"Damn right!"

"When am I getting it?"

"During halftime."

"Brad!"

"Why don't you get one of your toys and go entertain yourself? Show Susie Mae some love."

"Quit calling it that." I tried to hold back laughter. Brad called my coochie Susie Mae. "Besides, I don't want to. I have a living, breathing man in the room and I want you."

Looking around me and gently pushing me off his lap, he said, "Tonya, the game's back on. Go entertain yourself for a while. I won't be long."

"Brad? Brad?"

Once again, Brad's eyes were glued back to the TV screen. I wasn't sure if he heard me or even saw me leave the living room area to go into the bedroom of our suite to lie across the bed. I gave up. My man wanted to watch a football game more than make love to his woman. Whatever.

I decided to use my "free" time to call my mama. I knew she'd be at home because she never went anywhere. She still lived in the tiny—so tiny you'd miss it if you blinked—town in Mississippi that I grew up in. Mama was happy to attend church and babysit her grandchildren, my sisters' kids.

I pulled my cell phone out of my bag and dialed the number. The phone rang three or four times before someone finally answered.

"Talk to me."

"Who is this?"

"Malik."

"I thought that was you."

"Who this be?"

"This is your aunt Tonya. Boy, don't you have better phone manners than that?"

"Aww, Auntie. You just proper. You sound like a white lady."

"What?"

"I thought you were a bill collector calling for Big Mama."

"Well, I'm not. How are you doing in school?"

"Okay, I guess."

"What do you mean, okay, you guess? You should know what kind of grades you're making."

"Auntie, you crazy."

"Boy, put your grandmama on the phone. I'll talk to you during the Christmas holidays. Tell your mama hello for me."

A few minutes later, my out-of-breath Mama picked up the phone.

"Hey, baby."

"Hey, Mama. Why you sounding all out of breath?"

"Baby, these kids got me running ragged. I'm not a young chick; I can't do like I us'ta."

"Are all the kids over there?"

"Yes, your sisters dropped them by early this morning and I haven't seen or heard from them since."

"Mama, you've got to stop letting them take advantage of you like that." I had two older sisters who still hadn't grown up and who had children by four different men between them.

"Baby, I don't mind. I love my grandchildren to death."

"At least ask them to give you some money for babysitting and feeding them."

"I couldn't do that. Family looks out for family. But how you been doing, baby?"

"Okay."

"You still coming for Christmas?"

"Yes, Mama. You know I am."

"Good."

"Listen, Mama, are bill collectors calling you?"

"Who told you that?"

"Malik."

"I swear, if that boy won't place all my business in the street!"

"Well, are they, Mama?"

"I've gotten behind on a few bills."

"Mama! I've told you. Call me if you need anything."

"Baby, you always doing for me. Sometimes I want to do for myself."

"Like you said, that's what family does."

"You right. Next time I'll call if that will make you happy."

"Did you get the purse I sent you last week?" I asked.

"Yes, thank you, baby. It's still in my closet in the box."

"What? Why haven't you carried it?"

"You told me it cost you five hundred dollars."

"Mama."

"I told you I needed a new purse for church, but I'd feel funny carrying a five hundred dollar purse when that kind of money could buy groceries and diapers and pay the phone bill for some of our members, including me."

"Well, if you don't want it, send it back. I'll get you something else."

"Okay, baby."

"Well, let me go. I'll talk to you later, Mama. And I mean what I said—call me if you need something. Anything."

"I will, baby. Love you."

"Love you too, Mama. And tell Malik to help you with those kids."

I clicked End on my phone and laid my head down on the bed for a few minutes to clear my thoughts. I had vowed I'd never end up like my mama, and when I left my hometown, I never looked back. Calling home and making my one visit per year was always a reality check.

I must have dozed off because the next thing I knew, Brad was waking me up with light kisses to my lips, neck, and breasts.

"Wake up, sleepyhead."

I pulled myself up and shrank away from Brad's touch.

"The game is over, so I'm all yours."

"I slept through halftime? Why didn't you wake me?"

"You looked so beautiful, like Sleeping Beauty. I couldn't bring myself to wake you."

"Yeah right. You just wanted to see the halftime show."

"Shhh, stop talking so much. Get over here and show your man some love."

"I have a headache."

"You have a headache?"

"That's what I said."

"Well, I'll make it go away." He reached for me.

"Stop, Brad."

By now, he was on top of me, with my hands secured above my head in a playful manner.

"You don't want me to stop," Brad stated.

"Yes, I do. You didn't want me earlier, so you can't have me now. Can't have me."

Brad kissed me hard on my lips and lowered one hand to search between my legs. I tried to stifle a moan.

"This is mine and don't you forget it."

When he tried to kiss me again, I turned my head away.

"Tonya, did you hear me?"

I still didn't respond. I was purposely messing with him. Brad turned my head around with his free hand.

"This pussy is mine."

"Yes, Brad, I hear you. Loud and clear."

"Say it, then."

"I'm not going to say any such thing."

"Say it," he repeated, reaching for the nightstand, where it turned out he had placed handcuffs without my knowledge. He skillfully proceeded to lock my hands above my head before I could get away.

"Take these off, Brad." I twisted from side to side. "I'm not in the mood for your silly games."

With my hands cuffed and Brad's weight on top of me, I was immobile.

"Say it," he said again, sticking his meaty fingers deep into my womanhood and biting down on my neck.

"My pussy belongs to you," I recited in a robotic, monotone voice. "There, are you happy?"

"Very, and I'm going to make you happy too. You are a handful, but sometimes I have to let you know who's the man in this relationship." He rotated his fingers.

"Ohhh."

"Yeah, you like that, don't you?"

I didn't answer.

"Oh, now you can't talk," he laughed. "It takes a strong, forceful man to tame you, but I'm up for the challenge. Those young boys don't know what to do with you."

"If you say so."

"Open those legs up."

"No." I pouted.

"We'll see about that," he said jokingly through an onslaught of warm kisses.

Brad got up, walked over to his gym bag on the table, reached inside, and came back with purple silk ropes. I struggled to lift myself off the bed.

"Where you think you're going?" he mischievously asked, reaching for my legs.

I kicked and tossed, but Brad's power and strength won out in the end.

Brad gently and slowly tied each of my ankles to the bedposts, not too tight. We always tried to get this same room when we met because it had this huge bed with these tall, slim posts that almost touched the ceiling.

"Where's all that mouth now that you're lying up here spread-eagled and totally helpless?"

"I've never been helpless a day in my life."

"Well, I'm going to give you what you've been bugging me for all evening."

"Brad, untie me."

"When I'm finished," he gloated, running his hand lightly across my breast and flicking my nipple with his thumb.

Sliding down, Brad opened up Susie Mae with his fingers and lowered his mouth to taste the nectar.

A moan escaped me again. My right leg trembled.

He went down again and licked. Again and licked. Again and again.

"Oh, big daddy."

"Uh-huh."

He reached up to squeeze my breasts with his hand.

"This is mine." Then he licked. "Don't you ever forget it either. It's been bought and paid for, several times."

My hips lifted off the bed with a mind of their own. "Don't you ever, ever let anybody else touch this. You understand?"

"Yes, baby. Don't stop. Please don't stop. You're the best."

"You want this?"

"Yes, daddy."

"You gonna quit with all that mouth of yours and let me handle my situation at home?"

"Oh, baby. Ahhhh. Right there."

"Answer me."

"Yes, you take care of ho-o-ome."

"You want me inside you?"

"Yes."

"Tell me! Say it!"

"I want it. Now."

"What do you want?"

"You inside me."

Two hours later, we were both showered and dressed. I was lying across the bed and Brad was searching for his shoes underneath it.

"Why can't we stay longer?" I moaned into the pillow and turned over onto my stomach, with my arms stretched above my head.

"Tonya, I need to get home. You can stay if you'd like; the room is paid for. Stay here and relax for the rest of the evening."

"I don't want to stay without you, Brad," I cooed.

"You want some more. Sweetie, you trying to kill me. Remember I'm not a young man."

"No, I just don't want you to rush off. Come back to bed and cuddle for a while," I requested, reaching for him.

"Tonya, we go through this every time. You know my situation. You didn't enter this relationship with your eyes closed. Your eyes were wide open. I laid it all out on the table for you. Now, again, I need to get home."

"Fine." I pouted.

Brad sat down and pulled me close. "Don't be like this. I put some money in your purse. It's enough to get those ruby earrings you were raving about."

"Thanks, baby," I mustered without an ounce of enthusiasm.

"Nothing but the best for you. My little princess."

Brad kissed me and informed me he'd be out of town next week, but he'd try to call me. A couple of times in the past, I had taken a sick day and flown to whatever city he was in and spent the evening and night and flew back the next day.

As was our routine, Brad walked down to the lobby first and thirty minutes later I followed. I had my car brought around and drove away feeling empty.

lexie

E-mail: bigblackd@comcast.net

Message: Mystery, what's up? The last forty-eight hours have been hell. I've worked for two days straight and this morning we lost two children, a brother and sister, in a raging fire. We couldn't find them; I guess they were afraid of our masks and equipment, so they hid in a bedroom closet. When we located them, it was too late. The smoke had overcome them.

Damn, that's so fucked up! Man, I'm so tired. A five- and six-year-old aren't supposed to die.

Anyway, look, I'm sorry about the other day. You laid the rules on the table, and I broke one wide open. I of all people know how the game is played. So I'm very sorry that I went off on you.

Just wanted you to know. And whether you believe it or not, I'm not running game.

Derrick

E-mail: mysterywoman@msn.com

Message: Hey, Derrick! Apology accepted. And I apologize for not being honest about my feelings.

As for the fire, I'm feeling your pain. I'm sure you did the best you possibly could. Find consolation in that truth. Life is crazy; it's hard to watch children suffer and die. But you are a hero; I admire all you guys do. Like they say, when everybody else is running out of the building, you guys are running in. That's a hero.

E-mail: bigblackd@comcast.net

Message: Mystery, thanks for responding. After the other day, I didn't know if you would or not. Your words bring me comfort.

Now, I'm going to try and get some rest if I can get the image of those ash-covered, limp bodies out of my mind. This isn't the first time I've witnessed death, but that doesn't make it any easier.

E-mail: mysterywoman@msn.com

Message: Yes, get something to eat and then get some rest. Focus on happier times.

E-mail me tomorrow.

E-mail: bigblackd@comcast.net

Message: I will! I feel better already.

tracee

"What a beautiful day," I said out loud. "Gorgeous. There is nothing like Georgia in the fall." I breathed in the fresh, crisp air. In. Out.

Making sure my dreads were secure in the thick, black rubber band, I unlocked the door to my car and got in. I couldn't believe it was only two o'clock and I had the remainder of the day to myself. With all the research and long hours I had logged, I deserved today. Now I was off to the park to jog a few miles. I usually went to a local high school and ran around their track, two to three times a week. Today, I felt like trying somewhere different, getting back to nature. Even though it was out of my way, I felt like driving to the park where William and I had experienced our little adventure. I popped in one of my self-help tapes and off I drove.

After arriving, I got out of the car and did a few stretches and warm-up exercises to loosen my muscles. I adored the way my new pink and white jogging suit with matching shoes looked on me. It hugged my curves just right. Tonya and I had picked out matching sets awhile back. I chose the pink and white, and she picked up a red and blue and a black and white set. I breathed in and breathed out. I looked around to check out my surroundings. Since it was still early, I didn't see too many joggers from where I stretched. Good. I checked and secured my water bottle, turned on my stopwatch, and started out at a slow but steady pace, following the designated running trail.

I had run for about two miles when I finally stopped to catch my breath and to sip some of my bottled water. I was drinking and bouncing around so that my muscles wouldn't tighten up when I sensed another jogger coming up from behind me. Being a woman, I was always observant of my surroundings. A few years back I had even taken some self-defense classes.

Just as the jogger was passing my way, I looked up and then immediately back down to the ground. It was him. The jogger who had watched William and me have sex in the woods. Luckily, he hadn't recognized me. This was the second time I had seen him since that incident. What a small world we live in. The first time, he walked right past me and didn't blink an eye. Like Meshell said, I guess he wasn't really looking at my face that night.

I wanted to run at least two more miles, so I started back off at a brisk jog. The handsome stranger was up ahead of me. At least I had a view of that ass and what a view it was. Firm and tight. I could tell he was a true runner. He took long, sure strides and his form was excellent. Before long, I was caught up in my own personal daydream as I always was when I jogged. I went over the things Lexie had said to me and the more I thought about it, the more it made sense. Not everything, just some things.

I was so lost in my thoughts that I hadn't noticed the jogger had stopped up ahead until I was right upon him. I sped up so I could fly by him in a wave of white and pink. To my surprise, he caught up with me and was running alongside me.

"Good afternoon."

"Hello," I responded, keeping my eyes straight ahead.

"How many miles?" he asked.

"This is my third."

He looked back over at me. "Don't I know you?"

"No, I don't think so." My eyes remained focused straight ahead of me. My breathing was becoming ragged.

"Are you sure? I never forget a pretty face."

"Positive. Excuse me," I mumbled before jogging off ahead of him. I felt his eyes watching me.

Suddenly, I became very aware of my surroundings and realized I was so deep in the woods that there were not too many people around who could hear me if something went down. My focus was on finishing the last leg of the trail and getting safely back to my car. Meshell's and Lexie's words were coming back to haunt me. I had told them too many times there was power in words. Now their words had sent doom my way.

Twenty minutes later I was back at my car, standing in the parking lot. Only a couple of other cars had arrived since I drove up. I glanced around as I stretched and cooled down. I was perspiring and I wiped my forehead with the back of my hand; I didn't know if it was from the jog or from fear. I sipped on my water.

"I hope I didn't frighten you back there," a deep voice said.

It was him. "No, not at all," I stated, turning around to face him as he stretched and checked me out. I noticed his car was parked next to mine. What luck.

"Like I said, I never forget a face and I figured out where I've seen you."

"Where?" I asked, hoping he'd say the grocery store, church, or Blockbuster.

"It's really embarrassing and I'm ashamed to admit it, but . . ."

"But what?"

"I witnessed you making love to your boyfriend in the woods not long ago."

I immediately blushed and looked away. "Caught. I guess we got caught up in the heat of the moment."

There was a silence. I moved closer to my car.

"Man, this is awkward," he said, firmly looking back at me.

I nodded my head. "Yes, it is."

"I hope you don't think I'm a pervert of some kind—do you?"

I laughed. "I should be asking that of you."

"I don't make it a habit to watch people having sex."

"Hopefully you don't come across too many couples having sex in the woods," I shared.

"True," he laughed and his face completely lit up like a ray of sunshine. "When I first came upon you two, I had every intention of turning away and moving on, but then I looked at the sheer desire outlined on your face and I couldn't turn away. You mesmerized me."

"Don't remind me," I said, shaking my head and covering my face with my hand.

"No. Seriously, you were beautiful. You are beautiful."

"I could have sworn I saw you again not too long after that incident and you acted like you didn't know me."

"Oh, I saw you and immediately recognized you, but I was with my girlfriend."

"I don't remember seeing a woman," I said questioningly.

"No, she wasn't with me. She and I had had words and I had jogged off without her until I calmed down. She was one of the joggers behind me, and I would have caught hell if she noticed me so much as looking in your direction. She would have sworn I was trying to pick you up."

"Sounds like a piece of work." It slipped out before I could stop myself. "Oh, I'm sorry. I didn't mean to say that."

"No, don't be. That's why she's my ex-girlfriend. I can't deal with insecure women. Never again."

"Heard that." I smiled.

"You have a lovely smile."

"Thanks. Well, I've got to go. It was nice talking with you." I reached for the door handle, opened it, and got in.

"You too. I'd love to see you again. Is there any way I could get your phone number? Maybe I could take you out to dinner—or are you dating someone? The guy I saw you with?"

"No, I'm not dating anyone, but I'm not sure . . ."

"I understand your hesitation, but I guarantee you, I'm harmless, and I'm not the pervert you think I am."

"I guess I shouldn't pass judgment when I was the one showing off everything God gave me."

He laughed a good hearty laugh. It was so free and uplifting; I could get lost in that sound.

"What about this—could I give you my number and you could call me?" he asked.

"That's a possibility. Well, first of all, what's your name?"

"Excuse my manners; my mother didn't raise me this way. I'm Brandon Wells," he stated, reaching for my right hand.

"Nice to meet you. I'm Tracee Hinton."

"You too."

"Look, I really have to go."

"Wait. Let me give you my home number and cell phone number. Call me anytime; I'd love to just talk." He wrote his numbers on a piece of paper he pulled from his car.

"Okay."

"I'm glad I ran into you again," he said. "Literally. I guess I'd better get back over to Glendale Middle School before they come looking for me. My lunch break is definitely over." Brandon glanced down at his watch.

"Are you a teacher?" I asked.

"Used to be, but I'm a principal now."

"An educator, huh?"

"Yes, and I can sincerely say I love what I do."

"I hear you. Okay, this time, I'm gone for real."

"Take care, Miss Hinton," he stated, closing my door.

As I drove off, I glanced in my rearview mirror to get another look at him to last me through the night.

An educator? Small world. How come my middle school principal never looked like that?

After stopping by the grocery store to pick up ingredients for my famous vegetable lasagna, I pulled up into my apartment complex. It was still early. I intended to take my two bags of groceries into my apartment, pour myself some chardonnay, listen to a jazz CD, fix dinner, and relax for the rest of the evening. I had thought a lot about Brandon on the ride home. He appeared genuinely nice on the outside, but I was still going to proceed cautiously. Ted Bundy appeared nice on the outside too.

I locked my car doors, and with one bag held snugly in each arm, I started up the steps. I noticed a tall, lanky man coming down the stairs. He had on a basketball jersey with baggy jeans hanging low off his slim hips. I could easily see the waistband of his underwear sticking out. He looked strangely familiar, but I couldn't place where I knew him from. I moved over to let him walk by.

"What's up?" he said lazily, with hooded eyelids.

"Hi."

"Don't I know you, shorty?"

"No," I stated, taken aback.

"Yeah, I do."

"I don't think so," I said firmly.

"I seen you getting off on yo patio deck one night. I was like, yo, shorty shoulda called me over; I woulda set you straight."

"I don't know what you're talking about. But it obviously wasn't me."

"Ain't yo crib 104?"

"Yes, how do you know that?"

" 'Cause I came over and checked it out fo' myself. I was high that night, I 'member you was standin' at da 'partment that faced my cousin's. Big Ray Ray."

"So, you don't live here?"

"I'm crashing with Big Ray Ray until I gets on my feet; I just did a five-year bid."

"Oh," I said, moving closer to the wall and transferring both grocery bags to the arm closest to him.

"If that yo crib, it had to been you that I seen. I couldn't believe my fucking eyes, I walked out to get some fresh air, and I saw you playing with yo'self. That shit was wild. At first I thought da weed had me seeing thangs."

I hit my hand to my forehead. "Oh man, now I understand what you're talking about."

"What, shorty?" he asked, licking his lips and acting like he could gobble me up in one, maybe two bites. He was not trying to hide the fact that he was checking out my assets.

"You must have seen my twin sister, Bubbles."

"Bubbles? Shorty a stripper or what?"

"Yeah, Bubbles. She's my identical twin, and she was visiting from Chicago a few weeks ago."

"Yeah? Has a big, juicy ass and titties?"

"That's Bubbles."

"What yo name?" He was now cupping his dick through his pants.

"My friends call me Buttercup."

"Oh yeah?"

"Just between you and me, Bubbles is the one who is into a lot of kinky stuff like that. She even digs women."

"Damn! So, where shorty at?"

"Oh, she's back in Chicago. She caught some trouble, but now it's blown over and she went back."

He looked at me curiously. "Uh-huh. Well, if she ever in town again and lookin' for a good time, tell her to check me out in 304. Me and my boys will show her a real good time. Okay, shorty?"

"I'll do that."

"Cool. You sure you ain't down?"

"I'm sure. I've been celibate for five years."

"You been what, shorty?"

"I haven't had sex in over five years."

"Damn!" he said, walking away and shaking his head in disbelief. He looked back one last time. "Damn! Shorty!"

As I walked up the stairs, I breathed a sigh of relief. That was too close to home, literally. If dude had more brain cells and had been familiar with the Cartoon Network's Powerpuff Girls, I could be in serious trouble right now. Again, Lexie's and Meshell's words came back to bite me in the ass. If things had gone differently, I would have needed the Professor and Blossom's help.

lexie

E-mail: bigblackd@comcast.net

Message: For the last few days, we have talked about everything except anything personal. Why are you so afraid of opening up to me? Like I told you before, I don't bite, unless you want me to (LOL). I really like you, Mystery.

E-mail: mysterywoman@msn.com

Message: I'm not afraid of you. If I were, I never would have met with you. You seriously missed your calling; you are always trying to analyze somebody (smile).

E-mail: bigblackd@comcast.net

Message: You met me because you knew I was the man who could handle your situation (LOL). If I must say so myself, I handled it well. But, if you aren't afraid, tell me this. Have you gone out with anyone since we were together? Have you even had sex?

E-mail: mysterywoman@msn.com

Message: Even though it's none of your business, and if you must know, the answer is no. I haven't been out with anyone, and I haven't had sex.

E-mail: bigblackd@comcast.net

Message: Damn, girl! I'd have blue balls by now.

E-mail: mysterywoman@msn.com

Message: I take that to mean you've had sex? I have my career; that's what I'm focusing on. Again, sex isn't the end-all for me; I guess that's how we are different.

E-mail: bigblackd@comcast.net

Message: Sex isn't the end-all? Mystery, you kill me. People who aren't getting good sex say that type of shit. You mean to tell me if you had a brother like me hitting it every night, you wouldn't want it? Yeah, right! You just haven't met a man who can handle his business like I can. You been sleeping with too many stuffy suits who can't throw it on you.

E-mail: mysterywoman@msn.com

Message: Did your mama raise you to be this arrogant? Or did it happen automatically (LOL)?
    I'm not saying I wouldn't love a companion to share my life with. I'm saying that right now it isn't happening. My single, tunnel focus is my career. I don't go places to meet men. And to be honest, I'm sick of the lies you men can tell when I do meet one.

E-mail: bigblackd@comcast.net

Message: Hold up. Where did that come from? Men
tell too many lies. You can't possibly be talking
about me because I've been up front with you from
day one. You even know my name. I have nothing to
hide, baby, and have no reason to lie.
    Some dude has hurt you, hasn't he? So you
think the rest of us are bad apples. Typical,
typical, typical. I have to suffer because of the
transgression of some other brother that has hurt
you and get dumped in the same pot as a liar.
    Oh, by the way, it happened automatically. I
had too many women telling me I was da shit in
bed. Too many of y'all paying my bills, buying me
shit, and finally it went to my head and I started
believing it (LOL).

E-mail: mysterywoman@msn.com

Message: Yeah, I've been hurt. Haven't we all?
The man I thought I was going to marry and spend
the rest of my life with left me for another
woman. I never saw the signs, but I'm not bitter.
I choose to channel that energy into focusing on
my career.

E-mail: bigblackd@comcast.net

Message: That's too bad. His loss. Just don't
wake up one morning to a cold bed and realize
that's all you have in life—a career.
    I want to see you.

E-mail: mysterywoman@msn.com

Message: That's not possible!

E-mail: bigblackd@comcast.net

Message: Why isn't it possible? Did the airplanes
and trains stop running?

        Listen, you know what, don't worry about it.
I'm outta here. You are too much damn work for
me, Mystery.
        I have a lunch date with a nurse who isn't in-
terested in playing pen pal.

To my surprise, when I realized Derrick had signed off abruptly, I
was disappointed. And even more surprising, I was pissed off that he
had a lunch date with a nurse.

lexie

"Are you girls still having those ridiculous nights out?"

"Yes, we are, Mother. And they are not ridiculous. We bond, laugh, and have a good time as sister friends."

"Hmph. You can do that at church."

"No, I can't. Churchwomen are some of the most judgmental women you'll ever meet. They smile in your face and as soon as your back is turned, they talk about you."

"Child, quit talking that nonsense. See, that's why you need to participate in more church functions outside of regular Sunday service. There are several women you'd get along with."

"Mother, like I said, I don't know if I can attend the singles' night next weekend. That's our monthly Ladies' Night Out."

"All of you need to be up in the church that night. Maybe you can learn something about relationships, because all of you are thirty or pushing it, with no marriage proposals in sight."

"Mother, have you ever thought that we aren't looking for any?"

"What woman wouldn't? When I was your age I had already been married to the Bishop for ten years."

"No disrespect, but, Mother, you are living in the dark ages. Wake up. Fast-forward to the twenty-first century. Marriage is not a major goal for women today. We are independent, making our own money, buying our own homes, becoming single moms . . ."

"And that's exactly why the world is going to hell in a handbasket, I tell you. All these babies having illegitimate babies left and right. If you ever popped up pregnant without a husband and embarrassed me like that, I don't know what me and the Bishop would do."

"Mother!"

"What, child? Alexis, I expect you to be at church next Saturday at seven p.m. sharp. I don't ask much of you. For once, put your mother over your friends."

"Mother."

"Now, I have to go. Bring your friends, the more the merrier, they can learn something too."

"Mother!"

"Talk to you soon. Ta-ta."

I heard the dial tone. I couldn't remember the last time I got in the last word with Mother. She had a bad habit of simply hanging up the phone when she was finished with a conversation. That drove me crazy. Lately the church had been trying to come up with different events and outings for the singles' ministry since there were so many singles at the church. So far, this relationship seminar was getting a lot of positive press.

lexie

"Meshell, my mother is driving me up the wall. If I'm not careful, I'm going to be the one in a straitjacket, on my way to the nuthouse in Milledgeville."

Meshell laughed. "What has she done or said now?"

"She knows next weekend is our Ladies' Night Out."

"Shit. I had forgotten myself," Meshell shared.

"And if she didn't know, I told her, but she insisted on me attending this singles' ministry seminar. It focuses on being single, dating, sex, and relationships in today's society."

"Actually, Lexie, it sounds pretty interesting. I wouldn't mind going myself."

"Are you serious?" I asked.

"Yes. I've heard of those types of seminars before, and I've always wanted to attend one."

"Well, you are cordially invited. Mother told me to bring you guys too."

"Let me do this; I know you are emotionally drained after a phone conversation with your mother. So let me call up the rest of the Crew and see if they are willing to go to church as our Ladies' Night Out event."

"You are kidding, aren't you?"

"Why do you keep asking me that? Witch, I am very serious. Think about it. I've already told you I'd like to come. Tonya will want to go because there will be hundreds of single men in attendance, and she can dress up in her best diva wear. And Tracee's ass just needs to be there to let some religion rub off on her so that she can understand that showing your coochie to the universe ain't cool."

"Okay. Fine with me. Set it up and keep me posted. Be there or be square," I said with little enthusiasm.

"Be there or be square? You are so corny."

"But you love me anyway." I smiled.

"Are we still crashing at your place afterwards?"

"Always."

"Well, let me make some phone calls and get the ball rolling."

"Okay, tell them hello for me. Oh, ask Tonya to call me. I need a good deal on a bottle of wine for one of the psychologists at the office who's having a birthday in a few days."

"Will do. Talk to you later, Lexie."

At seven p.m. on the nose, the Crew strutted into one of the largest churches in the metro Atlanta area. My parents' church was absolutely breathtaking. It still amazed me every time I walked into the sanctuary, and I had been going there for years. It was huge, even though it wasn't the largest church in Atlanta. Out front, it had expansive white Greek columns with decorative designs that gave it a historical feel, and a giant white cross rested on the towering steeple, which seemed to reach toward heaven. Parishioners walked up several white steps to enter the building. There were four doors that led within. The inside was decorated in white and various hues of dark blue and the choir stand and pulpit were in shades of baby blue, which blended perfectly.

The church windows had artistically and vibrantly painted murals that showcased biblical scenes. When the sun set just right and reflected off of them, all spectrums of the rainbow shone through in a fabulous array of brilliance. There were fresh, colorful flowers in huge vases in spectacular arrangements everywhere the eye could behold. The sound system was state-of-the-art, and parishioners relaxed comfortably in an auditorium with theater-style seating. To top it all off, the ushers were friendly and helpful in their crisp, white uniforms. Visitors felt welcome, like they were returning home from a long journey.

Tonya had suggested we go all-out in our attire, so the previous weekend we had gone shopping. We had a ball playing dress-up. The Crew entered the church decked out in red dresses with matching gloves, and each of us had on a different color hat. I wore a purple one, Meshell's was red, Tracee's was blue, and Tonya's was burgundy. It looked like were were going to a tea party instead of church. When we walked in, all eyes were on us. The women were looking and whispering like *who do they think they are,* and the men were checking us out with admiration and delight.

Meshell led the way, with Tracee next, myself in the middle, and Tonya bringing up the rear of the line. Our timing was perfect; the seminar was just beginning.

"Huh, diva, it looks like a candy shop up in here. Look at all these sexy men in all shapes, sizes, and color." Tonya looked like she was in heaven.

"Girl, you are in the house of the Lord," I whispered. "Quit lusting."

"Diva, please. Somebody had to have sex for Christians to be here in the first place. What do you think Adam and Eve did in the Garden of Eden walking about buck-ass naked every day? So-called Christians kill me acting like they have never seen a dick or pussy before. I bet some of these women have stripper poles in their bedroom."

"Sshh, before somebody hears you," I whispered again.

"Dick, pussy. Dick, pussy." She was laughing hysterically now.

As we made our way up front to four empty seats, I saw Mother and Daddy—the Bishop—standing at the podium, eyeing us down. I waved and she nodded her head in acknowledgment. Daddy smiled his sly, charming grin. At the microphone, Mother cleared her throat and everyone started to quiet down and settle into their cushioned seats. I looked around and noticed many people had their Bibles, notepads, and pencils with them.

"Good evening, everyone," Mother said into the microphone.

"Good evening," people shouted back in cheerful response.

"May you be blessed for attending our first-ever singles' seminar: 'Everything you've wanted to know about dating as a Christian.' Our members asked for it and we delivered."

Tonya whispered, "What if you aren't dating as a Christian? What if you are dating like a whore?" We laughed like schoolgirls, covering our mouths and sliding down low in our seats.

Mother cleared her throat and continued, but not before giving us the evil eye.

"Just so you know, the Bishop and I aren't staying for your discussion. We came to welcome you, make introductions, and hand it over to our speakers for this evening. The Bishop and I have been married for almost thirty-five years—we don't need to know the secrets of dating. We're gonna let you young people handle this tonight. Now, when you're ready for the secrets to a long marriage, we have that one covered."

There was laughter.

"Now, without further ado, let me introduce our honorable guests."

Tracee leaned over to me. "Girl, your mama is wearing that suit."

"Always."

Mother did have a nice figure, and she took great pride in her appearance. At the first sight of a new strand of gray hair, Mother was at the beauty salon getting it covered up with a blue-black rinse. Looking at her standing up at the podium, I realized she was a very attractive woman. Daddy was big, handsome, and beaming beside her. It was obvious that he still loved her. And she him. I thought back to their years of marriage and realized I had never witnessed a heated argument between them. My father was a tall, broad-shouldered, quiet man of strength. Mother was definitely an old-school woman. She believed that the man was the head of the household; his decision was final. So she pampered and indulged my father.

"Our first guest speaker, Pastor Davis, hails from Memphis, Tennessee ..."

"The things I could do to him," Tracee whispered.

"Lord, help me," Tonya chimed in, fanning herself. They were looking at and admiring one of the guest speakers, who had just stood up.

Meshell joined in. "You could bounce a dime off that butt. I bet he is freaky in bed. Look at those lips. He has some soup coolers on him. He could do some serious damage."

"Reverend Dumas Davis received his master's degree from ..."

I would never forget the time Mother had the "birds and bees" talk with me. In her eyes, everything was black and white in regard to sex. One: Don't have sex until you get married. Two: Once you get married, act like a respectable lady in the streets, but satisfy your man in bed.

I remember asking about oral sex and she nearly fainted, but she did answer the question. She even went on to explain that oral sex with your husband wasn't considered dirty. Nothing you did with your husband should be considered dirty because your bodies belonged to each other. For the life of me, I couldn't picture Mother performing fellatio on the Bishop or him performing cunnilingus on her. It was a mental picture I didn't want to imagine. Ever.

Mother went on to explain that in the state the world was in, she had learned that men were weak. There were far too many free and loose women who were willing to do whatever for your man. So, as a wife, you'd better step up to the plate before someone else served it for you. That was Mother's only advice, but like I said, it only pertained to married women. As a young, single girl, she told me, I should keep my dress down and my legs closed.

"Check out the brother in the fourth row, third from the left, with the black sweater," Meshell said, boldly staring.

"Hmm, he's fine!" Tracee practically shouted. I saw a few women seated near us look at her like she had lost her mind.

I hadn't even noticed Mother and the Bishop had left the room. The first guest was speaking. "We are going to keep this very informal tonight. I thought we'd start with a question-and-answer session. Get a feel for what's on everybody's mind to open up dialogue. If that's okay with everyone?"

There was a murmur of okays and head nods.

One after another, sisters stood with questions: *Where are all the good men?* Aside: *Married, dead, or gay* (Tracee). *Should Christian women save themselves for marriage?* Aside: *If you don't give up the punani, you won't ever get married. Plus, women have to test the merchandise, so we don't get a dud and have to return it* (Tonya). *Why the sudden epidemic of gay men?* Aside: *There isn't an epidemic; it is just discussed more openly today* (Me).

The questions went on and on and each one was addressed. *I'm an attractive and intelligent sister—why can't I get a date? Why are today's women so picky? Is oral sex considered sex? What does the Bible say about divorce? Why will a woman choose a bad boy over a good man? What does evenly yoked mean? Why are women so materialistic?*

Then Tonya stood up boldly and asked, "Where are all these DL brothers coming from in the church? And what does a Christian woman do when she gets that special feeling?" At first, everybody was quiet, then laughter erupted all around us. Tonya had broken the ice and for the rest of the evening, the real questions were asked. When it was all said and done, surprisingly, the evening was informative and fun at the same time. It was uplifting to realize that most of the women had the same concerns and shared some of the same dating problems. Even more revealing, the men were looking for one-on-one relationships with the right woman. They craved love and marriage too. Go figure.

The speakers weren't too preachy and explained things from a biblical aspect but with a focus and understanding of modern times. All in all, it wasn't a bad way to spend a Ladies' Night Out. The evening ended with the facilitator asking us to write down what we were looking for in the opposite sex and see if we were being realistic.

As we were walking out to the parking lot, male attendees came up to us and complimented our attire and introduced themselves. I saw phone numbers being exchanged. I didn't take or give any.

"Come on. Let's get out of here before my mother corners us," I stated, walking rapidly toward the exit.

"Lexie, slow down. Don't you want to speak to your parents?" Tracee asked.

"No. Seriously, they are probably in their office working on something for tomorrow's service. But I swear to you, if we stop, Mother will give us the fifth degree about where we are going and what we learned tonight."

"I wanted to say hello. I haven't seen her in a while," Tonya said.

Meshell was staring at me. "Come on. Let's just go," she said, coming to my rescue. "I'm hungry and Lexie's right, they're probably busy."

I breathed a sigh of relief.

"That was pretty cool," Tracee said as we walked through the parking lot.

"It was. I enjoyed myself," Meshell said, clicking on her keypad to unlock the car doors. We had all ridden over in her Lexus and left our cars at my place.

"There were some cutie-pies up in there! I saw at least three I could take home and sop up with a biscuit. Diva, do all those men attend your church?"

"I guess. The church is so big, it's hard to know everyone. Plus, there are two separate services, an early morning and one at eleven."

"Well, I need to move my church membership to yours," Tracee laughed. "God, help me!" she shouted, throwing her hands up toward the heavens.

"I for one am starving," Meshell said. "When I see a lot of attractive men in the same room, it totally makes me hungry."

"I'm not really hungry; breakfast is okay with me," I said.

"Please, I'm starved. I need some real food," Meshell said.

"Okay, ladies, why don't we stop by Gladys Knight's Chicken and Waffles and satisfy everyone," Tracee volunteered. "Meshell, you can get a good meal and, Lexie, you can eat breakfast."

"Fine with me," I said.

"Cool. It's settled, then," Tracee said, checking out her nails.

"Meshell, I meant to tell you—I saw you on the news the other night talking about your new case. You looked sharp in that power suit; you were representing well," I told her.

"I try," Meshell said, pretending to pop her collar like in the hip-hop videos.

Twenty minutes later, as we entered the restaurant out near the mall, Tonya screamed out, "The Divas have entered the building!" All heads turned our way as women gave us the thumbs-up and men whistled and gave admiring stares.

It was on. Ladies' Night Out was just beginning. We had gone to church and gotten some religion; now it was time to get loose. Wild and crazy. Oddly enough, thoughts of Derrick raced through my mind, and I shivered as I hugged myself with both arms.

Two and a half hours and three drinks later at Dugan's, images of Derrick and me that night at the hotel raced through my thoughts again, causing my legs to quiver. What was this man doing to me? And what was I going to do about it?

tracee

Roughly two weeks had passed since
our outing at Lexie's church. I didn't consider myself religious, but spiritual. That night, however, was so much fun, and the Crew had received
so much attention based on the way we were dressed. Ladies in red never
looked so good. And we gave those church-lady hats a whole new look.
Sexy. Tonight was a Wednesday night and for once in a very long time,
I was sitting quietly at home with nothing to do. I had decided to take a
brief reprieve from the Zora article. Tonight, I had already taken a long
bubble bath to relax my mind and eaten a light meal, a simple spinach
salad with artichokes and a light, fat-free dressing. Now, already into my
third glass of merlot, I had some music playing and was sitting Indian-
style in the middle of my living room floor, with not a stitch of clothing
on, cleaning out my black leather Coach purse.

For me, it is pure heaven to lounge around in my birthday suit. It
is so liberating; most people don't realize that. I tried to visit Hedonism

resorts in Negril, Jamaica, every other year for at least a week's stay. I usually had to travel by myself and hook up with this group of black women I met years ago who are from England. They go the same time every year. I couldn't convince the Crew to go with me, but believe me, I had tried.

Twenty minutes earlier, I had gotten off the phone with Tonya and her crazy ass. She had me in tears of laughter over some incident that happened at her job; two of her co-workers were caught doing more than work in an empty conference room. Then Tonya received a call on her other line. She put me on hold, came back on, and in an excited voice told me she had to go.

Dumping out the contents of my purse, I didn't know how I'd accumulated so much junk in such a short period of time. I was cleaning out everything from chewing gum wrappers to cotton balls to clippers to half a dozen business cards I had received.

Brandon Wells. I came across the name and phone numbers of the jogger from the park. I held the torn sheet of paper in my hands for a few moments as if studying it. He had a very loopy handwriting; I tried to remember from my handwriting analysis class what that meant. I started to discard his numbers, but at the last moment I decided to call Mr. Wells up. I had a block on my phone, so it wasn't like he'd have my number or a way to get back in touch with me. The memory of the man across the way was still fresh in my mind. That fool had the nerve to leave a note on my door the other day. I came home from work to find: *Yo, Buttacup, I'm outta here tonite. Tell Bubbles to give me a holla if she ever wanna hook up. My cousin will know how to reach me. Peace.*

Brandon's phone rang and rang and rang. I was about to give up when a sleepy voice finally came on the line with a nasal hello.

"Uh, yes, I'm calling for Brandon Wells."

"Yes. Who's speaking?"

"This is Tracee, the jogger from the park."

"Oh, yes! Hi, Tracee. What's going on? I had almost given up on you." I heard a bit more pep in his voice now.

I laughed and laid my head back against the sofa, as I crossed my legs at the ankles. "Why is that?"

"Well, it's been almost three weeks and I haven't heard a peep from you, but don't get me wrong, better late than never. I'm glad you called."

"Is this a good time?"

"Actually, you caught me a little under the weather. As we speak, I'm in bed with a cold, fever, and body aches. I think I've caught the bug that's going around; a few of my students have been checking out with similar symptoms. But I'm shaking it off—this is my second day."

"I can call back some other time. Don't let me disturb your rest."

"No. No. Your sweet voice is already making me feel better. If I let you go, I might not hear from you for another three weeks, if ever."

"Okay. If you're sure."

"I'm very sure. I took some medicine an hour ago; so I'll be fine for a while. How has your day been?"

"Relaxing. Believe it or not, this is one of the first free evenings I've had in a long time. I don't know how to act," I stated, twirling one of my dreads around my finger.

"Enjoy it."

"Oh, I intend to. I've already pulled out the old CDs and merlot. I'm in for the night."

"I wish I was there to join you."

"You're pretty forward, aren't you?"

"You'll find that I'm pretty direct. I believe in speaking my mind. You appear to be the type of woman who respects that in a man, in people in general."

"I do."

"Good, because I got that vibe from you that day at your car," Brandon said.

"Oh, you believe in getting vibes or feelings from people?" I asked in curiosity.

"Don't laugh, as crazy as it sounds, I instantly know if I can get along with someone or not. People emit these vibes that I pick up on immediately. I don't know how my ex made it through my radar."

"I'm not laughing. I relate. You're preaching to the choir. What other vibes did you get from me?"

Brandon chuckled. "You don't want to know what I got from you the first time I saw you."

"I probably already know. A hard-on."

He laughed easily. "That too. Plus, I felt you were very giving in relationships."

"I am."

"You mentioned time restraints. What keeps you so busy into the late evenings? A man?"

"No. My job and research. Plus I volunteer one night a week down at one of the local homeless shelters."

"That's very admirable of you."

"I try. Some people have so much and others have so little; it doesn't take much to make them happy. A smile. A hug. Encouragement."

"What is your profession? A social worker?" Brandon sneezed.

"Bless you."

"Thank you."

"I'm a professor. English lit."

"I'm impressed."

I laughed. "Don't be."

"Hmm, a principal and a professor. I bet we could make beautiful music together."

"You're funny, but corny," I laughed.

"I have a few jokes. But hey, they aren't corny. Don't talk about my best lines," Brandon said, indignantly.

"Yes, they are. But you make up for it because you're so cute." I laughed again.

"You know, I love to hear you laugh. You have such a rich, throaty tone. Very sexy."

I thought to myself, if only he knew I was talking to him in the nude. His voice, nasal and all, was heating me up. I shifted around to make myself more comfortable on the floor.

"What are you listening to? I hear music in the background."

"I have a CD of hip-hop songs mixed with a jazz theme."

"Interesting, it sounds relaxing. Maybe you can make me a copy."

"Maybe."

"I'll accept that. At least you didn't say no."

"True. I didn't," I flirted back.

"Can I tell you something?"

"Sure, why not? Remember you are Mr. Direct."

"You are a very interesting woman."

My right thumb met a nipple as I thought back to how Brandon looked in those jogging pants. I gently stroked.

"You think so?"

"You know who you are. My ex-girlfriend didn't embrace her sexuality the way you do."

"Your ex? I know you aren't talking about your ex to me."

"I'm sorry, I don't mean to bring her up. I understand what that must sound like, but you are so refreshing to me. Gayle—that's her name—was so uptight about sex. I had to make love to her with the lights off."

"Damn."

"Exactly. You on the other hand are such a fascinating woman. Tell me more about yourself."

"What do you want to know?"

"Whatever you want to share with me."

"We could be up all night," I laughed, shifting my elbow on the sofa.

"I'm game."

Brandon and I stayed on the phone for another three hours simply talking. He got off the phone one time to take two more pills for his body aches and pains, but other than that, we talked nonstop. I hung up the phone anxious to know more about this man.

lexie

E-mail: bigblackd@comcast.com

Message: Mystery. How have you been? I'm sorry
about ending our last e-mail exchange so abruptly.
It seems like I'm always apologizing to you for
one thing or another. You are something else,
lady! You are making me do and say things I've
never done or said in the past. That's why I find
you so fascinating . . .

Yet, I still don't really know you. I'm going
off of the vibe I have when I do speak with you.
I'm going off of how I can't get you out of my
head. I can be working, riding on the fire truck,
when out of the clear blue, you pop into my mind.
And I smile. I see your face, I smell your skin, I
hear your sensual moans, and it drives me crazy.

I know right about now you are scared and anxious because you aren't used to a brother like
me. But hold on, hear me out. Mystery, I like
you, I like you a lot. I know what we said and

I know about your long list of rules, but baby,
life doesn't always follow a carefully planned
out script. Life just happens.

I know I'm not the type of dude your mama ex-
pects you to bring home to meet the family, but
those other men aren't making you happy. I think
I can make you happy. Hell, I know I can. Not just
sexually, but on other levels as well. I know you
were jealous that I took that nurse out (don't
even try to deny it). But don't worry, she didn't
compare to you. Other than the hot sex, she was
boring as hell.

I see this is getting sorta long, so I'll come
to the point. I need to know if you think there
is a chance for us to see each other again. I know
there are no guarantees in life. All I'm asking
is for the opportunity to get to know you better.
Who knows? I may end up hating you and vice versa,
but at least let's give each other the opportunity to find out.

As I told you before, I don't do friendships
with women well; it's not in my nature. I can't be
your pen pal forever. I can't talk back and forth
with you without telling you how I really feel. I
want you. I want to ease myself back inside you,
feel your warmth, and never let go. Baby, that's
real. That's life.

So, what I need to know from you is if you are
willing to give us a chance. To find out where
we really stand with one another. I'm sorry, but
I can't be your pen pal any longer. If you don't
think it is possible, that's cool. I'm a big boy;
life will go on, with or without you. But I also
won't ever contact you again or bother you in any
way.

When you are ready to let me know something,
holla back!
Derrick

What? What is this man doing to me? How dare he give me an ultimatum? The nerve of him. He can't be my pen pal? Then don't!
Derrick thought he knew me so well. Well, I had news for him—he
didn't. Why would I be jealous of some skank nurse he took out? Oh,

correction: bedded. He can screw whoever and whomever he wants to, wherever he wants to, however he wants to. I have no papers on the man. Just because he got me all hot and bothered, now I'm supposed to love him? Yeah, we've had fun, some interesting conversations, some great, mind-blowing sex, but now it's over. I got what I wanted.

See, that's why there are rules. Rules that are meant to be followed. When you break the rules, shit happens. What's a girl to do?

I tapped my French-manicured nails against my desk and looked at the clock. I had ten minutes before my next patient. God, this man had upset my entire day. When I first saw the e-mail, I was so happy to hear from him, and then he comes at me with this mess.

To make matters worse, Mother has been pestering me about dating some guy from church. Apparently, he is a new member and saw me at the singles' night and approached her the following Sunday about meeting me. Of course Mother worships him because he's an engineer, clean-cut, into the church, and never married, with no children. I don't know how many more ways I can say "Not interested!"

E-mail: mysterywoman@msn.com

Message: Derrick, I accept your apology, but please don't take this where you are taking it. You have no right to give me an ultimatum. I'm not your woman. I will gladly admit that if we don't have some type of contact, I will miss you dearly. You have quickly become a part of my life.
    Don't make me choose. Let's compromise in some way. Okay?
    By the way, I'm not jealous.

I didn't realize I was anxiously holding my breath and watching the clock until Derrick's message came back. I quickly opened it.

E-mail: bigblackd@comcast.net

Message: There is nothing to compromise. Either you want me in your life or you don't. You decide.

The ball is in your court. No pressure. You have complete control. Take all the time you need. Until I receive your answer, you won't hear back from me. So there's no need to respond to this e-mail unless it's with your decision. Understand, Mystery or whatever the hell your name is?

By the way, you ARE jealous. You can't stand the thought of me running up into somebody else. Admit it.

You can act like you are a prude to everybody else, but I've seen the other side of you (wild side) and it was free and beautiful.

I'll wait for your response.

My intercom buzzed and I almost jumped out of my seat. I pressed the Answer button. "Your next patient is here," my receptionist announced.

"Send Mr. Jackson in in five minutes."

With nervous fingers, I rapidly typed out a response.

E-mail: mysterywoman@msn.com

Message: My first name is Alexis. My friends call me Lexie.

I held my breath and waited for a response. None came.

tonya

"Damn!" I silently shouted, throwing up my hand toward heaven and flipping back my hair. I was behind closed doors, in my office, with reports stacked everywhere the eye could behold. Everyone thought being a buyer was glamorous, traveling to exotic places, but they didn't realize it involved analyzing sales, trends, and a host of other indicators and factors. Presently, I had about five stacks of reports that were about three inches thick lined up on the left corner of my desk. I had been going at this for most of the morning, stopping only long enough to drink some coffee and eat a bagel, and it didn't look like it would end anytime soon.

I heard muffled voices outside my door and then a couple of loud knocks. Damn! Couldn't these people leave me alone? Today wasn't the day to chitchat about weekend plans as we did sometimes when it was slow.

"Come in," I stated with mild irritation in my voice. "The door's unlocked."

"Hello, Miss Cunningham," a familiar voice said. "How are you?"

I looked up from my paperwork to find Brad strutting in with a big grin on his face. I could tell he had a recent haircut and trim.

As he closed my door, I smiled broadly. "Hello, Mr. Benson. What a pleasant surprise; I didn't know you were visiting the office today."

"You look beautiful," he whispered, walking my way. "I was in the area visiting a client and thought I'd come by and take you guys out to lunch. Company treat."

"Thank you, Mr. Benson."

"Come here," he whispered again, looking back toward the closed door. I walked over and met him halfway. Brad fondled my breasts through my silk blouse and exhaled.

"Brad, stop. Somebody might walk in," I whispered. We had always made a point of being very careful around others in the past. When Brad visited the office, I made sure I never went to lunch with him alone or slipped up and called him by his first name. So far, no one suspected. We were very discreet.

"No one is thinking about us. Everyone is in their office or already went out to lunch before I arrived."

"Still."

"Still nothing. Come here." He pulled me back to him and slid his beefy hand underneath my skirt and aggressively palmed my butt. Sometimes I got the feeling that Brad thought of me as a prize or possession.

Within minutes, he had the top two buttons of my blouse unbuttoned, while he fondled my breasts through my bra. I leaned into his hand.

"Miss Cunningham, are you going out to lunch with us?"

"No, I have too much work to complete before the weekend begins. Reports are calling my name.

"Oh, oh," I moaned. Brad was biting down on a nipple now and

still had his hand stuck up my skirt while he searched for the opening to my pantyhose.

"That's too bad. Maybe next time."

"Sure." I bit down on the back of my hand. "Sounds wonderful."

Brad had twisted me around with my back to him and had me up on my desk, pulled my pantyhose down in one swift move, my skirt next, and his fingers were working their magic.

"I could take you right here," he moaned into my ear, still working his magic with two fingers. He placed his legs between my thighs, which caused my legs to open even wider.

"Make sure you check out the sales figures for the Midwest stores. I'd like to discuss them with you later and get some feedback."

He stopped long enough to quickly place my reports on the floor with his free hand and turned me back around to face him. His fingers, still inside of me, lifted me onto the desk. I moved up and down on them. As I went up and down, he went in and out.

"Why are you so wet?" he whispered, teasing me with his moist tongue. He went back to sucking my breasts and neck.

I was trying hard not to scream out. I could tell this was amusing Brad.

"I want to taste you right on this desk. Lie you down, open you up, and feast."

"Hmm. That sounds good, baby."

I heard activity outside my door. I almost broke my neck pulling up my pantyhose and pulling down my skirt. I didn't know I could move so fast. I quickly walked to sit behind my desk and gain an ounce of composure.

"Mr. Benson, it was good seeing you again," I said really loudly.

"You too, Miss Cunningham. Have a wonderful weekend," Brad said just as loudly, with amusement in his voice.

Brad made the sign that he'd be calling me in a few minutes. I nodded my head.

"Enjoy your lunch." Then he opened the door and walked out

like nothing had happened. He even spoke to people in the hallway with my smell still on his fingers.

I breathed a sigh of relief. A few minutes later, my office phone rang.

"Hello."

"Hello, beautiful. I miss you already," Brad flirted. "Did I get you hot in there?"

"What do you think?" I asked, leaning back in my chair and running my fingers through my hair. "Where are you?"

"In the conference room, working on my laptop until lunchtime."

"Oh."

"You sure you don't want to go to lunch?"

"Yeah, I'm sure. I have tons of reports to go through—you saw them—and I don't want to take them home for the weekend."

"Okay, sexy lady."

"Plus, I wouldn't be able to keep my eyes off you, the others would instantly know something was up. They aren't crazy. Please don't underestimate them."

He laughed, but didn't comment.

"Where are you guys going?"

"They mentioned an Italian restaurant not far from here. Said we could walk over."

"Oh, I know where they're talking about. The food is really good."

"Can I see you tonight?"

"No, didn't I tell you? I have a hot date tonight," I teased.

"You better not. That would break my heart. Just the thought of someone else touching you makes me boil."

"Whatever, Brad."

"Can I?"

"Can you what?" I asked.

"May I see you tonight?"

"Where?"

"Where do you think? Our usual place."

"I'm sick of going to the hotel and not being seen. I like to dress up and be the center of attention."

"Tonya, I can't exactly take you out and show you off. I am married."

"That's the problem; I don't know how much longer I can live like this, Brad."

"Here we go again."

"Yes, here we go again. I'm not getting any younger and I'm not going to continue to wait for you to do what you need to do. One night you might call and I won't run to meet you. Maybe I'll start dating."

"Are you giving me an ultimatum?"

"If that's how you want to take it," I said coldly.

"These young boys couldn't afford you. You'd take them to the poorhouse."

"Whatever. Keep thinking that."

"You knew this would be difficult when we started seeing each other."

"I didn't know it would be this hard," I sighed.

"Just meet me at the spot tonight around nine o'clock. I'll make the reservations and set everything up."

"I guess."

"Oh, come on, sweetie. You don't want me to extinguish the fire I started in there?"

"What do you think?" I laughed a sexy laugh. I couldn't stay mad at Brad for very long. And he counted on that.

"I wanted this to be a surprise, but I want you to take a few days off to go to the Bahamas with me. Stay at the Paradise Island Hotel."

"What? When?" I screamed.

"You heard me, mon. Let's get away to the islands. Soon."

"Are you serious?"

"Very. I want to go to bed with you at night and wake up next to you. I want us to eat breakfast, lunch, and dinner without having to sneak around or rush off. I want us to really enjoy each other for once."

"How did you manage this?"

"Don't worry about all that."

"What about your wife? Where will she be?"

"Didn't I just say not to worry your pretty head about her? You were just bitching and moaning about not being able to go out in public with me. Now you can. Let me work out the logistics."

I squealed. "I can't wait. I have to buy a new swimsuit, maybe two."

"I'll give you the dates tonight so you can make arrangements on your end."

"Wait, I didn't say I was coming by tonight."

"You will," he stated boldly.

"You pretty sure of yourself, huh?"

"No, I'm sure of you. When have you ever given up the opportunity for me to go down on you?"

"Never?"

He laughed again. "That's what I'm talking about. I can't wait; I'm going to eat your sweet ass up."

"You nasty dog."

"And you love it."

"I do."

"Hold on for a moment." Brad clicked to his other line. Minutes later, he was back on.

"Was that her?"

"Tonya? You don't stop."

"Was it?"

I heard voices in the background.

"Listen, they are gathering for lunch, so I have to get off."

"Okay."

"Do me a favor?"

"What?" I asked.

"Tonight, when you come to me, I want you to wear your black trench coat. I don't want you to have on anything underneath . . . no bra, panties, nada. Wear those black high-heeled shoes with some black fishnet stockings for me."

"Why, Brad, I never would have thought you were so kinky!"

"Just do it. I'll see you tonight."

"Okay, I guess I can please my man."

"Sweetie?"

"Yes?"

"Don't be late."

"You gonna do it for how long?"

"As long as you like. All night if you want me to. I wanna please you. It's all about you tonight," Brad whispered seductively.

"Sounds good to me," I whispered with excitement in my voice.

"Can't wait."

A few minutes later, I heard them all gathering in the lobby to go out to lunch. Julie, a young white girl, knocked, stuck her head in, and asked if I was going. I told her no; I had too much work to finish. Ten minutes later, a renewed energy, and motivation, was surging through me. I knew Brad would live up to his promise to satisfy me for as long as I pleased. He could please me sexually, please me with expensive gifts and gadgets, yet he couldn't give me the one thing I so desperately desired. A title . . . *Mrs*. I knew that something was going to have to change. And soon.

I smiled and crossed and uncrossed my legs. For now, what Brad could give me tonight would be good enough. It had been a couple of weeks since we had been together. I was ready. The night couldn't come soon enough, and neither could I.

meshell

"Are you sure my personal information and service transaction will be kept strictly confidential?" I anxiously asked, as I paced back and forth in my bedroom with the phone pressed tightly to my earlobe.

"Why, of course. We cater to and retain very high-profile clients who stress confidentiality above all else. We are quite discreet in our business dealings," the young lady's voice over the phone guaranteed, reassuring me.

It was seven o'clock on a Friday night. It had been a long workday and already this new case was starting to get under my skin. I hated dealing with cases involving crimes against children, especially molestation. I could kill the bastards myself. With my bare hands.

I rubbed the back of my neck to release some tension. "So, what do you need from me?" Earlier, I had popped two Tylenol gel caps and they hadn't started working yet.

"Your credit card number, expiration, and an address," the voice chirped professionally and efficiently.

I gave the information and the voice on the other end repeated it back.

"That's correct," I stated.

"Thank you. Now, we just have the matter of where and what time."

I thought seriously for a moment. I knew I didn't want a stranger coming to my home and knowing where I lived. I quickly rolled off the address of my favorite Midtown hotel. "I will call your service back with a room number and particulars. Is nine o'clock okay?"

"Excellent." In the background I heard her keying my information into a computer. "Okay. I think you are all set."

I didn't say anything, because I couldn't believe what I was setting up; it was all surreal. However, that wasn't enough to make me want to discontinue or cancel my transaction.

"Just to verify, you'd like a black male, tall, preferably over six feet, muscular physique, clean-cut with a mustache or goatee, bald head or low-cut Caesar style, pretty, straight white teeth, well-endowed, between the ages of twenty-eight and thirty-four."

"Correct."

"Is there a particular service you desire?"

"Excuse me?"

"Oral, anal, bondage?" The voice professionally went down the list.

"No. I'll go with the flow."

"Thank you." I heard more typing. "Is there a preferred name you'd care to be called?"

I thought for a second and then a smile crept across my face.

"Yeah, Lil' Kim is fine."

"Lil' Kim," she repeated in a formal, professional tone. I heard her typing again.

"Yes."

"Excellent. Looks like you are all set. Our employee will be in the lobby, promptly at nine, to await further instructions regarding your room number. We appreciate your business and hope you will call again."

I hung up the phone and glanced down at my watch. I had two hours to make a reservation, shower, get dressed, and drive over to the hotel. I thought this was one of the craziest things, if not the craziest thing, I had ever done.

After confirming my reservation for the evening, I made a mad dash for the shower. I sought out my favorite bath products. In my mind, I was already planning what I'd wear. Something really sexy. I guess it really didn't matter because whatever I wore wasn't going to stay on very long. My discreet research revealed that this escort service employed some of the finest men in the city, and they were on point in servicing their exclusive clients to extreme satisfaction. They boasted of repeat customers.

I stayed in the shower until my hot water began to run out. Turning off the nozzle, I felt refreshed and amazingly some of the tension had been washed away too. Toweling off with a fluffy peach towel, I reached for my favorite scented body lotion and spritz. Some people were shoe people or purse people; me, I loved to purchase and try new fragrances. It was nothing for me to spend in the hundreds of dollars for a perfume that I liked or saw advertised.

I had finished up in the bathroom, applied my makeup flawlessly, and was going into my walk-in closet when the phone rang. I debated on whether I should answer it or not. After all, I didn't want to be late for my engagement. I looked down at the caller ID box and picked it up on the fourth ring.

"Hello."

"You are alive?"

"Hello to you too, Mama."

"I haven't heard from you in over two weeks, so I called to check up on you," she said in the very proper, crisp, clipped diction she always used.

"Has it really been two weeks? I'm sorry, but I just started a new case and got caught up."

"Oh, well, enough said. That explains everything," Mama said, dismissing my explanation as understandable.

There was a comfortable silence.

"Tell me about it. This new case."

"Not now, Mama. I was getting ready to go out. Unwind."

"Oh yes. Well, it is a Friday night and the night is still young and so are you," she said with resignation in her voice.

Now I felt bad. Daddy had died the first of last year and I knew Mama felt lonely at times. They had been together forever. I missed him so much myself, but I tried to keep those feelings at bay.

"I promise I'll call you first thing tomorrow."

"That sounds good. I look forward to it. I wanted to also remind you about the annual party that's coming up."

"Mama, how could I forget? I've been attending every year since high school." Every year Mama hosted this huge party, event actually, that consisted of pretty much the who's who among the black, intellectual elite in the Baltimore area.

"I know with your busy schedule, I have to remind you in advance to place it in your BlackBerry."

"I will be there, as always. I wouldn't miss it for the world. I have to see you shine," I said.

"I do, don't I?" We laughed.

My mama is an attorney and so was my daddy. And yes, you guessed it, my brother, Michael, is too. It's a family tradition; just like the women in my family all pledging the same sorority in college and the men the same fraternity. They would have disowned me if I had pledged that other sorority. We all attended the same historically black university and law school. My family is all about appearances, tradition, and serving our communities. Growing up, I attended private schools from elementary through high school, had a coming-out party, was a member of Jack & Jill, and was exposed to the best life had to offer. I had been to Europe before I was six. Growing up was all about being the best that I could be. Sometimes the pressure to live up to my parents' expectations was overbearing. My brother handles it by drinking and being a womanizer.

"That's my girl. It wouldn't be tragic either if you brought home a nice, brilliant young man for the family to meet," Mama volunteered.

There was a moment of silence.

"You are dating someone, aren't you? What man wouldn't want a lovely, intelligent woman like yourself on his arm?"

"I'm—I'm seeing someone," I totally lied.

"Well, bring him. I'm not asking you to marry the man. It just wouldn't look right for you to show up without a date like last year."

"We'll see." I didn't want to disappoint her and tell her that there wasn't a special man in my life. Hadn't been for quite a while.

"I love you and I can't wait until we go out on one of our infamous shopping sprees—and we have to get massages and try this new French restaurant that just opened. It's getting rave reviews. Plus, we must plan our ski trip for early next year."

I laughed because Mama could talk once she got on a roll.

"Mama? Remember, I'm going out? I'll call you tomorrow and we can discuss all this."

"Okay, dear, I'll let you go. Good night."

"Good night, Mama."

Fifteen minutes later, I was back on task. Since I was going to be buck-naked anyway, if things went as planned, I didn't waste a lot of time or energy on my outfit selection. I chose a black lacy teddy, threw a wife beater T-shirt on top of that, put on my black jeans and black boots, and called it a wrap. As I pulled my hair back in a ponytail, I sipped on the screwdriver I had mixed earlier. I needed something to calm me down a notch. My nervousness was making me bounce off the walls. I was like this the first day of a new trial as well. Lots of nervous energy.

Looking at myself in the mirror over my dresser, with my hair pulled back and bangs loose, I looked like a young girl. I had learned that looks were definitely misleading. What you saw was not always what you got. There was not a naïve bone in my body.

Before I could lose my nerve, I gulped down the last of my drink and felt it rush to my head. At the last minute, I packed another outfit and my toothbrush, toothpaste, and other toiletries. I grabbed my purse and keys, zipped up my black overnight bag, and headed out the front door.

The night was starless and there was a full moon. As usual, Interstate 75 was packed. On the drive over to the hotel, I had ample time to think. I considered calling Lexie because I knew she'd talk me out of what I was about to do. She had a similar experience a few months ago with her Internet lover and had backed down at the last minute. To be honest, I was shocked that she even made it as far as pulling up into the hotel parking lot. In the end, I didn't call her because I didn't have a need to be analyzed and critiqued regarding my actions.

I knew what I needed and I was going to claim it. I turned the music up on the radio and swayed my head to the hip-hop beat. I took a couple of sips from the white plastic cup that contained my third screwdriver of the night. Searching for a wintergreen mint and popping it into my mouth, I saw the hotel up ahead. I pulled up front.

By the time the valet took my car off to garage heaven, and I entered the front door, I was hyped for a night of partying and getting my groove on in a major way. Hopefully, I wouldn't see the face of a molested and murdered child in my dreams tonight. I stepped high in my three-inch black boots and peacoat. With my shoulder bag on my right shoulder and the overnight bag in my left hand, I smiled sweetly at the blond young woman at the front desk as I walked toward her.

As I checked in and waited for my scan card to be activated, I surveyed my surroundings. I always did love this hotel. It reeked of money, good taste, and the finer things in life. It even smelled expensive and it was. You never knew what celebrity you might see strolling leisurely through. Last year, I saw Aretha Franklin walking through the lobby like the queen she is and the handsome actor Blair Underwood waiting for his driver for the night.

It was eight forty-five when I called the escort service to give them my room number. They assured me that my date for the evening would arrive shortly. What? I rubbed my eyes and did a double take. I could have sworn I had just seen Tonya come from around the far wall, near one of the restaurants, and go up in the elevator dressed in a black trench coat and spiked shoes. By the time I looked again, the elevator doors were closing and the female was hunched over in the corner, with her face turned. Couldn't have been.

I made my way up in the elevator to the sixteenth floor, looking at my reflection in the mirror. I didn't like what I saw; I knew I was out of control again, but I didn't care at the moment. Self-gratification was the only thing on my mind. Seeing the scum of the earth, day in and day out, eventually took its toll on a person. I was only human. I needed someone to hold me close, devote his entire attention to me, make me feel special, and bring me some pleasure. Tonight was all about me. Pleasuring me. This "date" was on my dime, and a steep dime at that, so he was going to earn his money. On his back, or any other way I saw fit.

Unlocking the door and walking into my suite, I was once again overcome by the beauty and the exquisite detail that was given to each room. I strolled over to check out the bed. Sturdy, large, and firm. Tossing my bags down, I checked my watch and realized it was almost time. I quickly walked into the bathroom to change and freshen up. At the last minute, I changed into the outfit in my black overnight bag. I admired myself one last time and walked back into the front sitting area. I forced myself not to pace. Again, patience was not one of my virtues.

Perfect timing. There was a gentle but sturdy knock at the door. I exhaled, let it out through my nose, and walked over to open the door to my mystery man. The one who was going to help me forget my pain, for one night anyway. Before I could lose my nerve, I yanked the door open.

Wow! Standing before me was one of the most gorgeous men I had ever laid eyes on. He was everything I had asked for and more—much, much more. He had the face, the body, the smile . . . he was all that and then some. Lord have mercy, the things I could do to him. The things he could do to me.

"Lil' Kim?"

It took me a moment to realize he was addressing me. "Uh, yes," I finally answered, tearing my eyes away from the Boris Kodjoe look-alike. Suddenly I felt really stupid going by the moniker Lil' Kim. Wasn't the real one in jail somewhere anyway?

"I'm Sean. Your date for tonight."

"Please come in," I said a bit too formally, opening the door wider so he could gain entry.

Relax. Calm down, girl.

Sean walked in and I checked him out from behind. Buns of steel. I bit down on my knuckles. Sean turned around to look at me and I smiled innocently.

"Can I make you a drink?" he asked, as if he were the host of the party.

"Yes, please do. The glasses and minibar are over there," I said, pointing and taking a moment to compose myself by sitting down on the sofa.

Sean was dressed casually in black slacks and a black button-down shirt; he was very neat. He looked every bit the part of a businessman on casual Friday. And he smelled divine. And those muscles that bulged at each and every move he made. Those sexy, bedroom eyes were already doing things to my body that I couldn't explain. And those pretty, straight, white teeth. There was just something about a man and a sexy smile. I also tried to check out the bulge between his legs. I couldn't tell much, damn it, but he did have large hands and big feet.

"Here you go, Lil' Kim," he stated, turning to me with my drink and a drink for himself in hand. He was standing so close that I felt dizzy. I took a big gulp of my drink; half the glass was empty when I came back up for air.

"Sean, I'm new to all this. What now?"

"Your credit card has already been charged for tonight. You are set. Don't worry about a thing. Let me take care of you. I'm here to please you. Your every wish is my desire."

"My personal genie."

With that he took the near empty glass from my hand and placed it on the table near the nightstand. He came back over, gently leaned down and pulled me to standing, untied my white hotel bathrobe, and glided it from my shoulders. It fell to the floor. A small smile flashed across his face when he saw my attire. He instantly knew what was in store for the night.

I had on a shiny black leather outfit with black, thigh-high boots. My leather vest was cut out in the front, and exposing my breasts, and the pants were cut out in the back, exposing my buttocks. The shirt and the pants had small chains hanging from the front, near the zippers. The only thing missing was my black whip. However, Sean knew I was the dominatrix in charge.

"What can I do for you, Lil' Kim?"

"Show me what you're working with," I stated in a toneless but firm voice. I pulled up a wooden chair and gestured for Sean to take center stage. He immediately did as I commanded and went to work. He teased me and thrilled me, unbuttoning and taking off a piece of clothing at a time. By the time Sean unzipped his pants, I thought I'd fall out of the chair in anticipation of what was within. When he finally had everything off but his thong underwear, I admired his magnificent body.

"Come here."

He walked over and I felt him up and down. Taking my time, relishing the hardness of his male body. Inhaling his masculine aroma. Pulling from his strength.

"Show me. Take it out." I pointed.

"Yes, Lil' Kim."

Sean was playing my game and playing it well. He kept a tight face and obeyed my instructions. He released himself and I tried my best for my eyes not to bulge out of my head.

"Nice. Very nice." As I touched and kneaded the merchandise, I thought I saw a brief smile cross his face.

"Do you think I'm sexy, Sean?"

"Yes, Lil' Kim."

"Prove it. Touch me. Ignite my fire."

Sean took his time kissing me, touching my breasts and exposed nipples. Light kisses rained up and down my neck while he squeezed and sucked. Still sitting in my chair, I moaned and threw my head back. This man had skills; he knew all the pleasure points to push.

"Stop!" I screamed, pushing him away like discarded garbage. He almost lost his balance.

"Sean, I want you to take off my top and then my pants. I grant you free rein to do whatever you'd like. Please me."

Sean had me worked up in no time at all. His fingers were touching and prodding areas that had me in ecstasy. I closed my eyes and licked my lips and prayed that this wouldn't end. I wanted to feel him inside me, but not yet. I had all night to experience the pleasures of a pro. Especially one who looked like Boris.

"Sean, I want you to taste me," I stated, opening my legs in my nakedness.

He moved over and spread my legs even wider. He played with me. Teased me. Almost made me beg him to touch me with his tongue, but I didn't. His fingers worked magic going in and out and I struggled to get away from him, but he pulled me back to the edge of the chair. When his wet mouth first made contact, I gasped loudly. His tongue went in and out in firm, long, even strokes. I swear I purred like a kitty cat. Sean picked me up with little effort and carried me over to the bed. Instantly, my legs were over his shoulders, my back on the bed, and he worked me over. Two orgasms later, he finally released his firm grip on my inner thighs.

I shuddered uncontrollably while he wrapped his mouth around a nipple and bit down with just enough pressure to cause me to wince.

"Again," I managed to utter between shakes and shudders. "Speak. You can talk now."

"You like that, don't you? You like it a little rough?"

I nodded.

"I thought so," he stated, checking my wetness again. I moaned and almost came again.

He lifted my leg up high and inched himself down again and licked. "Hmmm. You taste heavenly." I found myself counting stars again as they danced and frolicked before my hazed eyes.

Finally I composed myself and took control again. "I want to feel you inside me. Be a good boy."

Sean did as he was told. He promptly climbed on top of me and entered me. I winced because he was definitely packing, long and thick. What a combination! I wasn't sure now if I could accommodate him.

"Talk to me," I commanded, harshly.

"You like this?" he asked, moving up and down. I shrieked. He smirked. "Think you can handle all this?"

He pushed himself farther in and my eyes bulged out.

"Where's all that talk now, Lil' Kim? Can you take this?"

"Yeah, that's right. Handle your business," I stated, smacking his butt cheek with my open hand.

"Damn. You're so wet. I can tell you like this. Don't you?"

I nodded.

Sean took it out and lifted himself up to place it between my breasts. I closed my eyes.

"Put it back in."

"You sure?" he asked.

"Yes," I answered, biting my lip.

He inched himself in. I felt my walls expanding to accept him and I inhaled.

"Yeah. Work it, baby boy."

"You can't handle all this."

I felt myself going into that other dimension and I couldn't stop myself.

"Act like my stuff belongs to you. That's right."

"Harder!"

"Oh, yes."

"Harder!"

"Work it, baby."

"Oh, yesssss!"

In the early morning hours, Saturday morning, Sean left my bed. Kissed me on the cheek. I couldn't move. He let himself out, but not before leaving his business card with his name and business number propped up on the nightstand. That man wore me out. He was worth every dollar. Before the door closed good, I was out like a light, and I slept right up to checkout time, which was at noon. I arose with just enough time to take a quick shower and get my ass up out of the place. Sexually, I was sated, but emotionally, the void was still alive and well. There was still a big, empty hole.

Once I turned the corner in my car, one block away from the hotel, big tears of shame and guilt spilled forth down my cheek and onto my lap. I swiped at them with my free hand. I knew then, I couldn't go on like this. Sex with strangers was empty, unfulfilling sex no matter how you looked at it. But why did I desire that over forming an intimate relationship with someone? That was a good question.

meshell

By the time I arrived home, my tears had subsided. But I still felt like hell. I imagined I was having a nervous breakdown. Was this what one felt like? I walked into my house, threw my overnight bag and purse on the sofa, and left a trail of clothing up the hallway as I jumped into the shower, yet again. I felt dirty. Wanted to wash the last remnants of Sean off of me, remains that I missed at the hotel.

I lathered up and scrubbed and scrubbed and washed until the hot water ran out. Then I pulled myself from the shower, didn't bother to lotion up, pulled a pajama top and bottom on, and climbed into bed. I glanced at the digital clock on the nightstand. It was only a little after one o'clock.

There was a dull ache, a soreness between my legs. Quick images of Sean, towering above me, saying nasty things to me, flashed before my eyes. I shook my head to dismiss them. I slipped farther beneath my comforter and reached for safety and comfort in the coolness of my silk sheets. Every time I closed my eyes, I saw myself with various men in different sexual situations. I couldn't remember some of their names. If the Crew only knew of my sexcapades, would they think differently of me? Probably. See me in a different light? More than likely.

I must have finally drifted off into a realm of restless sleep because the ringing phone startled me awake. I looked around at my surroundings in a sleepy haze. My pajamas and sheets were damp and my cover was on the floor beside the bed in a rumpled mess. The phone rang a few more times but I didn't have the energy or desire to answer it. The shrill sound annoyed me more. I knew I was supposed to call my mama back, but I didn't have the strength to move. I didn't even bother to pull the cover back on me from the floor. So I just lay there and stared at the ceiling. I observed patterns and designs I'd never noticed before.

Another couple of hours passed. I knew it was evening because darkness spread behind the partially opened mini blinds. I didn't care. I lay there. My stomach growled and I realized I hadn't eaten all day. The phone rang again. My stomach growled again in response. I struggled to sit up, managed to force myself to my feet, and walked into the kitchen to find something to eat. There wasn't much to choose from; I ate out so much that I didn't keep a stocked refrigerator. My milk was sour; I poured it down the drain and discarded the container. There was leftover Chinese and a bag of withered mixed salad greens; I tossed those as well. I finally settled on a cup of peach yogurt and orange juice that I found in the back of the fridge. It would have to do for now.

Walking back into the living room to check my messages, I turned the answering machine to play. I continued to spoon yogurt into my mouth until it was all gone and then licked the spoon.

"Meshell, please call your mother. Love you."

Second message: "Hey, it's Lexie. I really need to talk to you. Uh, concerning a personal matter that has me mixed up. Call me. Soon. Where are you?"

I walked over to the TV and turned it on, not really to watch it, but to at least have some background noise to relieve me from my jumbled thoughts. Big mistake. The ten o'clock news was focusing on the up-coming trial and jury selection; everybody in the metro Atlanta area was talking about it. There were the photos. Of him. Of her. I hurled the TV remote across the room, it bounced off the wall and crashed to the floor, and I burst into fresh tears. I must have cried nonstop for over twenty minutes. As I rocked my body back and forth, I wrapped my arms around myself and hugged and squeezed with all my might. My cries finally subsided.

The phone rang again. And again. And again. I lifted the receiver just to stop the noise that was driving me crazy. Flung it down next to me on the sofa.

Silence.

"Meshell. Hello?"

Silence.

"Hello?"

I still didn't answer. Just listened to Lexie's voice crying out.

"Is anybody there? . . . Meshell, say something."

Then, like a volcano erupting, my single sob, which started out as a silent meow, turned into a thunderous roar. I let loose and must have scared Lexie half to death.

"Meshell?! What's wrong? What's going on?" she screamed.

I picked up the phone. As much as I tried, I couldn't explain to her what was going wrong in my life because I couldn't understand it myself. I sobbed and mumbled like an idiot.

"Talk to me! I'm here.

"I'm coming over. Do you want me to come over? I'm coming over."

I managed to mutter a small "Yes."

"I'll be there. Call me on my cell. No, I'll call you on your home phone. Are you physically hurt?"

"No," I managed to murmur.

"I'm on my way. Hang on."

Thirty long minutes later, Lexie was rushing through my door like a cold winter blast, using her spare key, with a worried look on her sweet face. Even though my crying had subsided, I was still sitting on the sofa, in the exact same spot. The phone was lying beside me. I hadn't even bothered to hang it up. The TV was on, but muted.

"Meshell, what's going on?" Lexie asked, cautiously walking my way, dropping her purse on the floor.

I attempted to smile, but it came off as strained. Besides, it was too much work.

"You gave me a huge scare, girl."

I nodded and smiled sadly, as if to say I knew, but didn't care.

Lexie sat down beside me and looked me over. I saw her eyes checking me out from head to toe. Searching, looking for answers that I wasn't able to supply. When she saw I wasn't physically injured, she reached for my hand. I gave it freely.

"Tell me. What's going on? I'm here now and we can work this out together. That's what friends are for."

"I feel so alone," I whispered.

"Girl, you are never alone. Never."

With those soothing, caring words, I burst into tears yet again. I didn't think I had any left. Like a child, Lexie held me and rubbed my back until I was finished. Until I had released it all.

Finally, I pulled away. "I feel like such a fool," I said, wiping my nose with the back of my hand. She pulled a Kleenex out of her purse.

"Why? Because you cried? Because you needed someone?"

I smiled faintly. "All of the above."

"Girl, what's going on? Don't you ever scare me like that again. My hands are still shaking. I must have broken every speed limit there is driving over here like I was in the Indy 500. I was so afraid. I didn't know what I'd find once I got here."

I stared blankly at her. "You're a good friend."

"Duh!"

"Duh?"

"Yeah, duh. You heard me."

"I'm sitting here bawling my eyes out and you, the psychologist, all you can say is duh?" I questioned.

For whatever reason, I found that totally hilarious. I burst into loud laughter. Lexie just shook her head with a stern look on her face and after a while she couldn't help herself, she joined in too. We laughed so hard that our sides were aching and tears were streaming down our cheeks.

"You are stupid, just stupid. Sitting over there in some wrinkled-ass pajamas with your hair all over the place, laughing like an idiot."

"I love you too, witch."

"I know you do. Now, tell me what's wrong," she said, throwing her hands up in surrender. "Is your mom okay? Your brother?"

"Yes, Mama is fine. And Michael is probably screwing his wife's best friend as we speak."

"Well, what then? Why all the tears?" Lexie asked, searching my face for answers.

"Okay. Okay, I'll tell you. As long as you promise not to send me off to the loony farm. Have me sitting in a pure white room in a strait-jacket staring at the walls, screaming, 'I'm not crazy! Really, I'm not!'"

"I promise. Scout's honor," she said, lifting her fingers to her heart. I believed her.

I took a deep breath and, for the next hour, explained to Lexie as best I could everything that had occurred over the last few months in my life. I described how I was getting emotionally caught up more and more in every case I prosecuted. I dealt with stress by having wanton sex with strangers; a quick fix. Lexie listened without placing an ounce of judgment on me. She listened as a friend, not as a doctor. And before the night was over, I knew that I'd survive and this too would pass over the horizon like a springtime rain shower.

lexie

It was intervention night, another Ladies' Night Out! The last week had been a struggle; I never left Meshell's side except to go in to the office for a couple of hours a day. I had rescheduled and juggled all my patients so that I could stay close to home in case she needed me. I had insisted that Meshell move in with me until she felt better about going home and staying by herself. I even called her office and made arrangements for her to take a week off. I packed Meshell's suitcase with enough clothes and other essentials for a week and just like that we became roommates. I cooked for her, we went for walks in the park, and we talked and laughed and laughed and talked.

For a minute, we thought about canceling Ladies' Night Out, but reconsidered. If we were friends like we said we were, then we needed each other's support to see us through the rough times, not just the good ones. It was my idea, actually, to have an intervention night. Four heads were better than one. Plus, I had personally witnessed interventions before and they could be powerful. Tracee and Tonya had each been sent an electronic invitation to intervention night. They had both responded that they'd be in attendance. We were starting at eight o'clock and the attire was your most comfortable pajamas. It was now seven fifty-five.

"Watch those witches roll up in here around eight thirty," Meshell said, sitting on my sofa, watching me do all the work. She was pretty much back to her old self; she was going home on Sunday and returning to work on Monday. She had on a pretty pair of red silk pajamas that had such lovely intricate detail and flat, fluffy, black bedroom slippers. Meshell looked relaxed and well rested with her hair pulled back in a loose, casual ponytail. There were no visible signs of her previous stress.

I smiled at Meshell. We were closer than ever now. "It wouldn't be Tracee and Tonya if they didn't show up fashionably late."

"True. They'll never change."

I finished lighting the last of my candles and checking out the ambiance of the room. It was important that everyone feel relaxed and casual. Platters of snacks such as grapes, nuts, chips, and pretzels were arranged on the coffee table, along with empty wineglasses. I knew Tonya would bring over bottles of wine. She hadn't disappointed yet.

"Witch, sit down and relax. Everything looks great. You are making me tired just watching you."

I fluffed a pillow and sat down across from Meshell. I was wearing my faded blue and black plaid flannel pajama set. They were soft, warm, worn, and comfortable and I had owned them for years. I had thick white socks on my feet.

"Girl, Tracee and Tonya have bugged me to death trying to find out what our intervention theme is all about. I haven't talked to them this much in one week since . . . never."

"Nosy witches," Meshell laughed. "I wonder how they are going to react when they hear our reason."

The doorbell rang and I heard busy chatter on the other side.

"Speaking of, here they are. And on time. I guess we'll soon find out."

"I guess their nosiness got the better of them."

I ran over to answer the door. "Coming. Hold your horses.

"You ready for this?" I asked, looking back at Meshell, who now didn't look too sure of herself.

"Ready as I'll ever be."

I opened the door. "Hey, divas! Divas in the house!"

After exchanging hugs and kisses on the cheeks, the rest of the Crew walked in with their hands full. Tracee had a platter of sugar-free cookies and a veggie casserole she had baked—she was testing the recipes out on us. Tonya had two heavy bags that I assumed contained the drinks for the evening, wine and some liquor to make mixed drinks. She even included these cute tropical-looking umbrella sticks for the drinks. They set everything down on the kitchen table and walked back to grace Meshell with hugs and kisses. I noticed she had gotten a little quiet.

Before Tonya could even take off her coat, she was asking, "Okay, what's going on tonight? What's this damn intervention all about? Who needs intervention?" she asked, looking around at Meshell and myself.

"Yeah, what's going on?" Tracee asked as she struggled with her leather coat.

"Be patient, ladies. It will all be explained in a few minutes. Coats, please." I extended my arms.

"Tell me something. Trying to act all mysterious." Tonya was looking back and forth from Meshell to myself.

Tonya had on this sexy black floor-length gown with a matching robe and two-inch slip-on black bedroom slippers. To be honest, it would be more appropriate for her man, that is, if she had one. It was simply stunning. Tracee had on a hot pink pajama set that showed off her curves and exposed a bit too much cleavage, but that was Tracee. She slipped off her black Barbie slippers and made herself comfortable.

"Meshell, you've got to sample my casserole."

"I will."

"Mama gave me the recipe and I switched up some ingredients and left out the meat."

I placed their coats on my bed and walked back into the living room. I had the curtains pulled open, so we had a wonderful view of downtown. Music was playing quietly in the background and my candles were already emitting a fragrant aroma around the room. I paused in my tracks as I experienced a bit of déjà vu. The scene reminded me of a few months back, when everyone spent the night and the question was posed, *What's the freakiest thing you've ever done?*

"Everyone, help yourselves. There is plenty of food and drink. Dig in. There are no waiters here."

We started filling up my best china plates and glasses and chatting about things that were of no importance, embracing our sisterhood. I could feel the tension and curiosity rising in the room over what the evening held in store. I was sitting on the floor, over near the love seat, with Meshell stretched out on the love seat. Tracee and Tonya shared the larger sofa, at opposite ends. My largest candle glowed in the center of the coffee table, flanked by dozens of others, all creating a cozy, intimate setting.

"Okay, I can't wait any longer. What's up, divas?" Tonya asked again.

I sat up straighter and looked at each of my friends. "Ladies, Meshell and I talked about it and decided an intervention was appropriate for tonight."

They stared back blankly. "Intervention for what? For who?" Tracee asked.

"Be patient. I'm going to explain all that."

I took a sip of my wine to calm my nerves. "A lot has happened during the last week, both for Meshell and for myself. And we realize that true friends should be there to support each other through life's struggles and ups and downs. That's why we are here tonight."

"True, but I still don't understand, diva."

I held up my hand.

"Let her finish and everything will be clear in a few minutes," Meshell said in her usual authoritative tone.

"After some startling revelations, it became crystal clear to me that we consider each other best friends, have known each other forever, and hopefully will continue to be friends for the rest of our lives, but we keep a part of ourselves to ourselves. We hide behind masks and only expose the parts of us that are appealing. I found out some secrets about Meshell, and vice versa, that I couldn't believe and wouldn't have if she hadn't told me with her own mouth."

"Oh, shit," Tonya screamed, sitting up straight. "I smell some dirt." I had her full, undivided attention.

"It's true, you never really know a person; we are all so multilayered. But you ladies help to make my life complete in different ways, and I don't want to hide things from you for fear of you not understanding, for fear of you thinking differently of me, or for fear of you not approving. If you are a real friend, a true friend, you will accept me and like me for me. Plain and simple."

"I still don't understand what this has to do with an intervention," Tracee said, already working on her second glass of wine and munching on some chips and salsa. "You are talking in circles."

"I guess I started this mess so let me go first. When I finish my story, Tracee, you'll understand what Lexie is getting at."

All eyes and attention were now focused on Meshell. I crossed my legs at the ankles and looked up at her. When she first told me her story, I couldn't believe she had been living this double life that I was totally unaware of. I knew about some incidents in college, but I thought that was long behind her.

"I'm not going to beat around the bush." We all looked at her in anticipation. Tracee suspended her sip in midair and Tonya leaned forward on the sofa.

Meshell took a deep breath. "For the last couple of months, I've been having sex with strange men. My trip to DC wasn't business; I went solely to hook up with Charles and his friend. I even hooked up with some man at a swingers club. I have gotten so out of control that I paid an escort service for a date."

There was a stunned silence. Meshell looked over at the far wall. Couldn't meet our eyes.

"What?" Tonya finally questioned. "Diva, you do not have to pay anybody for a date. Look at you—you are successful and beautiful."

"Tonya, that's the thing. It's not about having a date or a man, it's about the sex and instant gratification with no strings attached," I said, sounding every bit the psychologist. I nodded to Meshell to continue.

"I've had this problem for a while, since my college days." Meshell paused for effect. "Whenever I'm stressed I seek out pleasure in the form of sex. My drug of choice is not alcohol or cocaine, it's sex. It's like a high; it takes my mind off the problem for a minute. In college, I'd stress myself out so much over my grades or an exam—and then in law school, the stakes were even higher. My family had such high expectations; I couldn't disappoint them."

Tracee still hadn't spoken; she looked absolutely shocked. "Meshell, I don't know what to say," she finally offered. "I didn't know. What can we do?"

"There's nothing you can say. I hid this from you guys. It was my dirty little secret. Just be here for me in case I need support, have the urge to vent or even cry. That's all."

Tracee walked over to offer Meshell a big hug. "I didn't know. Are you okay now?"

"I'm working on it. I realize this is a problem I need to get under control before I live to regret it. I've been very lucky I haven't met one of the creeps I help to put behind bars. I don't have an STD or HIV."

"So, what—how . . ." Tonya was for once at a loss for words.

"I've referred Meshell to a doctor I'm very familiar with on a professional level, one who is very qualified, and she's going to work with her. Help her to learn to deal with stressful situations in a more productive manner and to find out where her problems with intimacy stem from. And of course, we, as her friends and support team, will show love and understanding."

"Of course. That's a given," Tonya stated.

Tracee shook her head. "We just didn't know."

I glanced over at Meshell and she looked like a big burden had been lifted from her shoulders. I knew in that instant she would make her way through this, with a little help from her friends.

"Ladies, I really need a drink now," Tracee said, standing up and stretching. We all laughed nervously. "Whew! I never would have guessed this in a million years. I knew you were sexually adventurous, but this?"

"I know. I did a wonderful job of hiding it. I didn't want you guys to think less of me," Meshell said.

"Diva, please. I respect you even more for admitting you have a problem. Was the sex off the charts?"

Leave it to Tonya to break the ice. Everyone burst out in laughter. It was a welcome release.

"Off the chain!" Tracee and Meshell high-fived each other.

I nibbled on a salsa chip. "But there's more."

All eyes focused back on me. An uncomfortable silence returned.

"Damn, diva. There's more?" Tonya asked, looking over at Meshell. "What more could there be?"

"No, not from Meshell. I have a secret or revelation to share."

You should have seen the mouths that dropped wide open. Some wider than others. It was almost humorous. They didn't expect me to have a secret . . . not Miss Perfect.

I took a few sips of wine to get up my nerve. "I'm not going to beat around the bush either. Here's the short version. Not too long ago, I met a man over the Internet, agreed to meet him at a local hotel, and I had sex with him."

"Not our little Goody Two-shoes!" Tracee exclaimed. "Say it isn't so!"

"I'm afraid so. I did it to prove that I could be adventurous and sexy and spontaneous and plus I wanted at least one story to share like you guys had about your freakiest moment."

"Was the sex good?" Tonya asked.

I smiled shyly and then burst out laughing. "The best."

"You go, girl. Did he rock your world?" Tonya asked.

"Girl, he set it on fire."

"Did you practice safe sex?" Tracee asked.

"Of course. I'm no fool."

"You had good sex, you met a handsome man, no harm done," Tonya concluded. "Next!"

"He was fine, wasn't he?" Tracee asked.

"Yes." I smiled and couldn't help blushing at just the memory.

"Well, what's the problem?" Tracee asked, twisting a lock of hair around and around her finger.

I looked at Meshell. I had explained the situation to her and she knew the deal. She nodded and encouraged me to tell the rest. "The problem is that we reconnected a few weeks ago on the Internet, and he wants to see me again. To see if we could have a relationship."

"Hell no. Hell no, diva!" Tonya screamed. "Oh, hell no!"

"I don't think it's a good idea either," Tracee volunteered, sitting back with a scowl on her face.

"I don't know, witches," Meshell said. "At first I was hesitant too, but Lexie and I have talked at length about this man. He makes her happy. What could she lose?"

"What do you really know about this man?" Tracee asked. "What does he do for a living?"

I paused because I could already predict the reaction. "We've talked at great length over the Internet, so I feel I know him pretty well."

"Oh please, child. You can be anybody you want to be over the Internet," Tonya said. "What does he do?"

"He's a fireman."

"A fireman, diva?"

"Yes, in New York City. Brooklyn."

"Diva, have you lost your mind? You are totally out of his league. What could you possibly have in common?"

"For once, I have lost my mind. And you know what? It feels good. Wonderful. I wake up every morning with a smile on my face. What do we have in common? Not much, but so what? Opposites attract."

They looked at me with a variety of expressions, but I saw a new appreciation filter through. I saw acceptance slowly register on their faces.

"Just take it slow. Enjoy it, but take it slow," Tonya stated and they all agreed. "Miss Goody Two-shoes got sprung by a New York City fireman. What is the world coming to?"

"If it works out, good. If it doesn't, so what? At least you tried," Tracee offered up. "Life is too short to live with regrets. You have to answer for all your unlearned lessons in your next life."

Meshell and I looked at each other with smug satisfaction. It did feel good to have secrets off our chests. And to make matters even better . . . our friends were still loving us and supporting us. Nothing had changed.

"Open that other bottle of wine, Meshell," Tracee said.

"Where's the corkscrew?"

"It's on the end table."

Meshell reached for it.

"Since we are sharing and revealing secrets tonight, I have one I need to release to the universe," Tracee said, sneaking a glance at each of us.

We were silent. Thinking if we spoke and spoiled the moment, she may not go on. The candles cast an eerie glow upon our faces. This was the perfect night for revealing deep, dark secrets.

She took a deep breath. "I've been talking on the phone to the jogger from the park—the one who watched the professor and me have sex."

"Have you lost your damn mind?" Tonya asked, almost choking on her food.

"Tonya, give her a chance to explain how this went down," Meshell said. "Damn, you acting like your shit don't stink."

"He's really a good guy. And guess what? He's in education too. A middle school principal. If that isn't karma, I don't know what is."

I looked on in awe. Tonight was definitely a night of surprises. Unbelievable.

"I didn't intentionally seek him out; it just happened. And everything happens for a reason."

"Yeah, right," Tonya ventured. "It just so happened that he watched you fuck in the park and jacked off."

Tracee dismissed her with a wave of her hand. "I was jogging and Brandon was there, jogging too. That's his name. Brandon. He gave me his phone number and we've been talking since. Now he wants to go out on a date."

"You don't even jog in that park," Tonya said. "It's clear across town."

"Tonya, why are you dogging out Tracee?" Meshell asked.

"Because I love her and I don't want to see her hurt."

"We all love her, and Lexie and I don't want to see her hurt either, but we are not attacking her. I admit, I don't like the circumstances, but we keep forgetting, we are adults. Tracee, if you'd like to go out with the man, if you see something in him that's desirable, go for it. Please do it in a public setting and let one of us or all of us know the details of where you are going," Meshell said.

Tracee nodded in agreement. "Just be careful. Go in with your eyes wide open," I suggested.

"I will."

For a few minutes, we all sat back and took in all we had heard. There was a lot to digest. Some startling revelations had been made tonight. Just when I thought I knew my friends like the back of my hand, I realized I didn't know them as well as I thought I did. I guess it's true, you never really know a person or what goes on behind closed doors. Some mess was definitely happening behind ours.

"Since everyone is sharing tonight, and I find out my best friends are lead characters in a triple-X *Peyton Place* episode, I have a secret I've been keeping as well," Tonya said, looking down at the floor. "I might as well come clean."

"What?" Meshell asked. "Not Miss Diva? Miss My Shit Don't Stink?"

"Unfortunately, yes. I'm human too."

"Thank you. She finally figured it out," Meshell teased.

We all anxiously waited for Tonya to spill the beans. In true diva style, she stalled and built on her announcement. She refilled her wineglass, filled her plate up with more food, used the restroom, and took her precious time.

"We are waiting," Meshell said, as Tonya took her seat back on the sofa.

"Don't rush me."

"Witch, don't keep us waiting."

"Talk to the hand," Tonya replied, extending her hand upward with the palm facing outward.

We sighed and started talking about other things because we knew by now that Tonya would reveal her secret when she was good and ready.

She blurted it out, no fanfare involved. "I'm having an affair with a married man."

"What?" Tracee questioned. "Not you. I don't believe you. You have always declared how you'd never mess with a married man. We all have."

"You live and you learn. I've learned to never say never. I have to look out for my future."

"That was you I saw the other night at the hotel?" Meshell pointed at her. "I knew it! I knew it was you!"

"Look out for your future with another woman's husband?" Tracee asked.

"That's not my concern," Tonya stated flippantly and turned to

Meshell. "I thought I had gotten on that elevator without you seeing me. I waited behind a huge potted plant for over ten minutes waiting for you to do what you needed to do while checking in. Was that the night you hired the escort?"

"Actually it was."

"Damn! This is too much."

"Do we know your secret married lover?" I asked, turning the conversation back to Tonya.

"Yes. It's my boss." Meshell and I shared knowing glances.

"Oh, my God. Are you serious?" Tracee asked. "He's old and fat and boring. I met him that time he was visiting your office and you and I were going out to lunch."

"He's wealthy," Tonya defended him.

"Witch, you've got to be kidding! You'd break up this man's marriage over some money?"

"Well, it's not quite that black and white. He courted me, pursued me, and made promises to me of leaving his wife because they are in an unhappy marriage, have been for many years, but . . ."

"Let me guess. He offers one excuse after another as to why he can't leave," Meshell said.

Tonya nodded sadly.

"Witch, that man ain't going nowhere but where he's at. He's going to keep lying, showering you with gifts and trinkets, and you'll keep giving up the booty over false promises."

"But he loves me."

"Do you hear how pathetic that sounds?" Tracee asked.

"Yeah, he loves you. Loves your young, new pussy," Meshell offered.

"You are so nasty," Tonya screamed.

"No, I'm the truth and you can't handle it. Be for real—you aren't throwing it at him whenever he calls?"

"Well . . ."

"That's what I thought."

"I've given him an ultimatum. Either leave the wife or I'm gone."

"Tonya, do you love this man or his money?" I asked. "Seriously."

She took a long time to answer and that spoke volumes. "I don't know. He buys me nice things and treats me special, like a princess. And he knows exactly how I like for him to go down on me."

"But you don't love him," I stated sadly.

"No. But I could learn to. I could grow to love him."

"Tonya, you are a smart woman. We don't need to even discuss this one. You know what you have to do. Let it—let him—go," I said quietly.

"That's easy for you to say. You make a great salary as a psychologist. I grew up poor and I don't want to go back. Don't want to have to struggle for the rest of my life and pinch every penny until it bleeds."

"And you don't. You have a great career and are doing better than well. You're successful," I explained.

"True. But I want it all. I deserve it. I want the man, the house. I want it all."

"Well, you have to decide if you are willing to give up your soul to get that pot of gold at the end of the rainbow."

"Tonya, if he truly loves you, then let him handle his business and then come back to you," Tracee offered. "You don't want any bad karma coming back on you."

"But regardless of your decision, we got your back, witch," Meshell stated. "We love your selfish ass all the way to the bank."

"Thank you," Tonya whispered. "I love you too."

There was silence. We were all lost in our private reflections on life, love, and friendship. I for one had learned a very valuable lesson, one I would personally never forget. You never really know a person. As much as I loved my girls, as much as we had been through, there was this whole other side to them. Some freaky stuff had been going down behind closed doors. But you know what? I didn't care. Regardless, no one is perfect and these were my girls, my true friends, my crew, the divas . . . if I could help it, I knew there would be many, many more Ladies' Nights Out.

Suddenly, Meshell sat up straight. "Shhh. Turn that up."

I got up and turned up the volume on the radio.

"Uh-huh. Taking it back to the eighties. Salt-N-Pepa. 'I'll Take Your Man.' "

The Crew jumped up, moved the coffee table out of the way, and started singing the lyrics and dancing down our own imaginary *Soul Train* line.

"Hand me that bottle, girl," Tracee screamed.

"I'll take your man," Tonya screamed, taking off her robe.

"Ouch, witch, you stepped on my foot."

"Talk to the hand."

"Ladies, please behave. Please."

"Divas in the house! Divas in the house! Bow down!"

The night was young . . . and another Ladies' Night Out was just beginning.

lexie

Whew! Another successful Ladies' Night Out has come and gone. It still remains to be seen how everyone's situation will pan out in the long run. To be continued: Ladies' Night Out: Part II. But you guessed it, the Crew is as tight as ever. Our startling revelations made a small ripple but only succeeded in bringing us even closer together. Not too many people know your life history, accept your faults and imperfections, witness your joys and pains, suffer with you through your losses and low points, and celebrate your triumphs and victories. The Crew accepts me for me, unconditionally, without any hidden agendas; I know my girls have my back, now and always.

I've gained an even greater respect and appreciation for friendship and true sisterhood. Not too long ago, I read a short passage on the Internet someone had forwarded to me. It focused on advice an elderly grandmother gave to her only granddaughter the night before her big wedding. She calmly and cautiously told her granddaughter that, no matter what happened in life, she should never let go of her friends. The young bride reflected on how much she adored her future husband and how she couldn't wait to have his children; he was all she needed in her life. Then the grandmother wisely explained: *Husbands may come and go, children grow up and take on lives of their own, but friendship, true friendship, is everlasting. Cling to it.*

Sure enough, years later, the granddaughter and her husband had divorced, the children had graduated from college with careers and families of their own, but the granddaughter had adhered to her grandmother's advice and clung to her friends. They, her friends, were still there . . . through it all.

What's the freakiest thing you've ever done? LOL. Sure, I now have my very own story to share and even though it may not be freaky to some, it is major for me. I've learned what's freaky to one person isn't necessarily freaky to another. But in the long run, it doesn't even matter. What matters is loving yourself, being secure in who and what you are . . . and having a bunch of wild and crazy friends to cheer you on.

Acknowledgments

Today, I'm in a melancholy mood. Remembering. So much has happened since I sat in this same exact spot to write out my acknowledgments, over a year ago, for book three, *Almost Doesn't Count*. A lot can change in twelve months. Three hundred sixty-five days. Some good (new projects), some bad (family deaths), but it all makes me stronger. And wiser. As I sit in front of my PC, with my hands strategically placed on my keyboard, reflecting on all the people I'd like to thank for being here for me throughout this fantastic literary journey, I can't help but think about my mom. I've been doing a lot of that lately; especially since it's so close to Mother's Day.

For those of you who know a little of my real-life story, you know that I lost my mom, affectionately known as Dot, to breast cancer a few years ago—even though it feels like yesterday. Let me tell you, it's hard being an adult orphan. No matter how old you are, you still need a mother in your life. How I wish I could share this moment with her. Book four! Wow! I know my mom would be so proud of my many accomplishments. I'd give anything to hear her say those words, "I'm proud of you." You never realize how much you miss those words until you don't hear them anymore. But I know she is proud; I had a dream one night and she came to me and told me as much. Long story, true tale.

I realized I'm blessed with others who took up the torch when my mother crossed over. First of all, I always give God the glory for allowing me to follow my dreams and achieve them. I realize all things are possible through him who strengthens me. Amen. However, the following people have played a special role in my life, have touched my heart, and enabled me in some form or fashion to realize my dreams.

Special thanks to:

My husband and children, Tresseler Rome, Laymon Taylor, my nephews, DaJuan and Jordan, the Rakestraws and the Morrises, Sharron "Meshell" Nuckles, Tonia Davis, and Tracy Craig.

Much thanks to: my agent, Marc Gerald, and my editor, Kara Cesare, two people who have believed in me from day one, my former publicists Julie Samara and Angela Pickett Henderson, Earl Cox (Earl Cox & Associates), my book coach, and three very special women, Shunda Leigh (*Booking Matters* magazine), Heather Covington (Disilgold), and Tee C. Royal (Rawsistaz).

To the bookstores and book clubs, your support is greatly appreciated and highly valued. Without you, I don't know where I'd be; you constantly put the word out and hand-sell my books. Special thanks to the independent Atlanta bookstores Medu (Nia), Nubian (Marcus), the African Spectrum (Nzenga), Oasis (Fanta), B's Books and More (B'Randi).

Thanks to: Black Expression Book Club, Readincolor Reviewers, Peoplewholovegoodbooks, Nghosi Books, Radio First, and Marc Medley of the *Reading Circle* radio show.

A special shout-out to: Sistahs Unlimited, Nubian Sistas Book

Club, Mahogany Book Club, It's a She Thang Book Club, Phenomenal Women Book Club, Black Diamond Book Club, In the Company of My Sisters Book Club, Spirit Book Club, Simply Divine Book Club and Circle of Sisters Book Club, the Ladies of Kennesaw, Amigals, just to name a few. Thanks for your support and hospitality. Didn't we have fun?

Last but not least, to my readers. I love you guys! But you already know that. Until our next journey together, peace and abundant blessings.

Signing off, Atlanta, May 6, 2006, 9:18 p.m.

Much love,
Electa
www.electaromeparks.com

A Note from the Author

My dearest readers,

Hello! I hope all is well in your lives. I pray that you are in peace and God. As for me, I'm surviving, trying to do the best with what God gave me. Trying to fit a square peg (me) into a circular world. Praising God for every day that he gives me and for the many blessings he has bestowed upon me.

Readers, thank you soooo much for entering the relationship-based, drama-filled, and racy world of my vivid imagination once again. If you've traveled with me from the very beginning, *Ladies' Night Out* is our fourth journey together. Can you believe we are on round four? In *Ladies' Night Out*, I attempted to make it a little lighter, more fun, grown, and sexy than my previous novels, but to keep it real at the same time.

I've always admitted I'm a true people-watcher; human nature is simply amazing to me. At some point in time, we've all been guilty of lusting after what someone else has, e.g., their talent, money, beauty, man/woman, house, or car. Come on, admit it! That's human nature. But . . . we never really know what's going on behind closed doors because we are on the outside looking in. We all wear masks in one form or fashion; life is one big illusion.

Tonya, Meshell, Lexie, and Tracee were the best of friends, ace boom coons, yet they weren't aware of the double lives the others were living. From outside appearances, they had it all: six-figure salaries, education, beauty, and material possessions. However, if you stripped away the masks, the Crew had issues. By the way, Tonia, Meshell, and Tracy are the real names of some of my friends and we used to have a real monthly Ladies' Night Out. However, the similarities end there (LOL). *Clause: Any resemblance to actual persons, living or dead, business establishments, events, or locales is entirely coincidental (LOL).* There! Are you happy, Tonia, Meshell, and Tracy?

As always, last but not least, I'd like to thank my readers and give my sincere appreciation for all the e-mails, letters, and positive reviews I receive; it warms my heart to no end. You've embraced and showered me with so much love that it's indescribable; you guys make this all worthwhile. But, readers, y'all don't have to tell me all your deep dark secrets (LOL). Seriously, I can be having one of my "pity party" days and hear from one of you and I realize that I'm fulfilling my purpose. Your validation pulls me back into focus.

Please continue to share your feedback with me at www.elec taromeparks.com or novelideal@aol.com; keep me on my toes, but remember I'm sensitive now (Pisces trait) (LOL). Until our next drama-filled, sensual journey together, take care.

Big hugs *(spreading my arms)* and smooches,
Electa

ladies' night out

Electa Rome Parks

writing validates and elevates me to be in complete sync with my spirit. I thought that was so profound and so unbelievably true.

Bottom line, anyone who truly knows me will state that I'm real. I'm very approachable and have a genuinely caring nature (another Pisces trait). I have my "few" imperfections (control freak behavior, temper tantrums, and impatience, to name a few) and struggles just like the next person. However, I believe in order to really get in touch with our true spirit, we need to discover our gifts. I feel that we are all born into the world with a special gift and I've found mine. That brings me great joy!

What else? I pretty much suck at any sport, my favorite color is purple, I've never weighed more than 112 pounds my entire life, my all-time favorite movie is a toss between *Soul Food* and *The Best Man*, and I have tons of stories to share with my readers.

Q: I hear that your first name is a sensitive point for you. Your name is Electa. Do people often get your name wrong?

A: (LOL) I wouldn't say that it is a sensitive point for me, but it is a "big" pet peeve when people call me Electra, Electron, Electricity, etc. I've been dealing with this mispronunciation since elementary school, so I should be used to it, huh (LOL)? But everyone wants to be called by his or her correct name. I love my name, it's very unique. In fact, I've only met one other person named Electa in my lifetime.

Q: What do you want people to come away with after reading your novels?

A: Primarily, I'm writing for entertainment value first. I write for the readers who want a minivacation without ever leaving the sanctuary of their homes. I write for that reader who on a cold, wintry day wants nothing other than to curl up under a warm

A CONVERSATION WITH ELECTA ROME PARKS

Q: What can you tell your readers about Electa Rome Parks?

A: Umm, that's a hard question. It's not easy to define or describe oneself in a condensed version, but I'll try. I was born and raised in Georgia. So yes, I'm a true Georgia peach even though I lived in Chicago and North Carolina for many years. Basically, I'm just your average, down-to-earth wife and mother of two who has a great passion for writing and reading. Honestly, I don't think I could live without books and the written word. I've found that a pen with paper is a powerful tool!

Let's see, what else can I divulge about myself and keep you interested (smile)? Believe it or not, I'm actually kinda quiet and laid-back. I can be moody and oversensitive (Pisces trait). So . . . be careful what you say about *Ladies' Night Out* because I'm sensitive about my stuff (LOL).

I have a very vivid imagination, which is evident in my books, and I believe in a lot of theories that most people would think bizarre. Let's just say I absolutely love *X-Files* and the entire concept of spirits, spirit guides, guardian angels, and karma. I once had a palm reader tell me I was a writer in another life and that's why

afghan in front of a toasty fireplace, sip on some hot tea, and read about somebody else's life. Not just read about it, but get pulled in, engulfed by it, and feel the pure emotion. Feel the heat!

If readers take something away in the process, then that's great too; that's an added bonus. I've accomplished my goal and much more; it makes it all worthwhile. Every time I feel like giving up because the publishing industry is too stressful or the monsters (insecurity, impatience, and doubt) have reared their ugly heads, I receive an e-mail or a personal letter from an avid reader and it makes my day to realize I've made an impact on somebody's life. I can't describe that feeling.

Q: *Why do you think your writing is so well received?*

A: I'm an avid reader myself and I know what is entertaining for me to read. I feel that if readers crave elements of high drama, exciting relationships, smothering spiciness, more drama, compelling characters, and added twists and turns, then they'll embrace my books, which they have.

Also, with the correct blending of elements, I feel my books come across as real; i.e., my characters are ordinary people who are going through realistic "episodes" in their everyday life that readers can relate to in one way or the other.

Q: *What has been the most gratifying part of being an author?*

A: Hands down, the most gratifying part of being an author has been meeting and greeting new and interesting readers who are embracing my stories and e-mailing me and writing me and meeting me at signings and telling me how much they've enjoyed my books! We talk about my characters like they are old friends. No matter how many times I've experienced that, it always makes my day. Puts a big Kool-Aid smile on my face (LOL).

Their (the readers') feedback and reactions totally validate that my craft is a gift from God! If I can touch a number of people with my stories or even if I only entertain them and they don't walk away with a life lesson, then I've still done my job.

As you know, my stories are typically relationship based, very drama filled with an ounce of spice thrown in (well, maybe a pound of spice thrown in), and they usually cover a topical issue that is prevalent in today's society. Believe me, I have so many characters screaming inside my head, waiting to tell their story, that I feel like the lady from the movie *Sybil* (LOL). So, bottom line, I pray and claim that my readership base will continue to grow and I'll have wonderful opportunities to meet many more fans.

Q: Where do you see yourself as a writer ten years from now?

A: It's all about continuing to elevate myself to the next level. There's always room for growth and improvement. Ten years from now, I'd love to see myself as a full-time writer entertaining my readers with fabulous, refreshing, dramatic stories of love, life, and relationships. It's not about the money; it's all about the passion and joy you feel with each and every heartfelt word that turns into a sentence, then a paragraph, and eventually a completed novel. Being a writer is like being a creator of life . . . like giving birth. What can be better than that?

Q: How do you define success?

A: Good question. Personally, I define success as being able to do something you truly love on a day-to-day basis, getting paid for it in the process, giving back to the community (to whom much is given, much is expected), and being the best person you can be, which enables you to sleep peacefully at night. To me, those combined elements make you a successful person. And . . . if you place God and your family first, the sky's the limit!

Q: How do you deal with adversity and failure?

A: I stress out! I totally freak out, have a pity party, and take to my bed (LOL)! I'm laughing, but I'm pretty accurate. I'm so hard on myself, I'm my worst critic, and I've got to stop doing that. I can't enjoy my successes because I'm too busy worrying about what I could have done better or thinking about the next venture.

After I finally pull myself out of bed and stop my pity party (this usually lasts for roughly twenty-four hours), I analyze my situation like I'm breaking down a trigonometry problem. After all is said and done, I learn the lesson, file it in my permanent memory bank, remember I'm still standing, and move on. In afterthought, life lessons are wonderful, even the ones filled with adversity and failure; they make us stronger and wiser and who we are today.

Also, if I may add, I have a good support team in place with my family and friends. Plus, I have a solid spiritual foundation that keeps me strong and undaunted by the dream dashers.

Q: Has there been a significant life lesson for you?

A: A significant life lesson was my mom dying of breast cancer back in 1997. Her death at age fifty-two (my dad died at thirty-two) made me realize and appreciate how short and precious life truly is. After her death, I made the commitment then and there that I'd follow my dreams because I didn't know what tomorrow held. People are so caught up on playing it safe, sound, and conservative; much can be said for that. Unfortunately, sometimes we look up and our lives have passed us by in the blink of an eye and all we can say is "what if." I don't want to ever have to ask myself "what if."

Q: *What do you do to stay grounded and maintain a sense of balance in your life?*

A: By spirit, I'm a pretty grounded person, yet a person with a negative aura can throw my system totally off. I'm very perceptive and can pick up on and take in people's energies fairly easily. I try to distance myself from negative people (you know who you are) and their damaging energies; however, when I find myself losing my sense of balance I do several things. I meditate to clear my mind (I always picture myself near water because water centers me), I pray to God for guidance and strength, and I talk to myself. Yes, I talk to myself, but not in a "crazy" way (LOL). I give myself little pep talks and cheer myself on.

Q. *How can readers get in contact with you?*

A. My readers can keep abreast of my writing career through my Web site at www.electaromeparks.com. And please, readers, drop me a line, give me some feedback (remember I'm sensitive, now), just holla at a sista at novelideal@aol.com.

QUESTIONS FOR DISCUSSION

1. Which character did you identify with the most? Lexie, Meshell, Tonya, or Tracee? Why?

2. Did you feel their friendship was genuine and everlasting despite their differences?

3. Were their views regarding dating and the professional, single black female accurate? Is there a shortage of eligible black men? Are men intimated by a successful woman?

4. Have you and your girlfriends ever had a Ladies' Night Out? Describe it.

5. What is your definition of freaky?

6. Were you surprised at their sexcapades? Explain.

7. Would you reveal intimate details of your sexual life to your best friends?

8. Do you feel Lexie, Meshell, Tonya, and Tracee's friendship will survive their revelations?

9. Which character was the strongest? Weakest? Most insecure? Most in control?

10. How did their upbringing affect the women they became? How did their mothers shape them?

11. Is it possible to have it all? Career? Husband? Family?

12. What's the freakiest thing you've ever done?